GETTING BACK BRAHMS

Diana owns a bookshop, is thirty-something and is single again after a long relationship. The Brahms Requiem was once her favourite piece of music. Now she cannot listen to it without it stirring painful memories of her old love. She is determined to supplant the old memories with something new and, in her quest for a memory to superimpose on the past, joins the team intending to open the Academy of Forward Literature at Hassocks Hall . . .

GETTING BACK BRAHMS

Mavis Cheek

CHIVERS PRESS
BATH

First published 1997
by
Faber & Faber
This Large Print edition published by
Chivers Press
by arrangement with
Faber & Faber Ltd
2002

ISBN 0 7540 2493 8

British Library Cataloguing in Publication Data available

For Jane, Marianne, Ollie and Angus

I cried for madder music and for stronger wine,
But when the feast is finished and the lamps expire,
Then falls thy shadow, Cynara! the night is thine;
And I am desolate and sick of an old passion,
Yea, hungry for the lips of my desire:
I have been faithful to thee, Cynara! in my fashion.

Ernest Dowson, *Non sum qualis eram*

. . . This is the use of memory:
For liberation—not less of love but expanding
Of love beyond desire, and so liberation from the future
As well as the past.

T. S. Eliot, *Four Quartets, III*

Happiness is good health and a bad memory.

Ingrid Bergman

CHAPTER ONE

It is interesting how much good advice floats about from the Happy to the Unhappy. And all of it delivered in that same bright-faced way doctors ask, 'And how are *we* today?' When they have just removed a limb. You are required to smile, be equally bright-faced, and say, 'Never felt better. Leg got in the way as a matter of fact. Thanks doc . . .'

Well, not me. If it had been me in that hospital bed it would have been, 'Well, I don't know how *you* are, doc, but personally I've never felt worse . . .'

It was the emotional equivalent of losing a limb, being dumped by Teddy. Life became one long limp and I wanted sympathy, not solutions. And certainly not bright-faced ones. My mother, for example, said I should get a Project. What, pray? Knitting? Build Your Own Reflexologist kit? So easy for her, living comfortably in Spain and widowhood. Through and out the other side of her own grief, writing her well-received books, secure, safe, *happy*. And reminding me I was young. Young? So what, *Young*? Easy for her.

Easy, too, for all the others who said something similar. Don't dwell in the past. Never look back. I got quite scratchy with them. Friends' suggestions ranged from, 'Why

Not Just Pop Off around the world?' to the intensive pursuit, and therefore holistic effect, of providing balaclavas for Romanian orphans. I am not entirely sure, had I suggested adopting a few Romanian orphans, that they wouldn't have been rather taken with the idea. Sighs of relief, that's got *her* sorted . . . It was my bookshop that saved me. Without that to run they might well have paid for my ticket and thrown in a farewell party, too.

The other common suggestion was, 'Now is the time to grab your freedom with both hands and Go For It.' As if just turning thirty were moments away from the finale of a Faustian Pact. It is worth noting that the friends who suggested this tended to have a small cottage in Barnes, or a little flatfront in Islington, two children, large mortgage and a wide selection of herbal teas. The best they ever managed was backpacking in Sainsbury's.

It was the bookshop that gave me strength throughout all these wild ideas. It was my existent Bunbury, and was I grateful. I let the pals go for a time. Those who really cared about me would be there whenever I re-emerged, and those who didn't, wouldn't. It was hard enough to walk past couples in the street, without having to sit and spend a whole evening with them and their Dearest, Darling, Sweetie-Pie. Have you noticed that in front of the newly love-lorn, the warring or indifferent couple suddenly becomes magically transformed into Dante and Beatrice?

My own view during the deepest and darkest night-time of the soul was to end it all, but the usual irritating thought that I wouldn't be there to see the effect curtailed enthusiasm. Besides, in the early days it never occurred to me that Teddy would not come back. I thought, rather as I thought about my father until he died, that he would be there for ever. I also thought that he could love nobody better than me. So much for the Self-Esteem.

I gave it three weeks. I was still counting the calendar at four months. I was deeply hurt, deeply lonely, deeply uncomprehending but—more—I was deeply and inextricably *Angry* . . . When my mother rang and urged me to go and stay with her in Spain for a while I told her icily, and to good effect, that if she had not had me in the first place, none of this would have happened. She just said, 'Come when you are ready. You will recover, you *will*.' And rang off. Oh so easy for her. Older people don't feel things so deeply as the young. And anyway, thirty is hardly in the Springtime of one's youth.

Besides, Teddy was hard enough to find in the first place. Until I met him it seemed that single men of a suitable nature had found an underground carpark and decided to make a nest of it, chucking out the single men of an unsuitable nature to forage as best they could in the dung heap of the rest of the world.

Among which ripe midden dwelled myself. When I found him I was utterly grateful and utterly weary of the long and dreary search. This one is it, I told myself and the world. And he was. For five years. Which is, in case you do not know it, a very long time.

If only love were like a football game and you could bring on an immediate and qualified replacement. Since we parted I had not seen so much as *one* bright new hope. Not even one just with nice eyes to commend him, as I complained to those who would listen. Pearl said 'Eyes-Schmeyes,' disapprovingly, and shrugged. Pearl, having been married to the same man for thirty years and eventually burying him, seemed to have a more focused perspective on these things. 'Well I am sorry for you,' she said. 'But things move on.' Clearly her grief hadn't hung around her for too long, either.

Old women should not prognosticate, which I told her. Clearly, All Men Were Bastards (Teddy in particular), mothers were Not Much Cop, Pearl was Past It and I must rearrange my life accordingly. Which is why I determined, within the remit of having a bookshop to run, to *do* something about it.

I was therefore practising to be a Lesbian.

I was practising very hard and I was not, I felt, having a great deal of success, which led me to consider that those who practise the Sapphic Mode are extremely talented women.

Nevertheless, I was quite certain that with application I would get there in the end. And *then* wouldn't all those men be sorry.

Pearl raised her sparse and aged brows, a little shocked I fancied, and went on polishing. My mother I am not so sure about. She has an annoying propensity to be liberal.

So it was Practise, Practise, Practise, as my old piano teacher used to say. Though at this stage, and unlike Grade Two, there was nothing of a *hands on* nature. Begin by looking the part, I felt, and the heart and mind would follow.

Pearl, dropping the sparse and ageds, just rolled her eyes at the suggestion.

'Say nothing,' I warned her. And was irritated to see her lips clamp shut. She whisked the duster over the shelves with the maximum gestural disdain, paying particular non-attention to the more lurid titles, and remained quite silent, apparently not noticing my entirely denimed appearance and the erasure of the feminine (no earrings).

Nobody in the shop did either. Not the customers, not the occasional anonymous students helping out, not the reps. Not even the nun who comes collecting for Christian pursuits on what seems to be a regular basis. To them all I was merely a bookseller—not a woman with bruising for a soul. I felt extremely sorry for myself. Allowable because nobody else appeared to be. I am not quite sure what I expected—the emotional equivalent of beef tea I suppose. Anyway, it didn't seem to be forthcoming. Pearl said I didn't give anyone a chance. What, from out of her dim eye, did *she* know?

I read *Radclyffe Hall*, wore stout boots to dinner parties and did not have a badly needed legwax before a hot weekend in Hampshire. When I say hot, I mean of the sunshine variety, not hot as in car or date.

The book was dull, the boots were merely considered wacky over the Philippe Starck tableware, and not having a legwax kept me in leggings all weekend, despite the unseasonal sun.

'Harder,' my piano teacher used to say. *'Harder.'* Not easy when your dreams are filled with Lost Love, Male.

I was sitting in my horrible flat one evening, and I was at the third stage of Practise, Practise, Practise, which was to stare unblinkingly at a photograph of a macho young pop icon for a minimum of ten seconds and feel no lust—not very hard, since I had felt no lust these past months anyway—when Teddy rang. At the sound of his voice my stomach departed. Who needs bulimia?

Teddy the Ex. Teddy, for whom dear Radclyffe and the Doc Martens had been invoked. Teddy for whom the term shag could now apply only to the textural quality of my shins and my carpet . . .

The macho young pop icon's face—nay, the macho young pop icon's entire body—shrank to a handful of dust. Teddy's lovable, dear, familiar, countenance hove in its stead. Yearning broke damply out of every pore and I held the telephone tight to my ear, afraid his words would spill. Clearly my mother and Pearl were entirely wrong. This was to be suffering without end.

He spoke in the sepulchral tones of one who is fully aware that he has dumped the one to whom he speaks after several years of intense intimacy. The sepulchral voice of one who feels that the one to whom he speaks is of a volatile nature and might very well contemplate putting her head in a plastic bag and breathing deeply were he to show a hint of jocularity in his voice. The sepulchral voice of one who no longer cares one jot but feels he must sound as if he does . . .

And worse. The sepulchral voice of one who has somebody else in the room listening with him and who has said that this call must be made. Somebody else in the room with him, *Female.*

Teddy, sepulchrally: 'Diana? It is Edward.'

Edward?

I discovered an interesting baritone I knew not I owned. 'Teddy,' I growled. 'How are you old son?'

Sepulchral silence.

'Diana?'

Unable to speak, I gave a grunt.

'Diana? Have you got a cold?'

I could hear his urgent sub-question. *Old Son*? When did she ever refer to me as *Old Son*?

'Diana?'

'Teddy.'

Pause.

'Diana.'

'I think we have established that quite nicely. You are Teddy and I am Diana. Or do you need a little more time to bat the idea around?'

I was yearning to say, 'Come back, come back—take me in your arms . . .' All that caper. Instead I was rasping like a used razor blade and making Dorothy Parker look like Fanny Price. Perhaps he was ringing to tell me it was over between them? My happy fantasy. And that he *was* coming back? Joy made me lightheaded. I opened my mouth to speak. Joy was inclined to be perverse because for some reason I then said, 'How's it hanging?'

There was the barest sound of a parched throat swallowing. Followed by a whispering noise—a feminine whispering noise—Bootface was in the room with him. I had known it all along. Bootface was nudging him in his delightful, smooth, muscular ribs and saying Ring Her Up And Tell Her.

Tell her what?

My epiglottis went dry.

I felt the winged messenger of gloom, death or approximately similar.

Whatever this call had to do with, I had a presentiment it was something unpleasant. Something unpleasant and about which I could do nothing. I mean, if he up and announced he had a terminal illness I could have nursed him. I dreamed of such a thing occasionally—saw myself placing a cool hand upon his fevered brow, mopping his troubled eyes, reading aloud in the lamplight from books like *The Remains of the Day* and *I, Claudius* (sensitively not mentioning the author's surname) and administering little sips of water from a thin china cup. This was always a useful alternative to dreaming of humping like mad which could prove quite exhausting afterwards—especially if it achieved an inspirational overdrive.

I swallowed with difficulty. Commanded the epiglottis to gird its tonsils. Gave my bristling shins a quick, satisfying look, and grazed the back of one Doc Marten with the other. I began to think that thin, pale, hairy ankles disappearing into vast black leather footware were, really, very attractive. Kind of cute and different. For some reason I remembered a bit of Wordsworth and spoke it out loud. Teddy always loved my knowledge of poetry. Largely because he knew none.

'And I can listen to thee yet/Can lie upon the plain/And listen, till I do beget/That golden time again . . .' I sighed. 'So lovely,' I said.

'Mmm,' he went, noncommittally.

'From "To The Cuckoo".' Little pause, just long enough, before, 'And how *is* Agatha?'

'Agnes,' he corrected, not at all happy.

'Same root,' I said gaily.

Pause. Then, more sternly, 'Diana?'

'I am Diana. You are Teddy. This we know. And now, if I am not mistaken, we also have someone who is not Agatha but Agnes. Did you ring to say anything beyond establishing our nomenclature?'

I heard the phone rustle and scrape. A light, sweetly poisonous foreign voice came on. 'Diana?'

'For the umpteenth fucking time: Yes . . .'

But Agnes Yaudet was made of sterner stuff. With a face like hers she had to be. It could have fitted on the end of my thin, pale, hairy ankle quite nicely.

Paying no attention to my games she crashed straight on. 'We thought you should be the first to know that we were married yesterday. In Harrogate.'

That paid me back.

If I'd had him lying on a death bed I'd have whipped the thin china cup from his lips and cheerfully hurried him along.

Why should I be the first to know? And why *Harrogate*?

This last, only, I dared ask.

'Because we had never been there before.'

My heart lifted fractionally. The sub-text was: Somewhere you and Teddy have *not* been.

Teddy wrote for a motoring magazine so it was not surprising we had been to most places. Couldn't think how we had left Harrogate out of it, but so we had. It was fun before Normandy Nell *pied-chauded* it into view. Life was one long whirl. As I said to Teddy once, when he said he might go for the Editor's chair—Why? It was just hard work and settled ways if he did. Well, now he had. It was in all the papers last week. Him, smiling like a satisfied Grandee, and wearing a suit.

'Harrogate,' I said thoughtfully. 'Oh yes, I remember . . . Your husband'—pause, feel the pain, continue—'and I *did* stay there once—my birthday—nice hotel right in the centre—what *was* the name—' I knew Teddy couldn't refute it. Men seem to have a different focus on memory. I always found this useful if I bought a new outfit when we were economizing. 'Oh *this* old thing . . .'

Her voice took on a curiously strangled Frenchified twang; she always lapsed into a bit of an accent when under fire. 'The Black Swan?'

'That's it,' I lied triumphantly. 'Lovely place.'

Married, married, married.

Never, never, never.

Over, over, over.

'Ah,' she said. 'No. We stayed outside Harrogate at the Morpeth Arms.'

You see what I mean? Sterner stuff.

Somehow the telephone changed hands again and it was Ted, Ted the Newlywed. He had stiffened the sinews.

'Congratulations,' I said meekly.

He wisely ignored this. 'Diana—we have quite a lot of your stuff here at the flat still and—well—Agnes—and I—that is we both—feel that now we are married we should—um—do something about it.'

This was Agnes. Obviously a tidy tart. Teddy would have lived in a permanent pickle so long as he could find his wpc and write for his beloved *Wheels.* Anyway, there wasn't that much of my stuff. Just enough, I always thought, to keep a presence. Until this moment I was convinced that Agnes would be a short-term fancy, that she would lose her charm, that she would kindly do an Amy Robsart one fine day and that, stepping over her broken neck and trotting up the stairs, I would find my belongings were suddenly welcome once more as the sun in winter.

Oh how I longed to be free of loving him. How any old home counties buffer could rustle his *Sunday Telegraph* and say that young people are easily corrupted remained a mystery. Practise, Practise, Practise had so far left me cold.

My throat had gone dry again, the back

muscles contracted, the epiglottis stuck in limbo. I managed another sentence or two before total collapse.

'Sure,' I said. 'I'll come and get them.'

'Soon?' he said eagerly. 'Tonight?'

And I heard his voice from what seemed like a thousand years ago saying the same words, in the same way, when he first asked me to come to his bed . . . Tonight, he had pleaded then. Come tonight.

'Can't tonight,' I said jocularly. 'Got a hot date.' I wished I had replied like that those thousand years ago.

'Tomorrow then?' Cruel eagerness.

'Tomorrow,' I agreed. 'I'll come and get them then.'

CHAPTER TWO

Roberta Topp's dinner party was not exactly what you might call a Hot Date. But in those days of isolationist self-punishment (as in, if I do all the things I don't really want to do God might take pity and bring him back), I went. She rang to ask us both, not knowing we were no longer together. She rang at the shop, and with Pearl's eye on me I couldn't keep up the pretence any longer. I said, coolly, 'Teddy and I have ceased to be an item, Roberta. He has left me.'

'Damn,' she said.

As a matter of fact, it was quite refreshing after all the other suitably packaged responses.

Roberta liked Teddy at her dinner table because he was interesting, behaved well, looked nice and posed no threat whatsoever to her agenda. In short, he was level-headed, thoroughly normal. And in Roberta's rather facile, high-profile world, you didn't get many of *them* to the pound. Now that he was an editor, presumably, it added to his low-key cachet and made him all the more useful. We had filled in at several of her dinner parties over the years. I never minded. They were always fascinating—if for nothing else, for the sheer *con brio* of her calculations. I don't think she ever ate in company without her brain ticking over.

Mind you, this had its admirable side. When I set up the bookshop about six years ago, just after my father died, Roberta was a tower of strength—Blackpool, Eiffel, with Pisa thrown in. I met her at a book fair, when I had just begun to put my toe in the water, and she gave a talk entitled 'Being a Writer *Can* Mean Being Rich'. At the pre-talk drinks, emboldened, I asked her if that applied to Booksellers too, and was amazed when she inserted a little diversion into her talk all about Where Bookshops Go Wrong. 'Have you got a site in mind?' she asked afterwards. I told her. 'Hopeless,' she said. And rang me two days later with a much better one. 'I'll come and see you about it all.' She said. And she did. She had ideas, ways of getting publishers' discounts, cheaper money, events, and—of course—offered herself (much as the Godfather might gently offer Protection) as the Star of the Opening.

She was quite short, quite chunky, but somehow formidably stately. This came from within, from a deep, unchallenged belief in herself. And also from her imposing, most unsisterly, totally disproportionate bosom. Even her hair never dared venture out of place. She wore it like a helmet of black, in a style Mary Quant made her own, and which, with the honourable exception of Jean Muir, should have been buried along with flares and white plastic boots. Her eyes blinked like a lizard's when she was under duress, and flashed like black guns when someone really upset her. Like critics. Roberta made her money, and a considerable amount of it, as an entrepreneurial novelist. Her speciality was fictionalizing fact, the more gruesome or bizarre the better, and somehow she had tapped the secret soul's desire of a large number of otherwise normal women readers. When an aeroplane crashed in the jungle and the survivors survived by cannibalism, she wrote a novelization of it called *Jungle Fever.* The press renamed it *The Heart is a Lonely Luncher* and Roberta shot her ocular guns off and denounced their perfidy all the way to the bank. With many other such successes to follow.

She once said she looked on me rather as a daughter, a statement to which my mother took great exception. But I think she only meant it in a businesslike sense. If the meek were to inherit the earth, then Roberta was going to be destitute.

But even if the invitation to dinner was not five-star rating, there was something that was even less desirable—and that was for Teddy and Hagnes to be invited instead of me. Over my Practise, Practise, Practise Dead Body. Besides, the evening would be a good opportunity for me to try out my new Sapphic mode.

'Damn,' she said again. And then, with a note of hopefulness, 'Has he got someone else?'

I could picture the lizard eyes blinking. I repeated to myself, Over my Practise, Practise, Practise Dead Body.

'Yes,' I said. 'She's French—with a kind of *mysterious* beauty (God Forgive Me), very feminist in a Baroque way, and excellent at making her point about politics. No money and vegetarian. Unusual for a Frenchwoman. I'm sure you'll like her . . .'

Roberta groaned. I was in.

I wore black leather and Doc Martens and had cropped my hair very short. I'd *like* to say the effect was *gamine*, but I may just have looked ill. Anyway, I looked different. And being there was considerably better than sitting at home weeping and throwing darts at Agnes the Bidet's photograph.

I arrived late (small problem with lacing the Docs) and already the guests were seated at the table. With Roberta smiling down at them as she introduced me, as one might smile down at their prey. She was inclined to shift her bosoms around with the palms of her hands when she was being very earnest. She was mostly very earnest about herself. Sometimes conversation with Roberta was like chatting to Rommel, about Rommel, while he rearranged his big guns. She was doing it now.

'Here is Diana,' she said, plonking me down into a vacant chair. 'Now we can begin . . .'

Agenda flowed from her every pore. But what?

Pearl, who would never be asked to one of Roberta Topp's dinner parties in a million years, had a theory. Pearl's theory was that Roberta was about to launch herself into Good Works. For some time Roberta had been talking wistfully about Fame and Fortune not being enough. She also wanted Posterity. I blamed the Prince of Wales. Ever since he made his opinion felt on the subject of architecture, Roberta had been pensive. And in her speech at a recent Booksellers' Lunch she made full use of his name while declaring,

'Literature does not, necessarily, have to be modern and difficult,' adding with an extravagant simper, 'Take mine . . .'

Pearl, who had accompanied me, said it was a hope devoutly to be wished. Which caused me quite a coughing fit. Pearl does, occasionally, have wit. But no style. Absolutely no style. And she is never at ease with more than one set of cutlery. Put Pearl and Roberta in the same room together and they ignore each other. Pearl thought I should ban her from the shop's shelves. I pointed out that the profit was useful and Pearl merely curled her lip and said, 'Useful Schmooseful.'

Pearl had come late to literature and there was no stopping her.

Watching Roberta now, seated at the dinner table in her gloriously Italian minimalist dining room—which had been Spanish hacienda last time—I was fascinated all over again at the way she batted her breasts about.

Pearl says Roberta draws attention to them because they are the only large things about her and she is basically insecure. Pearl went through the psychology section once. In my opinion a great pity. Nevertheless, I have known leading male novelists lose the thread of their postulations completely when Roberta set to with the juggling. One leading Indian liberal writer once remarked that she was an argument for Fundamentalism, and should cover up. He had done a Uri Geller with a spoon handle during this little speech, and since we were dining at the Connaught after some book bash or other, they practically banned him. The Empire Strikes Back.

Our hostess tonight had, apparently, just learned about the Narrative Arc and was busy expounding it as 'one strong, unbroken thrust'.

To which I muttered, 'Not just a flap with a flaccid willy then?'

The man opposite me, an American, hid a smile, Americans being so polite.

Roberta finished her literary Road to Damascus and then looked about her with the light of Evangelism in her eyes. Here we go, I thought. Here we go. Agenda time.

There are those to whom networking is merely an arrangement of lines and interstices—or possibly a fireside pastime for the lonely fingers of an apple-cheeked maiden aunt. To Roberta it was Breathing. There were six of us sitting around the table, and those lizard eyes held us one by one.

To my right, at the end of the table, was a huge-eyed, hungry-looking woman; one of those eviscerated females who eye you hungrily because they are actually hungry; hungry because they eat so little and seem to be being eaten from within. Desperate. And just who was I to talk? Her copious blonde hair was coiled like snakes upon her head and her blue eyes blinked occasionally with a certain quality that can only be described as

Ill-Fitting Contact Lenses. Her name was Valeria.

She was an illustrator though she called herself an artist; bad ones always do. Illustration has nothing to do with art, of course. It is craft. This is not to say that an artist cannot illustrate—just that an illustrator cannot be an artist. My father was an illustrator, not an artist, and that is what he told me. He also said it was why he could live quite comfortably in Oxshott. An illustrator could, apparently, live in Oxshott. An artist never could. It used to drive my mother to distraction because she wanted to live in Chelsea. Well, she's in Spain now—which is certainly a long way from Oxshott.

That Valeria had designed Roberta's latest book jacket was a safe bet for her presence—but not an explanation—since to Roberta having the designer of her book jacket at table was rather like the Queen inviting the woman who made the curtains to lunch. Besides, it wasn't even a very good jacket. It was passable, but no more. And that was even odder. Roberta was usually very exacting about such things. Yet Ole Pink-Eyes was getting the velvet glove.

Odd.

She was seated next to the polite American, who kept smiling in a clean-cut college-boy way while she engaged him with all her heart, soul and evisceration skills. He listened to

Roberta. She of the blonde coils devoured him with her eyes. I was glad to be free of such indignities.

To my left, and therefore to Roberta's right since she headed the table, was a plump, pink little man with a spotted dicky bow and horn-rimmed spectacles who had done that very sensible thing of the ageing near bald and had his head completely shaved.

'It makes age irrelevant,' I said, by way of congratulation. 'You could be anywhere from forty to sixty-five.'

'I am twenty-seven,' he said, fixing me with the eye of a long-dead fish. A miffed long-dead fish. 'And I merely prefer it this way.' He ran his little plump hand over the dome. 'I have a very good head of hair should I choose.'

Completely humourless.

'Oh,' I said, scrabbling for safety. 'What colour?'

But he returned his attention to Roberta, the miffed fish changing to an adoring prawn.

Roberta had suddenly gone disgustingly girlish. Straining all the possibilities of her sky-blue *decolléte*, she reached over and straightened his tie. Which was already straight. On any other woman this sky-blue garment would have been a sky-blue turtle neck but in Roberta it had met with tension and plunged deep. So, clearly, from the way she eyed him and called him Peterkins, had he. Brought together, no doubt, by a twin lack of humour. They smiled into each other's eyes and I thought I was going to be sick.

'Peterkins is an Arts Oriented Entrepreneur,' she said to the table in general. And then she winked. Also disgustingly. 'More of which, anon.'

An Arts Oriented Entrepreneur with Shifty Little Eyes, I thought. But managed to keep it to myself.

Opposite Peterkins and eyeing me was a small, nut-brown creature called Erna. Wizened from the sun, with skin stretched across her tiny ancient skull, she stared wet-eyed and semi-focused. Most of her concentration was required in staying upright under large quantities of gold jewellery. An Inca princess could not have been more blessed, and she could certainly be that old.

Her glass was empty and not for the first time. We both looked down at it, clutched in her tiny, nut-brown hands, and then she raised it. 'Keeps me warm,' she said. 'Can't stand the cold. Do you know Cape Town?' The accent made me remember checking the provenance of Sainsbury's oranges.

'Nope,' I said sweetly. 'Do you know Mandela?'

Roberta coughed very loudly, filled Erna's glass, and gave me a Look. People are always giving me Looks. Sometimes I go with it, and sometimes I don't. This Look was one to go with.

Erna gazed at me uncomprehendingly for a moment. Then she threw back her head and laughed a cigarette and gin laugh. 'I know Nelson,' she said, 'I know the de Beers, I know the Bothas—I know *everybody.*' She leaned across, peering at me. 'Don't know you,' she said, and she raised her glass a little shakily and gave a smile. 'But I *like* you,' she said, leaning across the table and placing her chin rather precariously on her hand. 'I really *like you . . .*' She narrowed her eyes and tried to focus. 'Are you a boy or a girl?'

Now this, apparently, they *did* all find funny. Ho Ho Ho. Even the Polite American made amused noises. I impersonated a glacier round the table before returning my gaze to Erna, staying silent and looking condescending. She shrugged. 'Never mind, doesn't matter at all. And what is your job going to be?'

'I'm a bookseller. Already.'

She leaned back, smiling. 'Good one,' she said. 'If some people are going to write them then somebody else has to sell them I suppose. Welcome aboard. Roberta dear, I'm glad you've brought her in. I *like* her . . .'You know how a little drop taken can result in a complete stranger suddenly loving you madly. She leaned over and clutched my hand with hers. 'Good,' she said. *'Good.'*

Roberta and Peterkins seemed a little nonplussed by this.

Brought me in? In what?

I wanted to know, but the subject was changed.

Consommé bowls were cleared away. Roberta stood up.

'How's the house-hunting going?' Peterkins said, with horrible false cheer.

Erna waved a thin little wrist. The jewellery rattled. 'No hurry,' she said happily. 'It takes time. And anyway, I like the Savoy.'

Roberta paused at the door, gave a sweet smile and then snapped her eyes open and closed a couple of times like a till. 'You have the Midas touch, Erna,' she said.

'You certainly do,' said Peter the Bald, appearing to address her jewellery. He then gave a surprisingly uninhibited loud squeak. Explained by Erna's leaning across under the table, with a curiously long reach for one so small, and grabbing his manliness. Which she then gave a cheery squeeze. Even my eyes watered. 'I used to have a lot more than that,' she said wickedly.

I waited for his Beloved to smack her one. But No . . .

'Now, now,' said Roberta playfully, metronoming her finger at Erna, and shaking her head with astonishingly good-natured discouragement.

Erna, chuckling huskily, withdrew. The golden bangles flew back down her arm and clinked back into place like coin.

Of course. There was but one explanation

for such tolerance.

Money.

Let those amongst you without sin cast the first stone.

It was compelling. The starburst of rings on Erna's fingers, the shuddering of diamond dewdrops at her throat, and the golden wedges driven through her ears were certainly not without charm. Even I considered asking her where she bought her books.

Roberta looked down her stately nose at me warningly again. And changed the subject. 'Desmond was supposed to be here,' she said, 'but he was delayed on the way. Business I expect. He's in such demand as a journalist . . .' She fluttered her Disney 'n' mascara eyelashes at Erna. 'Ah well, ah well—friends in high places . . .'

Desmond? Friends? Souls in Torment in High Places, more like. The inmates of Kensington Palace or The Mother of Parliaments might smile at him across the tea cups—but mostly they had murder in their heart. And mostly, so did he.

Desmond was a journalist but it was highly unlikely that work or a high place had delayed him. He was camp as a row of tents and given to impersonating Joe Orton whenever possible. No bus queue was safe north of the river if it contained dark-eyed young men of ethnic countenance. No tatty bar was too dark nor too far for his sharp little eyes to go poke-about, and you didn't buy his kind of cottages in the country. He was like something out of Sheridan—but with one saving grace. He really liked women.

When he was working, he was good. His speciality was gossip and style all mixed into satire, and people strewed flowers in his path. An appropriate metaphor. He would choose to cruise, not turn up where he was supposed to be, go missing for days, and eventually manage to supply copy of a devastatingly enticing nature. It was his gift. That and attracting beautiful young men.

Roberta had now dispatched the dirty dishes, returned, and was stroking Peter the Bald's arm. She then peered at me—as if for the first time—eyeing my black leather waistcoat disapprovingly. 'Good Lord,' she said. What *are* you wearing?' She leaned forward, spilling her chest right into Peterkins's side plate.

'Gucci,' I said.

She nodded significantly. 'Very nice too.'

It was actually from Portobello Market.

She gave it a tentative little feel. 'It makes you look quite—well—mannish.'

I shrugged nonchalantly. 'Horses for courses, Roberta,' I said, and just so happened to wink at Valeria who responded like a rabbit caught in headlights.

'Well, well, never mind about Desmond,' said Roberta, leaning back and removing her breasts from the poor defeated Italian porcelain. 'Now I do so want you all to get to know our American guest, Jim Hite. He writes fiction, Erna,' she added loudly. And Erna raised her glass.

'To fiction,' she said, and drained it. 'Like what?'

All eyes were turned towards him. Roberta's, especially, were soft as a mother hen's. 'Go on,' she said encouragingly. And the college-fresh face went to work—deprecating half-smiles, work in progress, firm opinions on the feminine sentence—that sort of thing. Valeria gazed, Erna gazed, Peter the Bald (with hands somewhat protectively stowed beneath the table) gazed—Roberta nudged herself about a bit, thoughtfully, and metaphorically resettled her feathers. She then resumed the lizard mode and just went blink, blink, blink, with deep satisfaction.

Fortunately he was succinct. When he had finished, and it was delightfully clear that Erna was not even sure he had begun, our hostess fixed us all with a significant stare, ending with Valeria. Her palms rotated breastwards with pleasure. 'One should always have at least one literary American at one's gatherings. They do so bring the broader view . . .' She looked at me before I could speak. 'Jim is Yale,' she said. She looked at him. 'And Diana has a bookshop.'

I smiled.

He smiled and said very goodnaturedly, 'Do you sell a lot of American fiction, ma'am?'

Ma'am? How old did you have to be to look a ma'am?

I was about to speak—and quite sharply—when Roberta added, 'Diana sells a lot of *everything*, considering how dinky her little bookshop is.'

'That's just great,' said Erna, enthusiastically. 'I like dinky. Glad to have you in the team.'

Team?

I turned to Roberta for enlightenment. She coughed, looked away, and changed the subject. 'Now, Jim,' she said, 'help yourself to more wine.'

I caught Old Pink Eyes giving me a nervous glance. A slightly puzzled nervous glance. I considered flirting with her—after all, Practise, Practise, Practise. But what to say? Come here often? Take out your contact lenses and I'll make you mine? Courage failed and I offered only, 'Do you know why we are all here?'

'For dinner,' she said simply. Amazing what a private education can produce.

But our hostess was alert. 'Valeria's parents own Hassocks Hall,' she said, practically slinging her breasts earwards. She spoke as if such explanation were the end of the matter.

'Hassocks Hall?'

Roberta bridled magnificently. Peter the Bald coughed. Roberta fluttered the disgusting lashes again. She had obviously learned it as a new trick.

'Hassocks Hall,' she continued, 'is Robert Adam's masterpiece. *Still* privately owned, thank God, but fallen on straitened times. And about to become the centre for a new Academy, the Academy of Forward Fiction. It will be devoted to Clarity of Style, De-Mystifying the Word, and Marketing . . .' She gave Peter the Bald a fond look before fixing me with her Gorgon's eye. 'As with the Prince of Wales, it will not be interested in the *experimental.* Nor funded by government.' This last, apparently, being as disgusting as someone else's used tissue.

I knew the answer, but asked the question anyway. 'And—er—who is going to run this—er—Academy?'

Roberta's eyes widened. She put her small pointy chin in her hand and her reptilian eyes looked surprised. I suppose it was rather like asking Becket who was destined for Martyrdom.

'Why *me* of course . . .' she said. 'And Peterkins. And Erna will match our funding pound for pound.' She picked up a bottle and quickly refilled Erna's glass.

I looked at Roberta. She looked as if she was about to transubstantiate. 'Oh Jesus,' I said, and held out my glass, too.

'Valeria is going to teach illustration. Plain, straightforward *pictures*,' she said firmly. 'And

Jim will head structure and story-line. English and American. It will all be highly organized. And blessed by the most beautiful of settings. Absolutely inspirational.'

Valeria looked at Jim more hungrily than ever.

Roberta tapped the table with her forefinger and repeated, 'Absolutely Inspirational.'

'Or Else . . .' I muttered.

'Pardon?' she said, but I did not rise. She looked fondly at Yale and the hungry one. 'Of course, Lord and Lady Hartley are delighted with the idea.'

Valeria's parents, in my opinion, must be crowing at the idea. No dowry and two old piles off their hands.

The American?

I pondered.

He was talking animatedly to Erna who smiled hazily at his charm. It appeared to be pouring out of a tap. He extolled the virtues of popular New American Realism. He extolled the virtues of popular Nineteenth Century American Fantasy. *The Accidental Tourist* and *A Yankee at the Court of King Arthur* were married on the spot. He was beaming with passion. 'American fiction has a place, ma'am,' he said, 'in the straightforward stakes.'

Erna nodded, wonderingly. Her rings flashed as she groped for meaning in the air.

Yale beamed and raised a glass. 'Here's to

it,' he said, not altogether convincingly. He filled hers anew. He kept right on smiling. By comparison, the rottenness in Denmark was sweet as a bed of roses. Ah well, I sipped my wine, what wasn't corruptible nowadays? And, now that Teddy had gone, who, frankly, cared?

'And you?' said Erna to me suddenly, and with surprising aplomb.

I realized that the American had refilled her glass from a water bottle. I thought that was rather caring of him.

'Me? Nothing,' I said, for no apparent reason feeling close to tears. 'Me, nothing, nothing at all.'

Erna said, 'I used to talk like that when my Howie died. Somebody died on you?'

I tried to look butch and stern. And failed. A tear escaped.

'Not exactly,' I said.

She made a little thinking face and then brought the flat of her hand down on the table. Everybody jumped. 'I know,' she said.

'Know what?' said Roberta sharply.

'I know exactly what we need.' Thump went the little brown hand again. 'We need a Library.'

Roberta and Peter the Bald exchanged raised eyebrows. Patiently, Roberta said, 'They already have a Library at Hassocks Hall. A very *good* Library. Don't they Valeria?'

Valeria, tearing her eyes away from Jim, nodded vigorously.

'All stately homes have libraries, Erna,' she said, even more patiently, 'in this country.'

'Yes,' said Erna, quite patiently herself. 'But only with old books. Let's have a new one. Let's have the Erna Werner Foundation Library. And this . . . er'—she peered—'er . . . can set it up.' She clapped her hands together. 'Perfect,' she said. 'How about it?'

'No,' said Roberta.

'Yes,' said I.

'Good, good,' she said. 'Then that's all settled.'

I dropped butch and stern and opened my mouth to rescind. Then I thought, what the Hell—Teddy was Married, Life was Empty. Setting up a modern library might be really interesting. Better than the yawning gap called Future Plans, anyway.

'OK,' I said. 'OK. It will give me something to live for.' And I was only half joking.

Roberta stood up. 'Broken hearts are beastly, aren't they,' she said briskly. The effect being much as if she had remarked to Jackie Kennedy that the bang must have startled her.

Jim from Yale was looking at me and opened his mouth to speak.

'Now Jim,' said Roberta, with a definite edge of warning. 'You are meant to attend to Valeria.'

She exited.

Jim took care of Valeria by talking to her

about T. S. Eliot, apparently his hero. She responded with wide eyes and an expression that translated as hanging on his every word.

More drink was taken.

One thing was for sure—my feelings for Roberta would never be Sapphic. I thought about having a Practise with Erna but just then she took out her top teeth and stared at them speculatively; a feeling, wholly unakin to desire, entered my vitals. Compounded by her squinting at the pearl and pink-gummed gnashers before removing, with the nail of her little finger, a morsel of the pre-prandial Beluga.

I slid my eyes sideways. Now or never. 'Valeria,' I said, 'is a beautiful name.'

I saw Yale blink. But she of the beautiful name just looked at me nervously with her inflamed blue eyes and continued to look hungry. Could this be erotic?

'Very beautiful,' I added.

Erna smiled on benignly. In Erna's case twice, since she was still clasping her grinning dentals in her hand.

'So tell me, Valeria, about yourself . . .' I dwelled upon her name as if it were pure poetry.

She looked stumped, as women will. 'What do you mean?' she said.

I told her.

She offered horse-riding and sketching.

Yale leaned back, watching. I continued as

heartily as I could.

'How interesting,' I said. 'Do go on.'

She looked stumped again. It was not a pretty sight. Then, enlightenment. Fashion. She made her own frocks.

I leaned over and fingered the print of her sleeve, a fabric and garment in which a Hardy heroine pottering in the fields would have been quite at home. 'Lovely,' I said. 'Perfectly lovely.'

I did not *quite* have the courage to look deep into her eyes. My admiration for the hunting male rose in leaps and bounds. What they go through. Why not just say, Here's a pair of earrings/box of Milk Tray, now let's get on with it . . . ?

She blushed. I gave her a look but was not sure if, in her myopia, she could read it. I was just having another go, narrowing the eyes and whatnot, when Yale touched her sleeve and said, 'You look very beautiful in candlelight.' And her entire face glowed with pleasure.

A rival! We'd see about that.

I glared at him. He met my glare with bland and innocent eyes. I leaned closer towards her. 'Do you have your own horse?'

Unfortunately it came out considerably blunter than it had sounded in my head.

She wrested her hungering gaze from Yale and informed me she now used the stables near to Hassocks Hall. They got feed from Thurrocks.

Well that was jolly interesting. Thurrocks. Must remember that. Then we both looked stumped again. Perhaps I should take her hand and squeeze it?

'I'd like to ride while I'm here,' said Yale.

'Me too,' I said, grabbing at her fingers. And missing. She looked peculiarly startled and fastened them around her wine glass.

'Looks like we both want lessons,' said Yale cheerfully. 'In all kinds of areas.' And he tapped my glass with his.

I leaned back, brought my Doc Martened boot up so that I now sat in the careless pose of a Cornish Pisky, and tried to look above it all. Valeria was now uncontainable on the subject of withers and hacking and crops. ' . . . and Mummy and Daddy just thought it was Absolutely Not On to give up the Hall so we were terribly grateful to Roberta . . .'

Mummy and Daddy?

The Cornish Pisky, renowned for his ability to turn milk sour if he chooses, had entered more than my legs. 'Valeria,' I said, 'is the name of that vile-smelling shrub with the horrid little flowers that cats and dogs love so much. Isn't it?'

She blinked.

Yale made a noise, not altogether of approval.

'It's a charming name,' he said.

I squirmed a bit and felt obliged to add, '*Quite pretty . . .*'

He leaned forward and tapped my boot heel. 'You might at least be gallant.' he said. 'Or else stick to what you know in future.'

I crossed my arms, stuck out my chin, and sniffed.

'Here's a true story,' he said, suddenly. His open, goodnatured face became serious.

'Forward Fiction,' I muttered.

But he raised his finger for silence, and began.

'There is an Albatross, who should live quite happily in the Falklands with all the other Albatrosses. But instead, this Albatross wants to be a Gannet. So he leaves the Falklands and flies to Orkney and tries to be a Gannet along with all the other Gannets—but they don't want him and won't mate with him and beat up on him all the time. Kind people return the Albatross to the Falklands, and try to induce a sense of Albatrossness in him, but he will not hear of it. He returns to Orkney and makes more miserable efforts to fool those Gannets. Back and forth, back and forth. Miserable. He spends all his time being sad and confused and not quite knowing where he is.' He stopped and sipped his wine. 'Now isn't that a real shame?'

'Tiring,' I said. 'All that flying around. Anyway, all this is getting horribly close to a dinner party in an Iris Murdoch novel. Soon someone called Romilly will turn up and say something very dull about God.'

From then on I sulked until Roberta returned. Bearing food.

'I didn't understand any of that,' said Valeria. 'Those poor birds.'

And she went back to gazing at Yale.

Between mouthfuls of roast squirrel with walnuts, the latest and most ecologically sound dinner dish, he said, 'It's just about being comfortable with yourself. Knowing who you are . . .'

I kept my eyes on my plate. God those Americans can be earnest.

Later, Roberta sensitively asked, 'And how is Teddy despite it all?'

'I'll let you know. I'm having dinner with them tomorrow.'

At least it surprised her. 'That's very big of you.'

'Oh, no hard feelings,' I said, thinking this was true because I only had soft, limp, soggy ones.

She resettled her breasts and returned to her plate. 'Good,' she said, sawing into the dead flesh. 'He could be useful to us. Especially now he's the Editor. His subscription list would be very valuable. And then there's sponsorship.' Sometimes she really did stretch our tenuous friendship a mite too far. But at least, as I reminded myself, life around Roberta was always *interesting.* I suppose that was the attraction.

Peter the Bald raised his glass. He was really

creepy and made me think of the Brides in the Bath murderer at Madame Tussaud's with his cold eyes and pink damp flesh. Or Uriah Heep. 'To the most wonderful, clever woman,' he said. 'And to the marriage of Business and the Arts. Success to Her, Success to Clarity—and Success to Hassocks Hall.'

She chinked her glass with his, and looked down. 'Thank you,' she said, with a modest little flutter. 'But I would never have thought of it without you.'

'And *I* would never have thought of it if I had not heard you give that terrific speech . . .'

'*And* you found Erna.' She smiled upon her fondly, but the little wizened head, with its clouds of suspiciously black hair, was bent over her plate, and she was totally absorbed in trying to get a piece of nut to stay on her fork. Roberta returned her gaze to her beloved. '*Dear* Peterkins,' she said softly. 'It has all been because of your initiative.' And off went those fluttering lashes again.

I nearly fell off my chair. I had never known Roberta defer to anyone. At best, in matters of other people's ideas, she would claim joint first. If she had been even vaguely acquainted with Joseph Arkwright we'd have had a spinning-Roberta. But here she was, going all fluttery. My big, strong, shrewd Roberta Topp, after forty-odd years of avoidance, had fallen at the hurdle called Love. What an absolutely terrifying thought. If she was not inviolable, then what hope was there for the rest of us?

'Dearest Peterkins,' she went on meekly. 'We are in your hands.'

Whereupon she took his damp little paw and squeezed it to her breast.

If love had been a long time coming, she had certainly been saving up for it. I thought back to some of the blokes with whom she had dallied over the years—usually large, rich and foreign so they did not get in the way. And now *this*.

Romilly on God—how I longed for him.

I excused myself early, using Pearl's uncertain timetable as an excuse. Her unexplained status was always useful. Bugger Clarity.

Yale stood up politely as I left and said, 'Great to meet you,' Peter the Bald seemed not to notice, Erna said something approximating to See You Soon but it could have been an Afrikaaner greeting or a snippet from Zulu poetics. The only words of hers I could definitely make out were that it was nice to have some young folk on the team. At which Roberta bridled, and Valeria eyed me warily while leaning closer towards Yale. I gave her a wink. It was the least I could do. Practise, Practise, Practise.

Roberta made me declare myself publicly committed to Hassocks Hall and said she would be in touch. Rather than stay a moment longer I would have sworn allegiance to a small public convenience in Tonbridge Wells. I said Yes and ran. As soon as the front door banged shut, I was down the steps, out into the lonely, silent, starry night, and awash, yet again, with tears. I never wanted to see any of them again. It had just been a temporary madness.

And for dessert? A little madness of a more permanent kind. Tomorrow the newly-weds.

CHAPTER THREE

I arrived with one bottle of champagne inside me, and one in my hand, positively willing any pimply whey-faced young policeman I met during the drive to stop me. After all, if I was arrested, I wouldn't have to go. As usual, just when you want a policeman, there is never one in sight.

I wish I could say that I threw up on the new mint-green carpet. It is a very particular agony seeing strange soft furnishings in a place that has once been yours. But I only swayed about a bit.

Without benefit of much focus it was hard to see if the two lovebirds looked sweet or not. I suspect they looked frightened. After all, the shin hairs had grown, the cut-off trousers showed their springing abundance, and my eyebrows were now expressing the kind of enraptured greeting towards each other that Italian and French engineers make when their tunnellings meet perfectly in the middle of a mountain.

The walls, when I lived there, were white; the cornicing when I lived there was white; the windows were perfectly well endowed with shutters which were also white; and it reminded me of my theory that only people with colourless lives need to colour up their surroundings. We of the white persuasion are singingly vital enough. I believe I pointed this out to them.

Agnes was a florist. A florist who seemed not to favour flowers very much. I believe I also pointed this factor out to them. She tended to do things with bits of wire and twigs and distressed pots that all ended up looking like a brain on a stick. There were several of these dotted around. I think I remember leaning on one at some point and that it did not respond very stoutly. And I think I remember Teddy's face looking rather cross. I tickled him under the chin. I do remember that. I tickled him under the chin because it was the way I always cheered him up. Tickle, tickle, tickle, I went. He did not seem amused.

We spoke of many things. Harrogate was certainly mentioned because I recall asking them if they had brought me back any toffee. The answer being negative, I responded along the lines of their being a pair of mean old turds. It was shortly after this, I think, that I left. I believe I tripped over a defunct floral arrangement on the way and I think I found this quite amusing.

I remember realizing, as I struggled out into the night, how little he cared for me now, for was he not letting me drive home drunk? And was he not quite unbothered if I killed myself? In the past he would have hidden the keys or insisted, yes *insisted*, that he drive me. How horrible is the passing away of another's affection for it leaves you in the coldest, draughtiest corridors of life, shut out from that familiar, warm room within, the one that you thought would always be yours.

I tottered off to my car with two full plastic bags, one box, a small suitcase and an old Hermès shoulder bag—the first thing Teddy ever bought me when we went to Paris.

'Fuck Paris,' I said as I stuffed everything into the back of the Fiat and gave the Hermès a bit of a kick into place.

'Steady love,' said a passing bloke. 'We're in the Common Market now . . .' But he kept on passing. There was much to be said for dressing butch. Even if the heart and mind were less convinced after meeting Valeria.

I reached home in that shameful and miraculous way you do when you are completely plastered and put the car on automatic pilot. And then, of course, I had to go through all the wretched paraphernalia I had collected. It smelled of Agnes Yaudet, and I *swear* she had doused everything with her perfume. I thought I might just throw the whole lot away, unopened, but we humans are curious animals. If comparisons are odious, so are lists, but here is a selection: how she must have enjoyed putting this lot together.

old knickers with suspect elastic
framed photograph of me in Edwardian motoring outfit grinning from behind the wheel of a 1904 something
seventeen letters, Teddy's fair hand, in a fancy Italian chocolate box
framed ballooning diploma
menu from Ristorante Flavio, Amalfi
red leather jacket studded on back with the legend Ted and Di
spare packet of pills, contraceptive variety
a solitary expensive amber earring, other lost
a cassette of Brahms's Requiem
two brassières, not in the pink, which I would have publicly disowned, and which Boot Features had included in the bag to remind me what a disgusting old slag I was
a mug saying *Love is* . . . one of a pair . . .
art deco tulip vase, cracked
black suede boots, Armani, also present from Teddy; much decayed at heel
tweezers
book of Irish love poetry

Just the odds and sods left lying around when I moved out, overlooked in the magnificent and confident huff of my departure. Keep The Sodding Flat It Would Make Me Vomit To Continue Living Here, I said, and then fondly waited for the supplicatory telephone call in the night to my horrid, because temporary, first-floor flat in Putney.

It never came, of course, and now here I was, a strange assortment of articles strewn around on the tobacco-coloured carpet, the noise of the buses outside pounding the mushroom-soup walls, still in the horrid, now permanent, first-floor flat in Putney, fingering my way through a little heap of memories. Everything contains its opposite. Newton and Nature have their laws, I have mine. I wish it were not so—but there you are.

Great Joy: Great Misery
Great Love: Great Hate
Great Ease: Great Pain

The one can never exist without the other. As in the human condition, so in nature. Good contains its Bad. There are always mushrooms and toadstools, sweet blackberries and belladonna. And an end is also a beginning, as Eliot would have it.

I tried to think positive. I tried to think that these opposites can also be reversed. No Great

Joy, unless you have had Great Pain, etc. etc. And was doing quite well as I picked my way randomly through the pathetic pile of goods.

The menu, the chocolate box of letters. Such things were so tangible, so irreversible—caught in amber—I touched the earring. The memories hurt. And here was the cassette of Brahms's Requiem that my father gave me, years ago. I had played almost no music since I came to this new flat. Apart from the very occasional, very loud burst of something to blank out the silence. Mostly I just sat and stared, or went out, or scrunched up among the cushions on the slightly grubby taupe (a colour which should not exist) settee and watched TV detectives and soaps.

In my highly mawkish state that night it suddenly seemed entirely appropriate to play the Requiem. It was written as a consolation for the living, wasn't it, as well as the dead? 'Blessed are they that mourn, for they shall be comforted.' I knew it from happier, pre-Teddy times anyway, so I had a right to reinstate it. In fact, I had introduced it to Teddy so I needed to reclaim it. He loved it—and had bought a wonderful new recording which he no doubt now played for his horrible wife.

Well, it was mine. Not hers. And not his. It was mine from Before. I put it on. Volume loud. And waited for the consolation. Not a hope. As soon as it began, I no longer sat on a tobacco-coloured carpet, within mushroom-soup walls, a slight pounding in my head betokening a hangover. Now I lay in a white sunlit bed, beneath a familiar window: our flat one morning in spring. Beside me, glued to my shape as I was to his, lay Teddy—eyes closed, lips smiling, hand caressing my shoulder and the side of my neck.

I squeezed my eyes to eradicate the picture. I squeezed my cerebrals to stop the signals. And yet we were still there, together, lying in love, and it was far too real. The grandeur that is the human brain, unlike its wimpish computer counterpart, has a random, almost infinite memory that is quite beyond control. I did not want to remember but I could not forget. So I listened, right to the last final note, and not once was I anywhere but in that bed, with that man, on that morning. And now he was lying there with someone else. What was it Ingrid Bergman said? Or was it Ingmar? That to be happy a woman requires good health and a bad memory? I put the cassette back in its case. Was it to be no more Requiem too?

I went out for a walk, well, a bit of a stagger really, to think about it. It was cold enough to sharpen the senses and dull old Putney Bridge looked unusually appealing lit up and reflected in the black swell. This particular bit of the river, along the towpath, had seen much somnambulist action, many dark thoughts on sleepless nights. I flicked a stone into the water with my toe. And it had gone on long enough.

Something must be done. I had to get my life back.

I walked on a little way. I began to think of the Brahms Requiem as a metaphor for everything from which I had become excluded. If I could get that Brahms back—quite simply—I would be cured. Once I could listen to it again, with pleasure, and without the pain of memory, the future would shine. How to effect this was not forthcoming but for the moment I was content with the simple theory. Get Back Brahms and the rest of the world would fall into shape again. And on that hopeful, if somewhat inconclusive, note, I turned back and walked slowly towards the flat. Dark as it was, and empty of anything save myself and the rustling trees, the running river, I was not afraid. Grief made me invincible. Whoever was running my life from Up There was certainly not going to bother with hitting me when I was down. What they liked to do was to wait until I was happy—really happy—and *then* strike.

Bootface-the-frog met Teddy at the Earls Court Motor Show. That was a fact. My mother was in London with shingles at the time. That was also a fact. I did not go to Earls Court with Teddy because I played the dutiful daughter and stayed with my mother instead. Fact. Fact. Fact. My mother could have had her shingles in Spain perfectly easily. Just slipped back on the plane with a scarf round her face and no one would have been any the wiser. If she had done that, then none of this miserable, rotten, horrible stuff would have happened. I kicked at more stones. Mothers!

On having this rather shrilly pointed out to her, she had just said, in that *kind* voice of hers, 'It was probably Fate . . . You'll meet someone else. Someone who will suit you better . . .' And the famous phrase, so beloved of boring sages everywhere. 'You're young. You'll get over it.'

I ran that through my skull during the first days of separation when I parked my car in the old street and sat staring at the night-blank windows of our flat, imagining Teddy and Bootface bonking away inside. I did that for several nights in a row after I moved out. Until I got asked, once too often, if I was offering a French.

I thought about that bagful of nothingness I had collected earlier. All those objects, all those memories. It reminded me of a childhood game we used to play, of turning an unlikely group of objects into a composite tale. I was always very good at it, very inventive. For example, if you were given Mirror; Bucket; Vicar, you might combine it thus.

One day a French bint called Agnes Yaudet looked into her Mirror and was so horrified by what she saw that she immediately ran out into the garden and put her head into a Bucket. The Vicar coming along the road with his collecting tin was too late to save her and he buried her the next day. And everyone was happy again.

I smiled. Maybe all I needed was to exact some revenge. Tyre slashing, hate mail, that sort of thing—but no. That way lies Holloway or committal as a fruit cake. Things were bad. But not that bad. Getting Back Brahms was the solution. But how?

I mounted the steps to the dirty front door, which reminded me of T. S. Eliot—'Prepare for life, the last twist of the knife.' Yale had quoted it. By now Valeria was probably attempting to memorize the Complete Works. More fool him. If you love something, you should keep it to yourself. No more caring and sharing for me.

I put the Brahms cassette away in a drawer. It would not stay nestling among the spare lightbulbs and unnecessary horticultural equipment for long, I vowed, and meanwhile I would discuss the possibilities of its redemption with Pearl, though she would probably be sour. She never seemed to agree wholeheartedly with my ideas. Time the Great Healer was the best she had come up with. Oh, the *elderly.* Time may be the Great Healer, but you can short-circuit things.

I got into bed, remembered our happiness in Amalfi and the evening we dined at the Ristorante Flavio, and cried myself to sleep. Again.

CHAPTER FOUR

Brahms had his sorrows too. I had always been fond of Brahms's music, but impatient with him for suffering forty years of unrequited love over the priggish Widow Schumann. Over the next few days I began to have a creeping affinity with him. What if my feelings for Teddy endured in the same way? It was possible. Like Brahms with Clara, when I saw Teddy it was love at first sight. Like Brahms with Clara, it did not, exactly, seem to be diminishing. Like Brahms with Clara, it had become very much one-way.

Teddy came to my twenty-seventh birthday party. My father had just died, I had bought a bookshop, and painlessly lost my current boyfriend to a job in Leeds. The party was a way of announcing to the world that I was back in it again. He sat on the arm of my chair, broke it and blushed. I said it was my favourite piece of furniture. Actually it was one of a number of hired chairs, which someone eventually pointed out to him. I thought it was funny—I could be cruel in those days—but he was mortified. He walked away.

It took me all night to persuade him to forgive me. Usually I would have given up after half an hour. Once persuaded to stay, he promised he would never let me go. Come soon to my bed . . . Now he is with someone who puts dead foliar brains on to sticks and calls them floral art and they eat rocket salad in Tim-on-the-River. Nothing makes sense any more.

Teddy calmed me down. My mother said he did this too much, but what did she know? Only occasionally I might do something a bit outrageous at one of his press launches—like the old me, just to say I existed in my own right—but on the whole he tolerated it. He was probably the man to have babies with, but I wasn't ready for that. I liked the shop, and I liked spending money on fun. My mother always said Don't Worry About It Yet—but what did she know, running off almost as soon as she was widowed, tucked away twixt the Sea and Sierra Nevada? When Teddy and I talked about it I could always say that we had years and years and years ahead in which to decide. Grudgingly he agreed. It had seemed that way then.

Occasionally I felt dulled. I had one of those dullish feelings not so long before he met Agnes. On a whim, I went out to dinner with a publisher's rep without telling him—just for the hell of it really. No more than that. He saw us in the restaurant. He waited for me to tell him. And he may have seen me let the man hold my hand. Eventually he mentioned it. I shrugged it off. As I said, it was nothing.

But Fidelity. It never quite recovers, does it.

Though he said he was fine. If I could have my life reeled back again, this last is the action I would erase. Or maybe M. et Mme Yaudet's raw sex in Normandy, twenty-eight years ago. Sometimes things get dented and you never get the chance to straighten them out again.

At least Clara Schumann never went off and married a man with a face like a pig's boot, nor shoved Brahms's possessions back at him with a cheery wave of goodbye and who cares if you kill yourself as you weave your way home. And she certainly never flaunted a new lover in front of his nose at a Very Public Party. That was one of the worst moments of my life. I looked up, and there they were. One minute I was talking to a Scandinavian playwright about Ibsen's burden. The next I was down on all fours pretending to look for a contact lens. With my old friend Buffy saying loudly, 'But Diana—you don't wear them . . .' It was Hell. No, Clara might have rejected Brahms, but she never went and married anybody *else. She* knew how to behave, did Clara.

One of my recurrent nightmares was pregnancy. Not mine, Amphibian Features'. I went cold at the possibility. And this was another thing Clara Schumann did not do. Having already popped out the required children by her honourable, deceased spouse, she did not go on to breed more, adding insult to injury by flaunting them under Brahms's nose. In prospect of *that* he had a far easier ride than me.

I was convinced, in my dreams, that Agnes Yaudet was *barren.* Oh-dear-me-shame. Had they actually revoked Henry VIII's rules for that? But alas, I held out little hope in reality. If I know French women—they knock them out like rabbits in a field, slip into a little Chanel number, nip off to catch the 8.22 into the centre of Paris to continue their high-powered work in Finance, and visit their lover on the side before a quick blow-dry at the hairdresser. For which the Rout of Waterloo is no real compensation.

I feared there would be little tadpoles one day soon. And pictures of them all over *Wheels* in dinky little bonnets (two sorts of bonnets now, geddit?), presumably pulled down ever so low on their faces to hide any resemblance to their mother.

Angry? Hurt? Betrayed? Moi? How could you think such a thing? Had Teddy not, after all, been entirely honest about Agnes?

'Why?' I wanted to know.

'Lust?' he replied with a little shrug.

'Then have your lust,' I said. 'But don't leave . . .'

'Lust, turning into love,' he replied.

Why—if God is so keen on Truth—if God is so keen on Truth that He actually likes to think of Himself as Truth itself—does He make it *hurt* so much? Same reason chocolate is fattening, I suppose.

Well, I would get back the Requiem and I would *not* end up like Brahms. 'There goes poor old Johannes,' whispered the cognoscenti of Hamburg, Detmold, Vienna, for over forty years. 'Crusty old sod. He never recovered from Clara you know . . .'

I might also get back my libido. Since Teddy left I had forgotten what lust was and just sat around like a torpid houri past her sell-by date. Also, Pearl seemed to think I was drinking too much. She was none too sympathetic about my champagne headache after my visit to their flat and she said that I was beginning to have too many of them.

Very Chapel, our Pearl.

I wasn't what you would call a *serious* drinker; not what you would call a potential *lush*. These were temporary times, I pointed out, just temporary times . . . She folded her arms in that way of hers and said, just make sure: I might have sacked her, but it was her day off, which seemed unethical. Nevertheless, she had a point. She quite often does. Dignity, in my opinion, is everything. She Kept Her Dignity is what I should like written on my tombstone. Dignity is good for a broken heart. Take a little more water with it then, said Pearl. Pearl can be very *sobering* sometimes.

Heart is interesting. If we are going to endow that ugly lump of flesh with its pumping aortals as our seat of love, anything goes. Post-modernism all the way. The heart is second only to the long intestine for comic effect if you look at it objectively. I said to Pearl that I thought the kidneys were more appropriate—such pretty curves—such a sweet dark lilac colour laid out in their lacy caul—ready wrapped for the lover, so to speak.

Pearl looked at me as if I had a long grey beard and glitt'ring eye. 'Why don't you try it with the next one?' she said. 'Try saying, "Darling, take my life, my soul, my kidneys," and see where it gets you.'

Sour, as I say. Very sour.

*　　*　　*

Pearl, she of the pronouncements, is the cleaner and general factotum at the bookshop. The philosophical treasures that fall from her mouth are legion. Most of what she says I discount. She can be very obtuse, which I always tell her is due to her being working class and unable to grasp things. Take her attitude to My Great Matter.

She had a very soft spot for Teddy and a view of our relationship's demise that I can only say felt disloyal. When a friend and—more to the point perhaps—one whose wages you pay says, on hearing your ex-partner-over-whom-you-still-bite-the-pillow has married another, 'I'm not surprised . . .' You are brought up a little short in the entrustment stakes.

I could, of course, bring her to heel simply by saying we were going to springclean the children's corner, but the results of last night's champagne had left me no stamina for the fall-out. To have Pearl thumping about with the wash-o-wipe for those stubborn stains was a bad idea. As I said, she was not particularly sympathetic on the subject of my hangovers.

'Not surprised? Why do you say that?' I asked.

'Because I'm not. Surprised.'

Which seemed reasonable. The dreadful lateral logic of the cleaning classes. I rephrased it. 'Why are you not surprised?'

'Because people change.' She flicked a duster over the A-Ds. 'And he never really stood up to you.'

'Pearl,' I said. 'You're fired.'

'It'd be wrongful dismissal,' she said, back at the desk, gliding her duster lightly around the computer, which she never touches and refuses to go near.

'The screen is smeared, Pearl,' I say, from time to time, but ever since she found out they carry viruses she only hands me a cloth and calls them Nasty Things.

'I did not, by the way, take him for granted.'

'You did.'

'Collect your wages at the end of the week,' I said, leafing through *Publishing World*. 'And buy a pair of spectacles with them.'

I peered closer at the page. 'Ooh, look at

this.' There was a piece on Hassocks Hall: 'Roberta Topp fronts a new-style creativity centre in the heart of rural Heston . . .' Fronts, I thought, being the operative word.

I had kept a very low profile since that evening and had definitely changed my mind about being involved. Little and rarely was how I preferred Roberta, and I think she felt the same about me. I'll bet quite a lot of friendships are forged this way.

'Oh and before you go,' I said, not looking up, 'you can throw out all the Roberta Topps.' I went on reading.

There was a scuffling and a thudding behind me. I turned. Pearl had, indeed, cleared all the fat, garish books off S–Z, about ten of them, and was dumping them in a bin liner.

I gazed in astonishment. 'What are you *doing*?'

'Dumping the Topps. Like you said.'

I started to pick them out and replace them. 'You have no concept of irony,' I said. 'I cannot think why, for the lower classes once understood the likes of Hamlet you know.'

'Chucking out the Topps is about the first *sensible* thing you've suggested since he went,' she replied firmly. 'You must be on the mend.'

She made no move to retrieve the books. During her years at the shop Pearl has made full use of the facilities. I occasionally threaten her with a library fee.

I picked up Roberta's latest. It was about a

woman hostage in Beirut who after many jolly adventures falls in love with her captor, who fortunately returns the compliment and whisks her away to freedom, with many jolly adventures. Quite a few of the jolly adventures include jolly sex. It had sold jolly well. I looked at Valeria's illustration. A pair of lovers vaguely visible in the misty tops of an English cornfield that had a bit of Monet about it. Lovers naked, but nothing focused. I think it was meant to be somewhere near Hebron.

Valeria.

'Lovely man,' said Pearl, hand on hip and staring into the bin. 'Lovely.' Then she shook her head. 'But not for you.'

'Obviously,' I said sourly.

The cornfield lovers went fuzzy. 'Oh Pearl,' I said, 'I still love him.'

She went on with her dusting as if she were enacting it and found a particularly difficult spot on the shelf to rub. 'It's a good job for both of you in the end,' she said.

'And don't come back here asking for a reference.' I returned to the *Publishing World* article. 'So what can I do?'

'Forget him. Let it go. He was a puppy when you got him and now he's a full-grown dog.'

I looked at Pearl.

She looked at me.

She put her duster over her face to cover her confusion.

'Oh my Gawd,' she said.

And we burst out laughing.
Hassocks Hall indeed.
Roberta Topp indeed.
I peered more closely at the photograph. Mind you—the place itself looked *beautiful* . . .
I smiled. I shook my head. Plenty of other ways to fill my time.
As If . . .

CHAPTER FIVE

Roberta was persuasive. She called at the bookshop, first inspecting the shelves to see if her books were there. I gave Pearl a Look and glanced down at the waste bin. Pearl, quite unrepentant, merely sniffed and went out to the back to make tea.

As soon as she was gone, Roberta said, 'It's our first fundraising thrust.' And then, as if for emphasis, she thrust out her own proud chest and drew herself up to maximum height. Since this only brought us eyeball to eyeball, despite her high heels and my low ones, it was just as well she had the extra lateral. It certainly helped her to compel.

'Erna is very keen to have you,' she said. '*Very* . . .' She warmed a little, even showing a slight hint of respect and approval. 'And we need you on the team. You will be very good.' This last was said more as a threat than a compliment.

Roberta once gave a cub journalist One Look when a question did not suit her and I swear I heard his testicles drop off. So I agreed. I certainly had nothing to lose. And the greenness of early summer made me restless in the evenings.

'It's contemporary art. Very sexy at the moment. Nothing difficult. Get there early. Chat them up. Cheque books with menaces and don't let me down.'

'Will do,' I said, and practically saluted.

'Good *girl*,' said Roberta, as if to a well-behaved Corgi bitch.

* * *

I slipped off my sandals and felt the thick, damp grass with my toes. That very English dampness of evening dew after a hot early summer's day. Possibly there were still *some* things in the world worth getting up for, but only possibly.

I had not been getting on too well with Practise, Practise, Practise, and apart from the continuing, grinding pain of loss, I was bored. The thing that chroniclers of lost love tend to ignore is the unromantic aspect of boredom. Low spirits are dreary. *Continuing* low spirits are *ineffably* dreary. With not a high in sight, the *ennui* was crippling. Watching paint dry was a tempting alternative. I assumed that

Practise, Practise, Practise would produce a frisson or two. But alas—no.

I had honestly tried.

I had sat on a high stool in a wine bar looking purposeful, but the nearest I got to ecstatic union was when an unsmiling woman with short dark hair and a bad-tempered look about her moved her stool next to mine and asked for a light.

She stuck an extraordinarily long, thin, brown cigarette into her mouth, leaned forward, and gave me a Penetrating Look. I looked back with what I hoped was a Penetrating Ardour, only to hear myself whisper seductively that I did not smoke, that I thought it was a silly habit, and why didn't she just Give Up? Which, of course, she did. By moving her stool back to the other side of the bar and suggesting, none too politely, as she went that I go back to Sunday School.

It was no good at the gym, either. I had been around there for so long that I was just another piece of moving cellulite. If I had suddenly made a lunge at one of the female supervisors they would have laughed their Aertex polos off. You cannot do the *Daily Mail* crossword with folk one moment and try to get inside their running shorts the next. Well—not if you want to come back and use the Quad Kick Pulley again.

Besides, I had no idea who was and who wasn't. And when I asked my lesbian friend for some identification rulings—was there, for example, a special way of shaking hands or chewing gum—she, who had bravely gone to live in Wisbech because she would stick out for miles, apart from laughing, only offered the unhelpful suggestion that 'they come in all sorts, duckie, just like everybody else . . .' Which conjured strange pictures of just what really was in those boxes of liquorice nowadays.

So—here I was at Hassocks Hall. The fundraising evening had arrived and I had abandoned the boots and hairy legs on the basis that—despite being an ardent feminist to my pelvic floor, and one who would have stood on the right-hand side of Emmeline P, sword unsheathed, too—I was only prepared to chain myself to the railings if the shackled ankles I later displayed in Holloway while being force-fed were unhirsute.

I squidged my bare toes again. Difficult to slip off sixteen holes of bovver boot to do so, easy in my little Italian sandal numbers in pink calf.

Yes.

Pink.

Because, whilst a pair of strappy sandals clutched in the hand as you wander about *plein air* in polite assembly is acceptable, a pair of very large black boots strung about one's neck seems, to continue the theme, somewhat Albatrossian.

And because if, since the evening was warm, I was going to wear the snappy white linen number, of which there was not a lot, it seemed a burlesque to put on boots.

So—here, upon this cool terrace, sandals in one hand, glass of very cold champagne in the other, one could make a reasonable argument for the proposal that God was indeed in his heaven and all was reasonably satisfactory with the world. It was an enchanted setting, steeped in the pride and honour of centuries. No wonder Roberta was pleased with it.

Beyond the velvety lawn and ha-ha grazed golden cattle, sweet-eyed, glistening-mouthed, as pastorally perfect as any De Cuyp. None of your small-headed Friesians with their domino effect here. This was England in the eighteenth century—cows were cow-shaped and caramel-coloured and gave milk so rich that a breakfast bowl could see you through the day.

The sun, hazed by thin cloud, shone benignly on the early evening peace, and the red brick of the earlier Tudor outbuildings glowed like ruddy-cheeked country cousins next to the cool, austere countenance of the main Adam house behind me. In short, perfect evening, perfect vista and almost Et in Arcadia Ego?

Almost. But something had ruptured Eden. Well, some *things* actually.

Unfortunately, it was the Art.

Milton's 'Whence, and what art thou, execrable Shape,' was entirely appropriate. For placed around the dewy greensward were unmistakably execrable Shapes. Lumps of something. But lumps of what?

Graves's *Welsh Incident* also came to mind

> 'What were they then?'
> 'All sorts of queer things,
> Things never seen or heard or
>   written about . . .'
> 'Describe just one of them.'
> 'I am unable . . .'

But I'll try. Some were human size, some dog size, flat ones, undulating ones, stone ones, wooden ones, metal and glass—a few with their bits spread around like entrails and one or two spouting water. This was Roberta's mixed sculpture exhibition. Everything for sale. Rodin, Brancusi, Moore, might never have been.

Graves's *Welsh Incident* quite often came to mind when a Heritage Committee was let loose on the selection. Rather like Herod the Great being asked to choose the competitors in a beautiful baby competition, the resulting exhibits are nearly always unedifying. As if the selectors suffered from deep suspicion and a desire to strangle.

Each sunlit, leaf-dappled, indescribable lump had grouped around it, as if at a wake and viewing the remains, a handful of people in chic summer clothing. These people put their heads on one side, sipped ruminatively from their glasses, stepped back, walked round, feigned enlightenment and looked as if they could see *at last* what it was they viewed. They then sighed with relief as if the alien objects had spoken. What they should have done was to have fled screaming.

A little way off, flanked by the large nodding branches of ancient trees and directly behind this artistic obstacle course, stood a perfect, porticoed summer house—an eighteenth-century curtsey to the Grecian temple, yet unmistakably of its age—cool and grey and gently disapproving. The modernism of its day. Look, I wanted to say to the bogus lumps, see how beautifully it has spat in the eye of time.

I heard someone behind me, female, say to someone behind me, male, 'Oh *look*, Johnny—I do believe it's a bird table. What heaven!'

'Oh look,' I said to a passing tray, 'I do believe it's another glass of champagne.' And with a pleasurable squidging of the toes, I took off for the shaded steps of the summer house.

I sipped away and was just beginning to feel utterly relaxed when I saw the Topp frontage poking around the edge of what appeared to be a bronze dildo for a female dinosaur. 'You can grow a nice climber round it,' I heard her say to the straw-hatted aesthete who was standing in front of it, apparently entranced.

She was accompanied by Peter the Bald, her hand resting lightly on his arm in a gesture of absolute possession. She looked radiant, he looked smug and I just looked. It was two months since the dinner and they were clearly very much an item. Good for you, I thought sourly. In all the years I had known her, I had never seen Roberta looking so dewy. It was the twin achievements of Love and Glory that did it. She was so uplifted even her embonpoint seemed to be strung up round her ears. If she had been a kinder person I might have wished her well.

A third party appeared, half-shaded by the huge phallus—in a straw hat even more English-looking than the quasi aesthete's. I peered. It was Yale and he was obviously into it, English clothes and all. He looked ever so slightly posey.

I was not ready for any of this, I thought miserably. Not ready to give Roberta a nudge up with her Apotheosis and not ready to lure some poor old codger with no marbles and a healthy bank balance into buying a plastic tube with leather fronding and a purple perspex gimbal cunningly masquerading as art. With somewhere to put the tea things.

I heard Roberta say, 'Where *is* Diana?'

I considered hiding behind one of the summer house's pillars—decided it was too risky—and made a quick dash for an indescribable lump. Very gradually, and thinking French Resistance, sandals in one hand, empty glass in the other, and keeping my eye on the advancing group, I hid my way, via the larger obstacles, back towards the main house.

I reached the very last one; from here a quick dash across the gravel and I'd be in the door and out of sight. Unseen, I felt sure.

I bent double to creep along the length of a piece of four foot high concrete entitled Berlin Wall (why use metaphor when you can be brutally explicit?)—not pausing to take up its creator's kind suggestion to Make My Own Graffiti—when I came face to foot with a pair of large boots.

I looked up, feeling a little strange from the exertion.

A man wearing a badge saying Keeper gazed down at me. He wanted to know, quite kindly, if he could help. I handed him my empty glass, and fled.

Once inside the house I began to feel wormlike and depressed again. So all alone. Perhaps another glass of champagne? I followed the arrows across the hallway and down narrow stone steps towards Pictures for Forward Fiction and the sound of tinkling glasses and chatter.

Another glass of champagne was provided. All the downstairs rooms were given over to a highly catholic, not to say Huguenot, Zen

Buddhist or even, possibly, Small Cult in Shropshire, collection of modern paintings which made the Hyde Park railings look tasteful. A florid-cheeked lady in a dirndl skirt and a grey bun who should have been knitting was saying, and saying very loudly, how good it was to get the work *out* of her studio and *on* to the walls here, so she could see it with a fresh eye . . .

I had my doubts about this. Small pictures of pigs done in pointilliste fashion tend to look much the same wherever you hang them. Unless, of course, you put your head in a paper bag, which would improve them no end.

'Get one in the Academy this summer, Kitty?' called someone.

'Nope,' mouthed Kitty, wobbling her grey bun. 'Perhaps I'll do cats next time . . .'

Or a naked young girl in a big straw hat, *plein air.* My father used to say that the nipples should be just discernible. Cat or girl.

In the next room were very large canvases awash with colour. More committee art. Clean about the house abstracts. And again the same kind of groups of people were scattered about with their heads on one side looking perplexed.

'Can I see a giraffe's head?' asked one hopeful, bright, middle-aged thing in Betty Barclay. And nobody quite dared say Yes or No. Possibly, was called for. And Possibly was said.

Those painters whose works hung in this room were in an unfortunate position (or had won first prize in the lottery of life) because it also housed the bar. And one or two of them had obviously found it. Early. Leading to an inevitable and interesting loss of inhibition among the assembled artists.

Communication of the Giraffe's Head variety was likely to receive an interesting response as the bubbly went down. So I took a fresh glass and found a neat hiding place in a window embrasure. These plain grey-stone rooms were originally the service rooms to the main house and consequently barren of Adam's tranquil glamour. Just as well with the amount of sloshing going on. And they were wonderfully cool.

At times like this you miss a partner. When a posy chap in velvet jacket with acrylic paint splashed upon it and two glasses in his hand, drinking from both, says to a winsome female in Armani, 'Bollocks madam,' to her tentative request for artistic enlightenment, you need a mate.

And when a bearded man in worn corduroy grabs the passing buttocks of canary-yellow Ozbek, and canary-yellow Ozbek gives a loud squeak and becomes a startled faun, you long to share your delight.

Other fashionable punters were returning in droves from rooms full of paintings further on. They bore very bright smiles, those smiles so beloved of the British after Dunkirk, and immediately, too rapidly for comfort, made for a refill. I had no wish to investigate. Here I would stay.

The Ozbek canary squeaked again.

Beyond the window, hacking their way through the sylvan scene, I saw Valeria in the company of a pair of fierce-looking individuals, both of whom she resembled and who, being of one sex each, I took to be her parents. They stumped along the gravel, close to the mullioned glass. They had the look about them of people with murder in their hearts.

'Oh,' I heard Valeria say with relief. 'There's Diana. The bookshop person.' She peered and blinked. 'Good heavens she's wearing a frock.' To which her father gave a snort and said, 'I fail to see what is so surprising about that.' Valeria opened her mouth to reply and sensibly didn't.

I gave a little wave through the window. Too late to hide. Both sets of parental eyes were unreservedly hostile. I saw them take one, short, disgusted look at Milton's execrables upon the lawn, and hurry in.

I was torn.

Behind me the Corduroy had released the Ozbek Bambi who was checking her very small bit of canary-yellow, otherwise known as a skirt, for signs of paint or erotic tension. Her escort, meanwhile, had developed all the tension necessary and despite his cool suit was harbouring antlers.

The Corduroy made some reference to Ozbek Bambi's unfair coldness towards him. He then added, rather indistinctly, while jabbing at her breast area, '*And* you walked past my work without looking at it.'

Coming across, and artistic merit, were apparently one and the same.

'Why did you do that?' said the Corduroy with a thrust of his chin.

The irritated escort, having checked that his lady's rear was disengaged, stared down the bridge of his nose, squared his stylish shoulders, rattled his antlers a bit and said, 'Because I don't *like* it.'

'What? What don't you like?' said Corduroy.

The shoulders held their ground. The antlers swayed magnificently.

'It,' he said. *'It.'* And he encircled the quivering faunly buttocks, about to move on.

Corduroy took a step forward. 'Well—I don't like you,' he said loudly. And poked the Suit.

A little on the dry side poetically, but direct.

Beyond their jutting chins and sprouting antlers I saw Valeria and her twin hunters enter the room.

She gave a little wave and another myopic, peering smile.

There was no time to flee before Corduroy

let out an impassioned 'Fock you Johnny,' so I remained tucked out of sight.

Corduroy had gone very red. A fist was raised.

'I wouldn't do that if I were you,' said the Suit, with menace.

'No?' said Corduroy.

'No,' said the Suit.

Valeria advanced.

Her parents advanced.

They owned the place, did they not, and would therefore take the direct route towards me, which was through the debate.

'Not if you want to go on making that kind of crap I wouldn't . . .'

The Suit preened himself. The canary buttocks wiggled out My Hero. Corduroy, with a touch of the Hibernian flair for argument, threw a punch at the offending nose. Missed. And went for it again.

The Suit, who had perhaps not tasted of the grape so fully, showed wit enough to duck. Then rose again, putting up his fists.

The Valerians, firm in their feudal rights, marched on with chins held high. Which is exactly where Valeria, blonde beehive shuddering, copped it, right on her Held High Chin. She went down like a genteel sack, falling straight into her father's arms with a dainty little 'Oh', and her pink, blinking eyes fluttered and closed.

He held her torpid body firm while

managing to look as if this was perfectly usual behaviour—absolutely nothing untoward about it. Laudable, since the bearded Corduroy, visually confused and sobriety deprived, bent towards her recumbent body saying, 'And let that be a lesson to ye,' before sauntering off.

Valeria was fortunately out of it. Her father continued with the tableau Iron In His Soul. He was not here, never had been here, and this was not his daughter lying in his arms.

Only stiff-backed Mrs Valeria put her hand, fleetingly, to her head—a megaton reaction—and spoke. 'No more,' she said firmly. 'I would rather starve.'

Valeria opened her eyes, moaned, blinked, sat up straight holding one of her eyes and sobbed, 'I've gone blind, I've gone blind . . .'

Her parents' eyes met. An ageing unmarried on their hands was one thing. But a sightless ageing unmarried?

'Nonsense,' said her mother firmly.

'I have, I have,' cried Valeria—so that the crowd grew thick about her.

'Well just *try harder*,' said her mother, exasperated. 'Pull yourself together and have another go.'

Valeria blinked again and ceased to sob. 'Oh no,' she said conversationally. 'I've just lost a contact lens.'

Mrs Valeria was rock. Plantation Riots, Indian Mutinies, Mixed Sculpture Exhibitions.

It was all the same. 'Edward—they must all go. Send them away. Absolutely all of them. *Now!* It is not to be endured.'

Corduroy looked from the disappearing backs of Ozbek and Shoulders, to the recumbent Valeria, and rubbed his chin. Life, like Art, was a mystery. The general consensus was that it added to the thrilling enjoyment of an evening like this; one or two of the older cognoscenti decided it was a Happening. 'Clever Roberta. *Such* excitement. *Just* like the sixties.'

The excitement apparently spilled over into the cheque books. Pictures seemed to whizz off the walls. The dirndl beamed.

Meanwhile Valeria fluttered bravely back to life. She attempted to remove herself from her father's arms, saying, 'It's all right Mummy, I'm perfectly fine,' and promptly passed out.

A swathe was cut through the thrilled assembly.

Roberta Topp, flanked by Peter the Bald and Yale as spear carriers, strode forth, up to, and almost including, Mrs Valeria. The Topp bosom fairly quivered with menace. She might be on the short side but she was Valkyrie to her little pin legs.

Mrs Valeria repeated herself word for word. Enough, apparently, was enough.

Roberta went very pale, but only for an instant.

Valeria fluttered her eyes. Looked up. Saw

everybody looking down. Fixed her gaze upon the startled and for once smileless gaze of Yale. Gave a rallying Joan Hunter-Dunn grin, made odd by the accompanying rapid swelling of her jaw, and tried to rise again.

'I am absolutely fine.' She eyed Yale blindly. 'Just got in the way a bit . . .' Tears were not far away. 'No *Mummy*. There is really no need to get so het up. Please don't send *anybody* away.' And she passed out anew.

It was much like watching the end of a good Shakespeare—characters with swords sticking out of them making long, complicated speeches about metaphor. One thing was for sure. The daughter of the house was deeply committed to the literary aspirations of Hassocks Hall. Or one particular masculine part of it.

Roberta, colour regained, turned to Yale, pointed at Valeria, spoke in low tones. 'I told you to look after her,' she said crossly. 'If you want this to work take her somewhere safe and settle her down *nicely* . . . Make love to her if you've got to . . .'

At the very least I expected Yale to spit in her eye, but all he did was look sheepish.

Roberta was much ruffled. 'This is your opportunity,' she hissed. 'So Carpe bloody Diem.'

She then turned to Peter the Bald, pointed to Mr Valeria, spoke in lower tones, but gentler ones. 'Get Lord Hartley out of here,

Peterkins dear. I think he needs some advice.' Her lizard eyes roamed the room. I ducked. Where *is* Diana?' she said furiously. 'When you've seen to Valeria, Jim, you'd better find her.' And in true spear carrier fashion, he nodded assent.

Then, removing the peevishness and replacing it with a blood-chilling smile full of teeth, she put her hand gently under Mrs Valeria's elbow, and led her away. From my hiding place within a hair's breadth of her passage, I heard her say, 'But let us make no hasty decisions yet, Lady Hartley, let us make no decisions yet.'

Yale put a very tender arm around the shuddering beehive and slowly led her outside, parting the gathered as Moses the Sea. I had an uninvited lump in my throat as I watched them go, not helped by the dirndl beaming sentimentally as they passed. 'Ah,' she said, 'now isn't that sweet?'

I slipped past the pigs towards a narrow flight of stone steps. If someone had punched me, who was there now to scoop me up and bear me away so tenderly? I grabbed another glass and slipped up the stairs. Like St Augustine, I would do my fundraising bit for the Academy of Forward Fiction. But like St Augustine—not just yet. On the other hand, there was very little else on offer in my life. And there was an awful lot of life in my very little else. I heard a distant calling of my name and fled to the upper chambers. If it was the call of God, He could wait a bit longer.

CHAPTER SIX

Hassocks Hall is one of those piles so beloved by eighteenth-century gentlemen for their residences; close enough to London for Court and Administration access, far enough away to be considered countryside—and towards the west, indeed placed right by the Great West Road, when further travel to the Spas and Balls of the Season demanded.

Despite being stuck in a triangle of modern roads, grim housing and flanked by heavy-duty traffic, once in Hassocks Park the only disturbance from twentieth-century blight was relentless aircraft noise, Hassocks Hall being a mere flick of a hunting crop from Heathrow.

This fundraising event was to be the first of many. Art, fashion shows, soirées with piano and diva as the season progressed. Why people did not just post us their cheques and be done with it, rather than put themselves through these tortures, was another mystery. Condensed, I believe, into that very English word, *Form.* I could just imagine Valeria's parents' delight in an evening of schoolgirl bulimics teetering down the catwalk.

The season's Grand Finale would be an

open evening of jazz and fireworks. When I asked if it wouldn't be a touch noisy for such a tranquil scene, and what about the housing estate close by, Roberta just flapped her hand at such nonsense and said they would not complain. She was probably right. It seemed the only people prepared to live in the surrounding area, so close to the airport that Concorde knocked on their doors, were the desperate, the ignorant, the poor, the afflicted and the grateful immigrant. None of these was likely to assert their rights. It occurred to me that if Jesus Christ were due for a come-back he could do no better than begin in the densely populated area surrounding Hassocks Hall.

Roberta had organized things perfectly. How she managed to *know* all the right people, let alone make *use* of them, was beyond me. And why nobody minded that they were not exactly loved for themselves was also beyond me. Seems to me it's the first lesson you learn at school. Go in with a bag of sweets and everybody wants to be your friend. Next day, bag empty, they lock you in the lavatories and leave you there. Bad in childhood. Dangerous, surely, later . . .? But apparently not where the glitz of Good Works is concerned.

I opened the first door on the marbled landing, which led into the Grand Drawing Room, Adam's backwards nod to the long gallery. It was lined with portraits, and empty except for a lady attendant at the far end who had her nose in a book.

Opposite the pictures, a row of long windows sent in soft, golden light. They overlooked the gravel and the lawn below. I imagined Elizabeth Bennet gazing down on Mr Darcy. Or poor Caroline of Brunswick, half dead from childbirth, staring sad and lonely across the parkland and pondering her miserable fate. I don't suppose its being an Adam Gem made much difference to her misery. She might just as well have had mushroom-soup walls and a bus route too.

I removed the pink sandals again, not wishing to disturb the peace of centuries. Goggle-eyed eighteenth-century ladies looked down superciliously from their ovals; at least they managed an early death. I felt depressed. Fortunately there was a tray, with drinks, and—oddly enough—my glass appeared to be empty again. I helped myself. It was nice up here in this diffused light. Undemanding. Maybe I was almost cured? I tried humming a few bars of the Requiem but it gave me such a melancholy I gave up. The attendant read on, oblivious. Maybe what I should do was sit quietly for a while. There was a nice, worn, needlepointed window seat, so I did.

It was a magnificent room, spanning the whole of the first-floor front, and considered to be the most perfect Adam room in England. Certainly by its architect. Robert Adam wrote of it to his brother with little modesty. When James Adam remonstrated that a background colour of 'sunlit red wine' seemed in his opinion altogether too suffocating to live with, Robert merely said, 'So it would be, had another put his name to it . . .'

I suppose, if one were to argue that neo-classicism represented nobility, simplicity and calm grandeur, then this room was not—strictly—it. Motifs and screens made the space a little too busy. But if all one required was the rejection of Baroque trumpery for pleasing geometrical simplicity, here it was. You stood at its calm centre and your spirit was touched. The reverse of what you felt standing on the lawn among those execrable New Trumperies.

There was also damp in the ceiling, cracks in the mouldings, peeling of the sunlit red wine wallpaper, and a profound sense that decay had set in.

An aeroplane passed over. I looked out on to the gravel below. A window was slightly open, voices floated in. A woman with the tones of a glass-cutter and the air of one who will brook no nonsense, said to a plump, benign-looking man with white fluffy hair and a look of ill ease, 'Well Charles—it's all very fine—Genius *very* obvious. Brilliant use of screens and motifs and decoration inside and out—all that—' Her voice rose. 'But you'd have thought they'd have built it somewhere other than under the flight path.'

Charles nodded.

The attendant, who could not fail to have heard, looked up from her book and goggled. Indeed, we engaged each other's eyes and goggled in unison, joining our pop-eyed sisters strung about on the walls. People like that, I mused, *should* be made to purchase a purple perspex and leather gimbal for their garden.

Directly below, so directly that I could have spat on the top of his head and, indeed, for some reason had an urge to do so, was Yale's boyish haircut, now devoid of straw hat. Valeria stood next to him with what appeared to be a whole bag of toffees bulging in her mouth. She bore a terribly bright smile. Yale and Peter the Bald seemed to be engaged in a shrugging contest. They were scanning the horizon like a posse.

I moved to one side of the window. Not yet.

While I had another drink I watched Yale. He was quite pleasant-looking in an undemanding way. Having ceased to scan the horizon he took Valeria's elbow very gently and guided her towards the entrance porch. She smiled up at him with a pronounced squint, and her strangely lumpen swelling produced more of a leer. He, brave soul, continued to smile upon her. A kind man, I thought wistfully, a kind man. They probably all start out that way.

Peter the Bald strode off manfully with Mr V. Well, as manfully as his fat little legs could carry him, and talking hard all the way. Everybody in the world seemed to be involved in what they were doing. Except me. I was still adrift and spinning. Which thought quickly sent me from depressed to maudlin.

At least Clara Schumann had Brahms's devotion to keep her warm. And the tribute of a Requiem. I thought about sharing this information with the lady attendant, but found I was sobbing—which was quite a surprise really—so I kept it to myself.

Another bit of the glass cutter floated up. 'I believe he was very taken by Diocletian's palace, was he not? And absolutely *loved* Italy—well—don't we all. *Much* admired Wedgwood of course. Well—you can see it in the plastering. Superb . . .'

Plastering? I thought. Have another drink.

I looked out of the window again. Roberta was mingling with the great and the good, still with the Mrs V. attached, and looking thunderously about her. Yale, minus Valeria, joined her. Presumably the toffee-mountain jaw had posed a bit of a problem for erotic pursuit. Suddenly Roberta looked up. Too late to move out of sight, our eyes met. Without a hint of friendly delight.

I found myself giggling. It was fun playing hide and seek. I bobbed behind the window again, and peeked round. Roberta was still staring but Yale had gone. Pity.

Dignity being all, I attempted to put my

sandals back on. While I struggled with the straps (the holes seemed to have got smaller) I heard footsteps coming up the marble stairs, apparently two at a time. I felt a huge bubble of adrenalin—the kind of wild rising excitement children get when a game takes off. Securing the straps as best I could I made a run for the door at the far end, near the attendant, slipping a bit, presumably because the floor was so polished.

The door at the far end opened just as I reached the other one. Oh no you don't, I thought, and dodged on to the marble landing. It was the first time I had felt alive for months. Yale was just disappearing through his door into the long room, as I arrived back outside.

The chase was on.

I went swiftly along the landing, into another room, through its daffodil-yellow and Edinburgh rock walls, on to another, down some back stairs, across wide, cool, stone-flagged floors collecting another glass of champagne on the way, and back into the garden once more. I looked up. He was looking down from the open window.

I waved, raised my glass, drained it, turned, resumed French Resistance and fled across the lawns to the rhododendron plantation at the back. Suddenly the idea of hiding in its cool shade was enchanting. But once there, game over and no one following, I just kicked at the gravel disconsolately and wandered further into the thicket. Maybe I could find somewhere to have a sleep? I was suddenly a bit tired. Amalfi? Brahms? How futile it all felt. Futile, futile, futile—kick, kick, kick . . .

And then something caught my eye.

I peered.

I peered *harder.*

I peered very hard indeed.

As Emily Dickinson would have it, Hope is the thing with feathers, that perches in the soul. And here, it seemed, was Hope. Or at least the feathers of it. And tickling away at the libido, too. Sometimes our lowest ebb and darkness prepares us for light, even in a rhododendron dell, which came as rather a surprise. I peered *again*, *much* harder, and with a touch of disbelief. Quite suddenly I had rediscovered carnal oestrus.

A curve attended my lips. Quite a large curve. One of those facial geometries that are known, less prosaically, as a smile. Not something I had experienced very much recently. And certainly not over a sight like this. I straightened up. Got my bearings. And didn't feel sleepy any more. Suddenly things were beginning to look up.

CHAPTER SEVEN

Mostly I could wish D. H. Lawrence to the peak of a mystic mountain top, but there is that bit in *Lady Chatterley* when she spots muscly old Mellors having a bit of a wash-out behind the woodshed, which drives like a dowel through the feminine nerve endings.

Now, here in the shady damp of evergreens, was a similar vision. A youth—rather a large youth—rather a large youth whose mother had done all the right things with beefsteak and orange juice—coming down a winsome little path of dappled light, pushing a wheelbarrow and wearing only a smallish pair of shorts, a Walkman and—rather unfortunately—a baseball cap the wrong way round.

But thewy. Definitely *thewy.* And what matter if the blue eyes beneath the visor had a certain vacant quality? Or that the little, pursed mouth opened and closed to a rhythm that was unlikely to be Brahmsian? For the first time since Teddy, lust had stirred. He also looked pleasingly fuzzy around the edges—heat haze I decided. I stood still so as not to frighten him away. It was not exactly easy standing still because my sandals seemed a bit slithery, but I did my best.

So, how to introduce myself?

Should I lie down across the path and feign

injury? Er, no—the gravel had given way to muddy stones.

Should I feel moved to know the exact names of all the rhododendrons and azaleas and discuss their acidulated peat?

Should I ask coyly What is the difference between rhododendrons and azaleas?

Is there a difference between rhododendrons and azaleas?

How do you *spell* rhododendrons and azaleas?

Would you like to come back to my place and take off all your clothes and *discuss* rhododendrons and azaleas?

The conversational possibilities seemed endless.

I approached the wheelbarrow. When not puckering to the rhythm he chewed gum unselfconsciously.

I paused.

He smiled, and made to go around me. His smile transmitted friendly lack of erotic enthusiasm.

Irritating.

There are times when one wishes one had a chest like La Topp's. Or even a really decent pair of legs.

Well—God moves in a mysterious way . . .

I made to go around him, beaming my winning smile, delicately touching the edge of the wheelbarrow as if it might be his left thigh, took a calculated turn designed to entice, let the hips sashay around the rough wood as exotically as possible, slipped on the mossy path, and promptly fell in.

Difficult to know who was the more surprised really. Still, I tried to look casual in there. I didn't really mind. It was quite comfortable.

Something conversational seemed appropriate. I gazed up at him and said a rather velvety 'Hi.'

He went on chewing gum, absently puzzled.

I was just about to say something scintillating, not easy when one is prone among peat bags, when behind me I heard a familiar masculine voice say, 'Shoot.' Which was less a command to let fly with the arrows, than a Yale-like exclamation. I looked from the youth to the man and back again. The youth was now making a perfect O with his mouth, while Yale sported that infuriating campus grin.

I gave him a little wave.

The Yale grin remained but the Yale finger pointed, the mouth spoke, the signs were that the wheelbarrow was not to be my long-term resting place.

'Out,' he said.

With very little trouble, as much dignity as I could muster, and not showing my knickers, I obeyed, resisting the offered peaty hand with cool poise and retrieving my lost sandal. I held on to the wheelbarrow, toed my way into the pink calf, and had a thought. Peat. So I turned round to stick out my bottom at Yale and ask if it was a terrible mess.

He merely said Not Bad which did not seem altogether serious. I made some brushing gestures with my hand—*not* easy in a pair of spindly sandals on moss—and stood up properly by holding on to the barrow's handle again. Several of the rhododendrons seemed to be swaying rather more than the light breeze would indicate.

'Not to worry,' said the hunk through his gum, and he put out a hand to steady me. 'It's only forest bark. All dry. You OK?'

He gave a cheery wave, popped the Walkman headphones back in place, and rattled his barrow off down the winsome little path.

'Spectacular,' said Mr Yale.

'Yes,' I said, watching the shorts.

'I have been looking for you,' he said. 'I have been sent to look for you. And you have not been making it easy.' He sounded quite peeved.

'I am coming now,' I said meekly.

The rhododendrons had slipped again.

He took my arm which was helpful. 'Good Old America . . .' I said cheerfully. 'Star-spangled manners . . .' Which seemed rather witty.

'Have you eaten anything?' he asked conversationally as we pottered back towards the house. Somehow my little pink heels kept slipping sideways under me.

'Eaten?' I thought for a second. 'Oh—*Eaten* . . .' Odd question. 'No,' I said. 'Have you?' Philosophy, art, stomach contents—I was ready for any conversational turn.

At least we were back on the gravel now, approaching the sunlit greensward. I could feel those horrid little stones ruining my heels. I stopped and looked down. 'I love these sandals, you know.' Suddenly I felt desperately sorry for them. 'Poor, poor things . . .' I believe I shed a tear.

His grip increased.

He steered me towards two long white-covered tables that had magically appeared beneath the trees. Beyond the brooding shapes of the Execrables a quintet was playing Bach. Very pretty-looking canapés were laid out on trays and I suddenly realized that I was, indeed, ravenous.

'See if they can play the Clarinet in B minor . . .' I said, through a mouthful of goat's cheese gondola.

He stared.

'Brahms,' I added. He handed me a piece of salmon roule.

'Opus 115,' I said, to show off. An avocadoed prawn waved beneath my nose. 'Go on. *Ask* . . .'

I waited.

Nothing.

'Teddy would have done,' I said.
'This is fine,' he said.
'But I like Brahms,' I said, wistfully shovelling in a devilled egg. He was being very attentive.
Tears rose. I tried humming it but there was too much devilled egg in the way. 'Brahms,' I said, 'has not been given a fair ride. That's what I think.'
'Your privilege,' he said. Still not budging.
I thought, again, that Teddy would have gone and done it instantly. Teddy was wonderful. *Wonderful*. A tear rolled down. I gave a little sob, adding, 'And nor have I.'
He looked at the tear, less in sorrow than in acute embarrassment, and grabbed a small plate, piling stuff on to it, even stuff I didn't like. I stopped the tears for a moment. 'I don't like that.' I pointed at egg in aspic. 'Or that.' I pointed at something else just for the hell of it. He did not remove them.
When the plate was full he reclasped the elbow and guided me in the direction of the summer house.
'I hope those eggs in aspic are for you,' I said, trotting and slithering to keep up, 'because I'm *definitely* not eating them. I told you I didn't want them, and I *don't*.'
He gave me a look which I can only say made me change the subject.
As we passed the Execrables, I quoted Robert Graves at him. I am quite proud of my

capacity to retain chunks of poetry so I gave it my all. I could see he was impressed.

'I can give you Milton on the subject, too,' I said loftily, remembering how impressed Teddy was by such things. 'Do you know *Paradise Lost*?'

'Sure,' he said, hurrying me even faster. 'It's a small town in Tucson.'

'Oh no, no, no—' 'I shook my head kindly. 'It's a poem. A very old poem. As a matter of fact I regard it as the first sci-fi of literature, war of the worlds—but let that pass—'

A waitress bobbed by with a tray of drinks. I took one. His smile seemed to freeze a little more.

'Let *that* pass too, I think.' And he took the glass from me, exchanging it for an orange juice. 'You'll need this in the heat,' he said.

'But I don't *like* orange juice.' I could match that glass-cutter woman any old day. 'I want champagne.'

We reached the summer-house steps and I was extraordinarily thankful to be sitting down.

'Drink,' he said, bossily.

'How manly,' I replied. But he scarcely smiled.

He sat down. He offered me the plate. I picked up a dainty morsel. He kept the plate there so I took another. This went on for a moment or two. I was beginning to feel like a cuckoo chick. Suddenly, mid-fingerwards, the plate was removed. I had been finding it quite hard to concentrate so in some ways it was a blessing. On the other hand I was just about to negotiate a pink, prawny thing and was not entirely resigned to its loss.

He stood up. I gazed sadly at the plate that hovered somewhere just above my nose.

'Found her, Roberta,' he called.

I ceased to consider the bottom of the plate—Staffordshire, I recall, was stamped there—and focused beyond.

What I thought to be a little moving Indescribable with water wings became, on closer inspection, the downwardly bearing person of Roberta. She looked irate.

'She was in the long room,' said Mr Yale, 'talking to some folk about the pictures . . .'

'Who was?' I said interestedly

La Topp fixed me with a questioning look, her dark eyes snapping. Standing there tottering on her outrageously high heels I could quite see what my mother meant: Hit her with a good book, and she'd be over.

I might have said something along these lines but Yale put another goat's cheese boat to my lips. 'You were,' he said firmly. 'In the long room. With that couple.' He made stabbing motions with the cheese boat while emphasizing this so it was quite hard to get an oral purchase.

I tried to recall a couple. Ah yes.

'She had a voice like a glass cutter and he

had lots and lots of fluffy white hair . . .'

'The Scott-Moncktons?' said Roberta, giving me a look that seemed to require affirmation.

'Yup. The very ones.'

'And what were they interested in?'

How the hell should I know? This was all deeply boring. Like being at school.

'I don't give A-damn,' I giggled.

Roberta marshalled her breasts. They were encased in a navy and white spotted number and looked dangerous. 'I'm sorry?' she said, taking off the safety catch.

'Robert Adam,' said Yale. 'They were admiring Robert Adam.' He looked down at me. Not very nicely.

Roberta also looked down at me. None too nicely either. 'Well we aren't *selling* Robert Adam, now are we? We're selling all this—' And she gestured across the lawn. Never had the lumps looked more threatening.

Really, it did need saying. I opened my mouth to speak but it was filled with the long-awaited pink, prawny thing.

'Get those Scott-Moncktons and their cheque book,' she said. 'They ought to buy one of these at least. They've got acres. Just right.'

She spoke as if a purchase were a punishment. I suppose, in a way, it was.

'Oh absolutely,' I said.

She looked icy. 'And we've all got to work twice as hard because Valeria isn't up to much.'

'That's true.'

'She can't help it.'

'They never can.'

'She's had a very nasty accident, Diana.'

'Oh Roberta,' I said. 'How unkind. Some people are just born that way.'

Roberta did not find this at all funny. Neither did Yale. In fact, Roberta looked really peeved.

'All I have seen you do this evening is run around the sculptures like a Red Indian. What *were* you up to? The Keeper was quite bothered in case you were stealing things.'

Stealing things? Just slipping half a ton of sculptured bronze into my handbag?

'Measuring,' I said. Which I thought was brilliant.

Roberta looked puzzled.

'To see if it would go in their car.'

'Whose car?'

'Anybody's.'

'What, the Berlin Wall?' She rightly looked astonished.

'Well, they all have big cars,' I said lamely. Oh how I wanted to sleep.

Someone large in sky-blue Versace passed us by. He looked like a fat gangster and his moll looked like a stick insect in lime-green chiffon.

'Super,' he called out. 'The Canova went to Getty *and* that lovely little Sickert to the Nat.

Gal. so we need you darling . . .'

Roberta looked up from beneath her lashes, fluttered and woggled.

'Pinkie. Super,' she called. 'With you in a minute.'

'Measuring them,' I continued. 'Because you can't just sell something like that. You've got to know its dimensions—I mean—supposing our clients only have a little garden—maybe just a patio? It'd be no good flogging them the dildo for a dinosaur, now would it?'

Yale's hand began to shake.

Roberta whipped round and stared. 'I can assure you that none of these guests have that problem.' Her eyes went daggerish. 'And don't call it that. It is a Garden Love Totem.'

But her voice suddenly softened. 'Talking of which—there's Peterkins. I must see how he got on with Lord Hartley.'

And she teetered coquettishly back across the lawn, waving to Pinkie and the stick insect as she went, telling them to go and look at the bronze, she would be with them soon, and wouldn't it look good with a nice Montana climber going round it?

'That's right,' I said to her disappearing back view. 'Piss off.'

He was suddenly kneeling at my side. He was suddenly completely serious. He was suddenly about a nose-bite away and kept making me go cross-eyed in the effort to focus.

He looked and sounded oddly desperate.

'Now just listen,' he said. Definitely desperation. 'Please.' We looked at Roberta, cooing in the distance with her beloved.

'Do you know,' I said, 'I have never seen her like this before.' I sighed. 'All right for some.'

'Well I'm glad she's happy. Because that,' he pointed, 'is the woman who will get this place off the ground if anyone can, and give employment and succour to at least one exiled American academic who needs it. *You* might not—*some* of us do.'

'Do prawns make you sexy?' I asked, remembering young Mellors.

'They give you high cholesterol,' he said impatiently. 'Now look—'

'How like an American to know that . . .'

'Do you want to get thrown off the team? I thought we were all committed. Saving a great old house like this and doing no harm to anyone.'

'No harm?' I sat up. 'We're peddling crap.'

'We won't be peddling anything unless it gets funded. So far your only contribution is drinking the profits. You'd still be flat on your back if I hadn't pitched up.'

'I can think of worse things . . .' I said wistfully.

I reached for a crab tart and leant back against the cool stone pillar. 'My hero,' I said, biting with relish. 'Is that the only reason you've been so helpful? To Save the

Academy?'

He stood up. Removed his hand. Brushed his silly English striped tie into place. And smiled that offensive boyish number again. 'Yes and no,' he said.

'Well I think that's disgusting. What a charade.'

He raised an eyebrow. 'I thought charades were the English national pastime?'

'I loathe it,' I said. 'I loathe dishonesty in all its forms.'

Stage two of drinking with me quite often produces a strong moral line about something.

He gave me a very odd smile as he pulled me to my feet. 'Really?' he said. 'But then—I have always admired the honesty of lesbians.'

'Ah,' I said, raising a finger. 'Er—' I still felt strangely wobbly.

From behind a shoulder-high rendering of a fan-tailed turkey-cock, made from laminated coal sacks and copper wire, appeared the Keeper man. I velcroed the bouche.

'There are some seats inside. And soft drinks,' he said. 'All this heat. Very unexpected for May.'

Yale nodded significantly. I saw no reason to pass, and joined in nodding significantly too.

'Come on,' said Mr Yale. 'A sit in the cool, more juice and you'll be fine.'

'Brahms,' I said, as I followed behind him, dodging the lumps. *'I want Brahms.'*

But he only repeated, 'More juice.'

Feeling inclined to sulk, I said, 'I don't want to be part of this any more.' I ran my finger over the Berlin Wall as he hurried me along. 'I was only bored,' I said. 'Bored and broken-hearted.' I waited for lots of sympathy and I was disappointed.

'Didn't think the two went together,' was all he said.

'I didn't think they went together,' I mimicked. 'Well, what about you?'

'I like England. I've got my Magnum Opus to write and I'll be paid while doing my own thing: English creative writing courses are a breeze.'

'This isn't creative writing—it's Roberta writing. It's rubbish.'

'Oh—and you're not the only one with a broken heart. They happen in the States, too.'

I looked at him suspiciously but he seemed quite serious. 'Who broke it?'

But he hurried on ahead and disappeared through the main door.

'About lesbians,' I said.

He seemed not to hear.

We went into a little ground floor anteroom which contained the perspiring, semi-dozing form of the erstwhile Charles. I went over to him to have a closer look, if not an exploratory prod.

'*Don't touch him*,' Yale said sharply, and pulled me back.

'It's only Charles . . .'

We smiled at some pearl chokers of a certain age and their earnest, dark-suited husbands who were shaking their silvery heads in another part of the room.

'We'll have to do it, of course, though frankly I prefer the Lord Leightons.'

'Roberta's very persuasive. We'll get our names on the plaque I suppose. And Royalty's interested.'

'What have you put yourselves down for?'

'Just the one. We'll put it in the paddock. And you?'

'Farm animals. For the barn conversion.'

'Oh, *love* the pigs . . .'

'Might take the turkey cock too. Will it stand up to the rain?'

'One sincerely hopes not.'

Yale handed me another glass of orange juice. We sat. He was not *exactly* radiating affection. Well, I thought, crossing my arms, and then my legs, with Attitude. I can wait.

I waited. He seemed to be suddenly very far away and quite unmoved by either my twitching ankle, or the considerable amount of thigh thrown in.

I was disappointed.

'Drink up,' he said eventually. 'Got to get cracking.'

Interestingly, and obediently, Charles stirred and sat up. We acknowledged each other with a nod. I drank the glass of orange juice. Much more and I'd be talking Spanish. I went on twitching my foot.

'Better get back out there,' said Yale.

Twitch, twitch.

'Feeling better?'

'Never felt ill.'

'One for the road.'

I let him fill my glass. 'What was her name?'

'Who?'

'The one who broke your heart.'

'Carrie,' he said shortly. And stood up.

'Tell me about her?'

Silence.

Asking a man to talk about his feelings is like suggesting he pull his own teeth.

'Do you want to tell me about it?'

'Nope.'

I leaned forward and whispered, 'The fact of the matter is, I am *not* a lesbian.'

'Oh, it's OK,' he said, patting my arm. 'I'm broad-minded. Now, let's get out there and sell.'

The bastard was laughing at me. I was stung.

I'd show him.

I went over to Charles, who bore the facial expression of one being approached by a pterodactyl, and slipped my hand into the crook of his arm. I gave him a lovely smile. 'I'm Diana, your minder,' I said. 'Shall we take a stroll around the exhibits?'

Over my shoulder I winked at Yale, who looked quite shocked. 'You've got dirt on your butt,' he called.

But I clung to Charles and headed off in the direction of the purple perspex with gimbal. If Charles bought it I *might* let him brush me down.

The pink sandals stayed upright *reasonably* well.

CHAPTER EIGHT

At the end of the evening Roberta was beaming and her breasts were pneumatic with joy.

Even I had done well. My only blunder was agreeing with someone that all the exhibits were appalling. She meant all the exhibits *except hers.* Oddly enough, as I said to her, *Oddly Enough*—hers was the *only* piece with any merit at all . . .

Charles bought both the perspex with gimbal and the Berlin Wall to grace the lawn at Evesham. After all, I pointed out, John Constable was considered a revolutionary once. Artists were often ahead of themselves.

We, the Team, sat in Valeria's parents' drawing room sipping coffee from old Japanese cups. Peter the Bald on the sofa with his beloved, me on a high-backed Important something or other, and our Transatlantic friend crouched on a little stool near Valeria's feet. She certainly looked rough. Another pound of toffees, at least, had been added and one of her eyes was closed. The other gazed yearningly at the top of Yale's head. Mr and Mrs Valeria sat side by side, straight-backed, in a pair of threadbare Chinese Chippendales, staring ahead like frozen reeds.

Roberta praised us all and said that darling Peterkins would let us know the sums as soon as possible. 'If this evening is any yardstick, we will do very well indeed . . .' She handed out the list of future events and looked disgustingly smug.

Yale clapped.

We, being English, froze at the untoward show of emotion. Roberta looked a little disconcerted and hurried on. 'This was a dry run tonight.' She looked pointedly at me. 'For some of us.' More than this she could not say because I had achieved most sales.

Yale smiled at me, very brightly.

I put out my tongue.

Neither gesture escaped Long John Valeria.

Valeria's parents were quite rigid. They were hating every minute.

'You have a very fine library here,' I said.

'Thank you,' said Mrs V. graciously.

'We will be moving that—carefully of course—and installing our own,' said Roberta.

Both parental backs went rigid again.

'As discussed,' said La Topp, consulting a piece of paper from the sheaf on her lap, 'your books will go into the east wing green room. They will be professionally moved, of course . . . Along with your furniture and whatnot.'

Mr and Mrs Valeria showed the distaste usually reserved for a disease.

'We are on course,' said Roberta. 'And our Open Day will feature jazz and fireworks . . . It will be so *chic* . . .' She leaned forward and tapped the now thunderous Mr Parent of Valeria on his knee. A terrifying experience.

'I can see you're remembering Beatniks and whatnot, aren't you?'

He remained unmoved, merely blenching.

'And dope,' I said cheerfully.

Roberta pretended not to hear and Yale frowned.

'Well,' she said, 'the jazz and fireworks won't be like that at all . . .' She leaned even further forwards so that the imbalance of frontage and lap was startling. 'The jazz group comes from a *very* exclusive public school . . .'

'*Definitely* dope,' I said, even more cheerfully.

'Well—thanks, Team,' said Roberta, wisely ignoring this. She and Peterkins smiled like a pair of very unpleasant lovebirds. Yale went to clap again but thought better of it. Gradually England was teaching him very proper restraint. The parental Valerias had never looked less Teamlike in their lives. Their daughter squinted at them anxiously.

Roberta gave a proud little cough and said,

'Now Peter darling, tell them about Erna, our Patroness.'

He released her hand with an absurd theatrical flourish. Suddenly he was brisk. 'In a nutshell,' he said to the Valerias, 'none of the relocation or building upgrades required by the Academy will cost you a penny. Work will begin at the end of the month. Your own apartments are costed in. It is all underwritten.'

'Super,' said Roberta.

The responding smile from Chinese Chippendales could not have been glassier if Mr Valeria had been carried here from a waxworks show. His wife resembled one who has just learned that the Empire has gone, the new Archbishop of Canterbury is black and Winston Churchill was gay.

Roberta leaned back, pointing her devastating frontage like a pair of well-aimed cannons. 'Of course,' she said with studied ease, 'the little bit of dry rot in the new library room can very easily be dealt with. And the roof at the back, *not* strictly our remit. And the damp. Some of those window frames . . . All that. Immediately? Mmm?'

Mr V.'s back remained ramrod straight against the faded silk, but his eyes had yielded. What Agincourt and Flodden could not do, decay and income tax had achieved. Even his companion lady registered the briefest of glimmerings of relief.

I, Tiresias, saw it all. Roberta had got them in the impoverished aristocratic wallet. Was this better than opening a butterfly house and serving cream teas? Mrs Valeria, now standing, seemed not so sure. She walked to the door, opened it, then turned and asked if anybody wanted more coffee. Since the coffee pot and the tray were all on the small central table and nowhere near the door, and since the door was the way to make exit, I assumed it was another example of that superb politesse—driven completely without sentiment and fuelled by good taste—for suggesting we leave. Well, she could hardly stand there and say Fuck Off Out Of It, now could she? But it came to the same. And we did.

Valeria followed us out to the stone steps. By now the Execrable Indescribables were moonlit and the cows beyond were only huddled things. Roberta and Peterkins clung together and scrunched down on to the gravel. 'You were wonderful,' he said to her proudly

I ached. Now that *was* love.

The air was chill and my snappy linen number inadequate. A tremor went through the breathing statuary that was Roberta and immediately Peterkins took off his jacket and draped it around her shoulders. I shivered and watched them saunter off, arms around each other, dark shapes in the silvery light, and felt very sad.

'Well, goodnight,' I said to Valeria, as

cheerfully as I could muster. 'Hope the face clears up.'

Take that which way you like, I thought, and was about to ask Yale if I could borrow his jacket until we got to my car—but he did not move from the top step. He and Valeria returned my wave, and they both went in. *Oh!*

I suddenly felt rather foolish and walked off very briskly in the direction of my car. 'How do you like *them* potatoes?' I asked the steering wheel. The answer was Not Very Much. But it was only pique.

I cheered myself up with thoughts of the young woodsman, but minus the reversed cap and Walkman. Perhaps, as all this madness unfolded, there would be an opportunity to get to know him. It would make a positive stepping stone in the sluggish waters of my life. My head began to throb. Pearl, damn her, might be right.

Well, at least I didn't live here, I thought, as I drove back past rows of deadbeat housing. Council architects never seem to have heard of Robert Adam. Or is it just a plot to keep the proles in their place? If so it succeeds. One decaying stately home containing one mouldering, miserable ancient family—or this lot? Speaking as one who knew the depressive power of surroundings, there did not seem much in it. I whistled a note or two. Found it was Brahms again. And stopped.

Valeria?

Surely not. He was just being kind.

Arriving home I was surprised at how much I had enjoyed myself. Even if the pink sandals were ruined. And I had promised the dreaded Roberta to be part of the Team, had I not? So—conscience aside, I *had* to oblige . . .

I recall that I slept rather well.

CHAPTER NINE

'Pearl,' I said. 'What do you think about older women and younger men?'

She paused, Windolene in hand, and gave me a look. I faced her out. A customer came in and stood between us, unaware that he was in direct line of the High Noon bullet. He asked for the Sartre/de Beauvoir letters.

Just for the moment I could not remember if we had replaced it on the shelf—just for a *moment* you understand—and in that moment Pearl stepped in, gestured in the direction of the biography section with her pink-stained window cloth, and said—if you please—'*Very* well-edited selection,' urging him towards the right spot.

'Pearl,' I said when he had gone. 'Please don't talk to the customers.' I remembered the dreary council estate of last night. 'Come to think of it,' I added, 'why aren't *you* living in Hassocks Lee? It'd suit you very well.'

'There isn't a direct bus,' she said. 'So I moved.'

'You could have taken a taxi,' I said. 'And while you're about it, eat cake.'

There were one or two browsers looking through the shelves, but apart from them the shop was very quiet. She crossed her stringy arms over her flat bosom and said, 'How old?'

'How old what?' I said, being cool.

She did not waver. She has an unfortunate habit of not wavering. Quite disconcerting sometimes. 'How old?'

'Eighteen . . . nineteen . . .' I shrugged.

She shook her head. 'You're not old enough. You need to grow up.'

'Me? I'm more or less old enough to be his mother.'

'That's not age. That's biology.'

Talk about Sybil in a pinny. Or Sphinx with duster.

What does *that* mean?'

'You'll know one day.'

'Pearl,' I said. 'Shut up. And answer me this.'

'Can't do both.'

'What do you mean *Grow Up*?'

She shrugged and began putting away her things. 'Birthdays,' she sniffed. 'If you know what I mean.'

I should never tell Pearl anything.

Last month I decided not to celebrate my birthday. Just ignore it. I did not get a card from Teddy which, in my book, meant that the year had not been worth acknowledging anyway. I would resume celebrating birthdays once I was perfectly happy again.

'I have simply delayed my birthday.' I said with dignity. 'Which is my privilege. "What though the field be lost? All is not lost . . ." '

Pearl shrugged. 'She who lies on the ground cannot fall, I suppose. Who is the youngster?'

'Don't know his name.'

She stopped folding her duster and stared at me.

'Yet.'

'Well, you'd better find out. Whatever happened to being One of Them?'

'One of them, what?'

'You know—*Them.*'

She never approved of the Radclyffe Hall approach, and clearly she did not approve of this new one. Which made it all the more enticing.

'I am now deadly serious about having a fling with a boy,' I said. 'It's more appealing. For one thing, I know where his bits are.'

She put her hand to her head, said, 'Oh my *Gawd*,' and then reached for a book of sex tips. 'You'll be needing this,' she said. 'And you'll need to be fit. Yoghurt and exercise and some early nights.' Coming from her, desiccation row, that was rich. 'Youngsters are lethal, *lethal* in the you-know department . . .'

Was she laughing at me?

‘Just *clean*, Pearl. *Clean*,’ I said airily. But fear ate the soul and I was trembling inside.

I went home that night with the book in my bag, six organic yoghurts and a detour to enrol at the gym for something called step aerobics.

* * *

The fundraising progressed well. And though I only caught glimpses of the youthful gardener in the distance over the next few weeks, I kept him in my sights. He was certainly not forgotten.

Roberta sent us long, oblique Up-dates On Progress, emphasizing the corporate culture perspective of the scheme and the as-is analysis of feedback. She also hinted that she had a New Promotional Idea for the Academy. Something that would consolidate the identity of our Mission. A scheme which we, the Team, would all have an opportunity to buy into.

The memo ended with her suggesting that in the meantime we consider our individual strategy input, and ask ourselves: What Is Culture?

Frankly, at this stage, I preferred not to.

I asked Pearl. ‘Pearl,’ I said, ‘what is Culture?’

She pointed at the shelf of Topps. ‘Not that,’ she said.

I asked her if she would like to come to the Hassocks Hall jazz evening. ‘You could check out the boy for me.' I winked. I had done the course in step aerobics, had I not, so I felt very confident. A bit painful. But confident.

Fortunately she declined. 'I have no wish to see you make a fool of yourself,' she said crisply. 'You'll be wiped out in the first round.'

'You are wrong,' I said to Pearl. 'Stamina is not the issue, it is style.'

She watched me limping about. She shook her head. She smiled a smile. She said, 'No, My Lady—*you* are wrong: a youngster eats like a horse and makes love like a donkey on roller skates.'

'Well, I'll be ready for him then,' I said.

She just gave me another of those looks.

'He's a gardener, Pearl,' I said. 'Not a bloody marine.'

'Is he now?' She looked a little startled. But I skipped off to the gym.

*   *   *

By the time the jazz and fireworks came around, though I still limped a little I was no longer, quite, an example of the living dead. For some reason I had to sit down rather gingerly. I had not realized before this that I had half a dozen slothful, poker-playing, gin-swigging muscles secreted in my buttocks and that to them, in particular, step aerobics is nothing short of Armageddon. Worth it though.

I had it all worked out. Get there early while he was still working. A little gentle courtship ritual. A little desultory flitting through the trees, perhaps, a little draping oneself upright around a useful trunk. A knowing smile, a touch on the arm, a wishful hint of future intent—that sort of thing . . . None of which required much shifting of muscles in the posterior department. As long as he didn't become crazed with desire and hurl me to the ground I would be fine.

Buoyed by the thought, I drove towards Hassocks Hall on yet another perfect evening, and wondered, idly, what Roberta's new idea for a Promotion would be. She tended to be very good at that sort of thing. Very small people, I reminded myself, always feel they have a lot to prove. Tinkling around in my mind was the as yet unconsolidated reclamation of the Requiem. It will happen, I told myself, and put it on the back burner to simmer, while bringing young Mellors very firmly to the fore.

CHAPTER TEN

It was no cooler, but after the drive through Hassocks Lee, I had to admit—if grudgingly—that coming through the gates of the great house past bowing trees and the silvery rippling lake was like breathing again. Even the notion of its decay seemed less depressing, more right. No wonder Yale was so enchanted. If he was suffering from a broken heart—and I was not entirely convinced, given his near-permanent smiling arrangement—then this was the place to be.

I, of course, still living in Putney, could take advantage of Hassocks Hall's magic only sporadically—most of the time I continued deep down in the glooms. No wonder people chew arsenic. Progress is entirely selective. If they could put a man on the moon and and grow a human ear from a hog's back, surely, *surely* they could invent a selective forgetfulness pill? I found the unfolding summer hard to handle, given the memories it brought. I even had trouble with cow parsley. Every time I saw it it reminded me of happiness.

I curled the car round the drive and began to think positive. At least the prospect of Young Mellors brightened the load. Though I was not quite sure how. The world will sometimes throw together two disparate forces that make a surprising and beautiful whole (the murderous Medici, the Sistine Chapel), but not often. Young Mellors and Getting Back Brahms seemed a dauntingly unlikely combination. On the other hand I quite liked the idea of *daunting.* It smacked of something difficult, absorbing—Take Your Mind Off

Things—which lust alone would not achieve. I decided the best thing was to wait and see, that useful and very adult requirement.

Erna was apparently a jazz fan. She was tottering around the grounds beaming with a proprietorial glow and looking like a danger to herself.

I could not quite approve of the way Roberta overlooked Erna's little problem. She referred to it as her 'celebratory life style', and she became quite sniffy when I suggested we might never get the money if her liver packed up.

The celebratory life style included some very odd dressing. Tonight Erna was in jeans piped with gold, and a little navy top with a gold anchor logo over one tit. Very *Elle*, very her, very pantoland. She looked like a nautical Simple Simon. A nautical Simple Simon with jewellery—and jeans that made her shrivelled derrière look shrink-wrapped. It is at times like this that one wonders why women were not granted mirrors in their behinds. As for her shoes—they made the memory of my now ruined pink sandals positively nun-like. They were *statements.* Completely unsuitable statements. Venetian glitz without benefit of constraint—small, dark blue pointy things with a slender heel striated with gold and so steep that she tottered. Roberta's had nothing on hers.

Valeria had been seconded to care, but she

was having difficulty staying at Erna's side since Erna, perhaps in celebration of her nautical logo, appeared to be tacking rather than walking. Valeria kept up as best she could, while shredding the tassles of her Indian print shawl as if she were shelling peas. They made an interesting pair.

The jazz ensemble—saxophonist, guitar, bass, trombonist and drummer—were setting up on a podium under the trees, and were all women. They looked so down at heel that they had to be Debs. Erna slewed up to them as they unpacked their instruments, and stood there jiggling her feet and tapping away at her glass to the silence. Valeria caught sight of me and waved. It was the gesture of a drowning woman. She came towards me towing her charge as if she were on reins.

Not surprisingly, Erna was much hampered by her heels, which dowelled into the sod at each step, securing her fast, like a wobbly woman. Valeria, shawl swinging, had to pause every so often to hoick her out. She left a little trail of molehills behind her, adding to the strange yellow shapes remaining from the sculptures. The once springing emerald turf did not look at its best. Poetically, it looked as if an army of gnomes had encamped there and dug all over it for fairy gold.

Valeria reached me first, giving me a quick up and down garment appraisal. Her jaw was back to normal, though there were vague signs of bruising. She seemed to approve of the jeans.

'Hallo,' she said with an uncharacteristic rakishness. 'You'll be pleased with the jazz group.' One of her eyes appeared to twitch.

'Er, yes . . .' I said, wondering if I should wink back. 'I like jazz . . .'

She shook her head. 'Not *only* the music,' she said, even more rakishly.

I smiled.

No? What then? Should I venture a compliment or two about the spanking shine on the trombonist's slide?

She went mysteriously conspiratorial, her voice lowered. '*All* women,' she said knowingly. 'The ensemble . . .'

Ah.

All women.

'I must say you types do ring the changes,' she said, eyeing me up and down again. 'No boots today? And what about those little pink ones. Sandal thingies.'

Thingies? They were State of the Art.

'Yes,' I said, a little defensively.

'Very dainty.' She said this with disapproval.

'Small feet,' I offered cautiously.

She looked down at them, nodding significantly. 'Difficult.'

We looked at them together. 'Not *very*,' I said, feeling quite affectionate about them. I was not exactly sure where we were heading. Girl-talk seemed appropriate.

'Yours are very nice,' I said warmly to a pair of unremarkable navy courts. 'And not at all big, either.'

She blushed. 'Oh thank you.'

Her eyes met mine in a horribly suggestive manner that had me gabbling on nervously. 'Oh—I like shoes . . . flat ones, high ones, sillier the better—those pink ones for instance . . .'

'Very feminine,' she said. 'And the dress. Do you often wear dresses?'

'Oh—Er—*Ah*—' was approximately the next beautiful sentence I wrought. 'Quite often,' I said, even more cautiously. 'Nice shawl . . .'

'When did you first . . . ?' she began.

I tried to go.

She moved a little nearer. Her pinky blue purblinds widened. Instead of pupils they sported huge questionmarks.

I knew exactly what she was going to do. She was going to ask me what we did in bed. I know because my friend in Wisbech says she is always being asked this. And occasionally she gets cross enough to answer. She was once followed home by a comely traffic warden on the strength of her description.

Valeria continued to look enquiring. And lubricious. 'Jim told me all about you,' she said. And came a step closer.

For some reason I could take no more of her eyes and found myself addressing the bridge of her genteel nose. Easier to lie to I suppose.

'And skirts,' I offered brightly. 'Sometimes skirts.'

Valeria considered. Valeria was torn. What to do? Which way to go now? Sartorial or Sexual?

'Long and short,' I trilled. 'Pleats occasionally. *You* know. Even a kilt—my word yes.'

She looked disappointed. But Sartorial had won.

'*I* said I couldn't really believe it, but Jim said you don't all go around in battledress every day.'

'Did he now?' It was not pleasant to think I had been discussed. 'What does he know?'

'Oh, a *lot*,' she said reverently. 'He's wonderful.'

'Is he here?'

'Who?'

'Jim . . .'

'Why?' It was a pounce rather than a question.

'Just asking.'

'It's very early,' she said, in a voice that implied she was doing a temporary fill-in for Sisyphus. 'And I'm already wiped out.' We both looked at Erna.

'Poor soul,' I said.

'Poor?' hissed Valeria. 'She's rolling.'

And indeed she was.

'Nearly there now,' I muttered, as she made the final lurch. I did not like Valeria's tone. 'Pity,' I said, 'that he isn't here.'

Her eyes narrowed. Who?'

'Jim . . .'

. . . and narrowed some more. 'Oh? Why?' she spat. Even more suspiciously.

Which told me all I needed to know. I'll take you on any time, dearie, I thought, any time. 'Be kind to Erna, won't you?'

'I can hardly be anything else,' she said stiffly.

Erna was smiling trustfully at the empty distance and tapping her feet at nothing again. Sweet.

'How's the jaw?' I asked politely

'Fine,' said Valeria. She was tassle shredding again. 'Jim has been looking after it. With ice-packs. Americans are very keen on ice. He's absolutely wonderful. Don't you think?'

If her eyes went any dewier she'd be shedding tears.

'Oh wonderful,' I said.

'You're not an extremist, then?'

'Pardon?'

'I didn't think you could be. Not with those pink sandals . . .' she said wistfully. Then she brightened. 'Jim says you don't like men. Is that true?'

If ever a woman wanted an affirmative answer, here she was.

'Well—er . . .'

'Do you think he's attractive? For a man? I don't suppose you think about it really.'

'Well—er . . .'

'I wonder if men look at people like you and find you attractive?'

People like me? People like me?

I clapped her playfully on the back. Perhaps a *little* too hard. Then I smiled a big smile for Erna, gave her a wave, and bounded off towards the rhododendrons. Contact must be made before the evening commenced. Roberta was going to make a Big Announcement later and my life would be worth but a snowflake in Hades if I did not attend.

* * *

In the distance I could hear the sound of a merry hoe being struck, or shears exuberantly clipping, or at any rate, *something* of a cultivatory nature. Good. The drape, the winning smile, the older woman as panther seemed a sensible arrangement. I straightened my back, stuck out my chest, took my courage in both hands and ran down the dappled little path. The distant sound of hoeing grew nearer. I was just congratulating myself on having got away from them all, when, from behind me . . .

Stasis . . .

'Diana?'

A voice, calling. A very familiar voice.

Who was it, in mythology, who turned to

stone?

At the sound of that voice I was as rock in the winsome eye of Medusa.

Perhaps I had suddenly cracked? Literature is filled with heroines driven mad by lost love and hearing voices. But I didn't think so. It was real. The stone continued.

Not here . . . Not now . . . Not just when I'd got myself some sort of survival plan . . . *Surely* not.

'Diana?' called the voice again.

'Teddy?' I whispered to the darkness of the rustling rhododendrons. 'Teddy?' A little louder.

The merry hoe went on a-merrying somewhere in the distance.

'Teddy?' I shrieked, so that birds flew out of the darkness and the rustlings all around me.

CHAPTER ELEVEN

Pearl and my mother like each other and agree on many things. 'You should go and stay with her,' is Pearl's current anthem. 'She's offered to pay your fare.'

'Bribery,' I said coldly. 'Downright bribery.'

Plenty More Fish In The Sea, Time Is The Great Healer, All Part Of The Learning Curve—I could just imagine her dishing up that lot every day on the Costa. It was bad enough having her book jackets winking down at me, without going and staying with her. Customers are always telling me how wonderful she is. I long to lean across the counter and say, Yes, but she never baked me a tray of scones like Polly's mum. I might say such things when I reach the menopause. I am saving up quite a lot of stuff for the moment that arrives. Like the fact she thought Teddy was too dull for me. What did she want? A daughter dating Papa Doc?

Pearl and my mother also agree about Roberta Topp. My mother is fond of telling her that she 'wasted no time in reading her books' which satisfies honour for both. Roberta is not one to look for secondary meanings in language. She's too busy scouring the newspapers for plots. Privately my mother says her work is all structure and silly coincidence. People don't just happen to pop up in the right or wrong place or the right or wrong time in books. They only do that in real life. Both she and Pearl hold this view. And it is quite unbearable how often, how *very* often, they are right. I was moved to think all this as I heard my name called again. It was exactly like appearing in a Roberta Topp novel.

Teddy it was.

Really here, in living Technicolor and if-you-prick-him-he-bleeds. Roberta, with her usual sensitivity, had finally invited him. With no thought for me. One day, I vowed—one day

God would punish her, and if He didn't, I certainly would.

In fourth-dynasty Giza they produced something called Reserve Heads. Just a few alternative bonces, dotted around the place, in case you felt like a change after passing on. What sensible civilizations we have lost. How good it would have been to be able to whip one of these out of my shoulder bag and put it on. It would have smiling eyes, artfully windswept hair, and a dewy look about the lip area that said This Woman Has Just Been Fucked. Extremely Well. Think pheromones, I told myself through artfully clenched teeth, for he may be alone. I turned around.

Naturally, he was not.

Well—that was it then. That was bloody well *it*. So much for the little demon of hope.

Standing next to Teddy, who waved and smiled at me as if he had just spotted a favourite aunt, was something resembling the Caucasian version of a prehistoric fertility doll. One on whom the bust had slipped a bit southwards. There was more than a tadpole or two in there.

Agnes was bloomingly, billowingly—and in my opinion *blowsily*—pregnant.

I breathed in. I stood erect. At least *my* stomach was nice and flat and tight. For some reason that made me feel sad. And for some reason, when I feel sad, I tend to shed tears. Which are noticeable. Accordingly, I set off in their direction and, with a merry wave, deliberately walked myself into an overhanging branch. This took quite a detour. Funny how you think, under stress, that the maddest of actions will look convincingly sane. I could now hold on to my legitimately streaming eye and advance.

Once upon a time Teddy would have rushed up with a clean white handkerchief and made it all better. Now he—and Fatty—stood uncertainly, waiting for me to reach them.

'Daft thing to do,' he said conversationally.

I looked pointedly at the fatly fertilized bulge and then back at him.

'Yes—wasn't it?' I said sweetly.

Strangely enough there was a bit of a pause after this. Behind them I suddenly saw Yale, in all his campus sweetheart meets T. S. Eliot glory, cross the top of the gravel path, glance down, notice us, and stop.

'Hi,' he called, beaming that smile.

'Hi-i-i . . .' I called back, waving like a lunatic with semaphore. 'Well—Jim—*dear* Jim—hi-i- . . .'

He looked puzzled, as indeed he might. The natural conclusion to be drawn from my greeting was that I had mistaken him for one who had been abroad for some years. Possibly somewhere dangerous. Like the shores of an alligator swamp. Whence he was unable to write or telephone, had been given up for dead and was, in fact, my deeply adored, surprisingly restored, husband.

He came towards us, looking strangely uncertain. He was wearing baggy cream flannels and a most unpleasant navy blazer, but at least he was hatless—and he would just have to do. Sartorial advice could come later.

'Well hallo Jim,' I said, patting him on the back and giving him a huge kiss on the lips, a real smackeroo. 'I wondered where you'd got to . . .'

His eyes had gone a very peculiar size and he smiled uneasily. Opting for the safer ground of fact concerning his provenance, he pointed behind him, about to be deliciously literal. 'Well—I—er . . .'

I tucked my hand into his arm. 'Never mind, never mind,' I said gaily. 'Let me introduce you to two very old friends of mine—Teddy and . . .'

I ceased the introductions. Something was wrong with my hearing aid, had I been wearing one, for I heard, repeated, as if in echo of my words, 'Well—hallo Jim—I wondered where you'd got to,' repeated.

And, unless one of the party was a part-time ventriloquist, the statement had not issued from them.

I looked beyond the pair.

Shit.

It was Valeria.

Smile clamped on lips, eyes lowering, tassels swinging with determination as she scrunched towards us. Gravel flew. She came right to the heart of us, smiled up at the new arrival from the alligator swamp, and only *for* him, in that way I can never manage and which he and the rest of his sex would kill for, and then looked enquiringly from Teddy, to Agnes, to me. Well—not *exactly* to me in the full sense—more to me in the sense of my hand, which was still in the crook of Yale's arm.

Valeria—perfectly legitimately I grant you—hooked her hand into Yale's other arm. So we were both—as it were—attached and resembling something out of a Hollywood movie. *On The Town* perhaps? Frank Sinatra with a couple of smiling broads?

I casually slid my hand away under the watchful stare of four pairs of eyes. I prayed not to blush, but of course I did. Caught with your fingers in the till, came to mind. Despite their bovinity, Agnes's eyes said she understood entirely. Agnes's eyes also showed a degree of sympathy.

And kindness. Madonna to my harlot. Perfectly intolerable. Hormones most likely.

Teddy just stood there looking wonderful. And silent. My eye was still watering, and in a moment of supreme forgetfulness I rubbed it. Oh good. That was the mascara done for. A one-eyed panda loose in the rhododendron dell. Reserve Head? Reserve Head? What I needed was a Reserve Brain.

You know that moment when everyone

looks at you and nothing is said? When everyone looks at you significantly and nothing is said? And when the range of looks goes from It Might Bite to Deepest Sympathy? You know it. I know it. And there it was.

'Your poor eye,' said Agnes eventually.

'What have you done to it?' asked Valeria. Which was rich coming from her. 'It's watering rather.'

'Walked into a tree,' said Teddy.

'That,' I said icily, 'is what battered women say when they daren't admit to the truth.'

That was *really* good.

Nobody said a word.

Somewhere above my head a bird trilled its evening song and the metallic leaves rustled anew. Gloriously free things, birds, soaring away, unreachable, wings on the air. A short life but an untrammelled one. A short life made joyful by its ability to bomb anyone it might choose.

'Oh, listen to that bird,' I said lamely.

More silence. Everyone strained to look as if they were straining to hear. Four necks were dutifully arched. Teddy's adam's apple, that darling and entirely masculine appurtenance, bobbed.

'Mmm,' he said. Bob, bob.

Struggle on, I thought, since speech is called for. And smiling my gay, one-eyed smilc, I declaimed, 'Ethereal minstrel! Pilgrim of the sky!' Of which I was rather proud. Nature and humanity, essential Wordsworth. For a moment I felt as uplifted as the skylark.

'It's a pigeon,' said Yale, as something grey flapped its way out of the branches.

'Pigeons coo. That was song.'

'Well,' said Teddy in that conciliatory tone I knew so well, 'it was probably a blackbird.'

'*Not* a skylark, I'd say,' said Yale, pointedly.

The trouble with getting World Domination for Women is that we never will. And that is because, apart from economic and biological factors, men are very good at staying the course in matters both big (splitting the atom) and small (fucking ornithological speculations).

I have been likened on occasion, and when sulking, to one of those game tribeswomen who stick a plate in their lower lip to get an attractive dish effect. This, apparently, wins over the tribal boys dramatically, and you've soon got all the beads you can handle. But not, apparently, in Middlesex.

'How about an off-course albatross?' I asked brightly.

Yale's mouth twitched.

I looked pointedly at Agnes. 'A very *large* albatross?'

Saying this proved so enjoyable I prepared to continue the theme.

Smooth as butter, Valeria got in first.

'I'm sorry,' she said, extending her free hand to old Fertile Features, 'we haven't met . . .'

'Albatross?' said Teddy wonderingly, looking up cautiously at the trees.

I continued the soup-plate pout and my eyes sought Yale's. He looked away. But not before I caught a trace of amusement. Deeply irritating.

He looked skywards again. 'Brahms, skylarks . . .' he said to the air. 'Never satisfied.'

'What?' said Valeria, who had the nose of a hornet.

I should have ignored him. But couldn't.

'Well we wouldn't have got very far in the world if we'd been *satisfied*, now would we . . . I mean—what would have happened to Mother Theresa's destitute if she just sat there looking at her pious fingernails and saying, "Oh well, mustn't grumble." Mmm?'

Another well-rendered silence.

Teddy stared. '*Albatross?*' he mouthed. I could begin to see what my mother meant about him not always being very bright.

The silence was broken by Agnes who took Valeria's profferred hand and introduced herself, adding, 'And this is my husband . . .'

Husband is a very terrible word. I heard no more because of the rushing wind in my ears—as if a thousand pigeons had been loosed upon the air, a million albatrosses flown off course. Something punched me very hard in the solar plexus only nothing was near enough to take the blame. I may have gone scarlet, I may have gone white, but I definitely, *definitely* did not look a normal colour.

Yale's face, concerned now, and Valeria's so polite, were well out of focus. I believe I squeaked. 'Hot,' I said. 'So *hot* . . .'

Agnes said that she, too, felt a little warm and would like to sit down.

I then watched them walk away slowly with their arms around each other, through the dappled sunlight, the soughing trees, the dancing air, out into the brilliance of the lawn beyond. How kind of her it was to go. Kind. Kind. Kind. But then, she could afford to be kind—and generous—and sensitive—and all those heartwarming things—could she not?

Now,' said Valeria with horrible playfulness. 'I have a little job for you.' And she tugged at Yale's silly sleeve.

'See you later,' she called, in a voice that carried the confident triumph of one whose ancestors fought on the winning side.

He merely nodded at me before scrunching off beside her.

Exit two couples. And I was alone. I could remember exactly how that arm felt when Teddy used to hold me like that. There was no refuting it. Memories were the biggest albatrosses of all. Strung around your neck for all eternity unless you *did* something about it. So do something I would.

For some moments I stood there feeling things and then I got a tissue and a mirror from the bag which had let me down so cruelly in the spare head department, and dabbed my eyes so that the mascara should be neat.

In the distance continued the sound of a woodsman a-wooding. He was haphazardly yelling out the words of what seemed to be a rap song, and despite its rawness of rhythm his voice was, suddenly, very dear to me. No skylark. No blackbird. Not even a pigeon. But a raven, I fancied, and croaking away to his doom. One hoped it would prove a pleasant experience.

CHAPTER TWELVE

The Brahms Requiem certainly would not sit well with the singing I heard as I approached: something about all women being bitches out to get you so you had to screw them first . . . The kind of up-to-date lyrics so beloved of Cultural and Media Studies in the better class of Polytechnic.

Fortunately Young Mellors was thinking nothing as he sang along. His beautiful eyes were quite, and wholly, vacant and he was raking to the rhythm. A nice, muscular activity. Earphones were in place, which accounted for the choral offering. Rap today, I thought, Brahms tomorrow? One must have faith.

'Hi,' I said, going round to the front of him

so he could see me. I tried That Smile.

He slipped off his headphones eagerly and his eyes lit up.

So it really worked.

I smiled even more.

He had the sweetest face beneath the stubble. Young and undamaged. A fresh plain upon which life had not yet stamped its miserable rune.

'Hi,' he replied, clearly delighted.

How confident I felt. It was in the bag. Whatever it was.

He disengaged the Walkman. He opened his mouth. He spoke. I waited for some kind of tryst, some kind of boyish banter.

He said, 'Are you one of the teachers, Miss?'

Well—you keep smiling, don't you. It's the only way. First Old Frogspawn, and now I was being mistaken for a blue-stocking. An old blue-stocking.

I shook my head.

He looked surprised. 'The lady in charge'—he made a sort of chestward gesture—'er . . . small lady, big . . . er . . .' He thought better of it. 'She said you were one of them.'

I looked at him askance. Was this some kind of joke?

But no. He was quite serious. No Sapphic pun intended.

Teacher? Lady in charge? 'You mean Roberta?'

He looked unenlightened.

'Miss Topp . . . er . . .' I gestured in the same chestward way. 'Little with a big voice. Writes books?'

'That's her. Runs this school thing.'

He put down his rake and got a look in his eyes that was highly unexpected. A look called Enthusiasm.

I responded immediately, and I hoped attractively. 'You like gardening? I must say I—'

'*Gardening?* Oh fuck no. I want to be a writer. I've enrolled. I will enshrine your vision.'

Continue to smile, I urged. It could be worse. He could have declared marriage with six children and a loving wife.

'Enshrine my vision?'

'That's what she said. There is a storyteller in every one of us. And she's going to help me to prove it.'

He took a scrumpled piece of paper from his shorts. 'Got an idea already,' he said. I listened in a kind of fog. He wanted, it appeared, to create a hero not unlike the Terminator. In fact, you could say, exactly like the Terminator. A computer-game hero brought to life.

'Good idea, eh?' he said eagerly.

I listened. I did not say that I thought it had been done and at least twice. I am not entirely stupid.

'Like Schwarzenegger movies,' he added.

And looked at me enquiringly.

I nodded, thought, and then posed for a photograph called Inspired.

'Terminatrix,' I found myself saying idly. 'Terminatrix . . .'

He paused and looked puzzled.

'Female,' I said. 'Why not?'

'A woman couldn't do that stuff,' he said, almost kindly.

'No,' I said. 'But then—neither, really, could a man. You have to have an angle, that's all. You can't just repeat somebody else's success. Jane Austen might be able to stand still at the centre of the same world. You have to go out and create one.'

'Jane Austen?' he said, and pursed his lips thinking. 'Who she?'

The breeze around us was gentle. The smell of the damp, warm earth was seductive. You could almost feel the squirrels holding their breath. And then the Idea came to me. To Get Back Brahms, yes, but to get back Amalfi too. *And* the Ristorante Flavio. Reclaim all three memories. Why not? Providing I didn't do an Icarus and attempt more than that—it was perfectly possible.

In olden days and with similar desires, the lady of the manor would have invited him in to her home and offered him an education in return for his favours. Well—so would *I*. He would have the sublime delight of Brahms, the beauties of Italian food and landscape, and the sensuous pleasures of my bed. Perfect. I beamed at him. He beamed back. So far, so good. Stage two, consolidate.

'Look,' I said. 'Are you serious about this book and the Academy?'

'Dead serious.'

'Then I'll help. You'll need a location first. All the best writers do.'

He looked puzzled again.

'Dickens, Hardy . . . ?'

He thought hard. He looked very sweet.

'Forster, Hemingway . . . ?'

Blank—very attractive—but blank.

'Fleming, Forsyth?'

He began to look hunted.

'Blyton? Dahl?'

Still he looked hunted.

I racked my brains. Only connect.

'Where's Wally?'

He nodded at last.

'All writers need something to hook things on to,' I made hooking gestures with my hands. 'Like a castle or an island or something.' I'd have been great in *What's My Line?*—hook, hook, hook I went.

A little light seemed to penetrate. 'Oh,' he said, 'like in *Dracula*?'

'You've read *Dracula*?'

'Didn't know they'd made a book of it.'

Deep breath. 'Perfect example,' I said. 'You need somewhere atmospheric—full of danger—somewhere high up, jagged with rocks, real Terminator country, with a boiling sea below.'

He seemed only half convinced.

'Where people can be hurled off forcefully and dash their brains out on the crags?' I said firmly.

Oddly enough, Agnes Yaudet's visage swam through my mind.

'Sounds good,' he said, brightening.

'Sounds like Amalfi,' I said. 'Italy.'

'Sounds like Sheppey as well,' he said. 'Kent. That's nearer. My Nan's got a caravan there. Don't know about a boiling sea, though,' he went on. 'It's fucking freezing all year . . .' He shuffled. 'Sorry to swear.'

'That's all right,' I said, practically crying inside. It was the word Sheppey I objected to.

I looked around me at the waving, rustling trees, the gravel path behind, the sunlight delicately lighting on the new-laid sod, and I thought—Tell me, Fate, why you had to let me choose him. Not only does he have pretensions towards Art, but he has a Nan with a Caravan and, apparently, a mind of his own. Why, Fate, why?

Fate was feeling conversational. Oracles sound strangely like mothers. She went into full flow immediately, as oracles will. 'Everything you are is a memory. Don't mess with Fate, dear, and do realize this is Life. Not yours to control. Frankly, all you mortals can do is to tinker with the engine. The design is unalterable, try as you might.'

Listen, I said, nobody objected to Jason and the Argonauts. Did you say to him: Don't bother to go for the Golden Fleece, my boy—just stay at home and suck vine leaves? Of course not. So don't try it with me.

The oracle went silent. They do when faced with irrefutable pluck.

It'll end in tears, was all she added, before disappearing into her bed of burned entrails. It'll end in tears. For somebody.

And the other thing They always do is hedge their bets.

I looked at the Fleece substitute. 'What's your name?'

'Dave Barnes.'

'Well, Dave, won't it be a bit expensive to join?'

I was brought up very sharpish by his reply.

'Oh no,' he said cheerily. 'I'm getting a scholarship. The lady said.' He smiled. 'Got to go in a minute. She's going to introduce me. She says I am her Promotional Plum.'

No *wonder* Fate backed off fast. She had wafted him beneath my gaze and then plucked him from me.

Clever Roberta. A Promotional Plum indeed. He was malleable, with the essential requirements of youth and good looks. Plucked from me, be damned. If she could have her agenda, I could have mine. Honour was dead anyway. Somewhere in an unmarked grave alongside Dickens, Hardy and Dahl.

I smiled at the victim.

'In that case,' I said, 'I am sure we will meet again.'

'You are a teacher then?' He looked hopeful.

'No,' I said.

He looked disappointed.

'But I *am* an Expert.'

'An *Expert*? Ah,' he said, and looked impressed.

'So ask my advice any time. Will you?' I stepped nearer. 'Promise?'

In the distance the band struck up its first number, 'Putting on the Ritz'.

'Shit music,' he said, almost apologetically, and quickly stuffed his Walkman back in his ears.

I watched him go. Had the downtrodden agricultural classes worn cut-off Levis rather than rough old smocks, the lady of the manor might not have retained her wimple so resolutely. We might have had our revolution hundreds of years before.

The libido was definitely stirred. And while the libido was stirred the past began to pale. The Idea was good. Amalfi it would be. Somehow. I would just have to deal with the appalling prospect of Sheppey later. In some respects a site close to Southend was not, *necessarily*, a bad thing. The sludgy brown mudwastes of the Kent coast were not unBrahmsian. Barren of all charm, of course, but there *had* to be cliffs, didn't there? And swirling waters as promised. In fact, I could make out a great case for Sheppey being second only to Amalfi for locational perfection. In short, with one lone straw clutched in my hand, and the depressing proximity of the fecund Agnes, I was—to mince no words—*desperate.*

'See you then,' he called. 'And thanks for the offer.'

'Don't mention it,' I said cheerfully.

In fact, I thought, *please* don't mention it. And set off back towards the music and the madder wine.

CHAPTER THIRTEEN

As I crossed the lawn towards the gathering hordes I passed Erna, oblivious of the music and peacefully unconscious in a deckchair. Even in sleep she had a smile on her face. I had become quite fond of her.

Near the band Peter the Bald, in a very silly straw hat, cousin to Yale's, was holding the fort with a famous actress of indeterminate years who had mastered the art of Polyfilla. Every time the *Wotchacock* photographer got her to pose, Peter the Bald stepped smartly out of the way. Which seemed commendably self-deprecating. Polyfilla tried her best to encourage him by giggling and acting frisky, a very horrible sight in a woman of such years, but he refused. 'I am merely the Eminence Grise,' he said finally, looking Eminence Pink, 'and would rather stay out of the limelight.'

Of Desmond there was no sign. Rumour had it that he was in India, tracking another Windsor scandal, but wherever he was, Roberta was much miffed at his absence. She had given him at least two lunches and one dinner to report progress along the way and she expected him here, now, for the Grand Finale and her Night of Stars. She had been irritated by it all week, and she looked even more irritated now as she beckoned me over. She stood defiantly, hands on hips, chin up like a furious daisy, apparently giving Mr and Mrs Valeria what-for.

I fought my way towards her through half-dead rock stars with fabulous wealth and a yen for immortality, rakish ex-politicians who had run away to join the media circus, women who lunch and have liposuction, *les enfants terribles* of every quarter from painting to sport to violins. Each one had something in common. They had all been published. They were the proof of what the Academy of Forward Fiction stood for: That everyone has at least one book in them. This was the Star-studded Authorial Crème de la Crème.

Roberta's theme was Englishness. The

Englishness of a perfect summer's evening at an English country house. With jazz. The gathered were therefore obliged to venture into deckchairs if they wished to sit. This had separated the indigenous from those beyond Calais. One forgets just how peculiarly English they are, deckchairs. So redolent of the English lawn and Betjeman country. And how mysterious to the foreigner, like golliwogs in jam. I was reminded of this as I passed a flushed-looking Jim and Valeria.

She stood to one side of him, hands clasped, watching anxiously as he attempted to resurrect the wood and canvas mystery. He, meanwhile, went through several perplexed convolutions in the course of my short walk across the green, and Valeria held the pose of she who suffers one of the most terrible agonies known to woman—how *not* to wrest something from the inept hands of the struggling male, with a cry of, Oh Let Me.

Valeria was wise, for such behaviour bids farewell, immediate and for ever, to the diamond, second finger left . . . A tribute that was surely never far from her thoughts. Hence she kept her hands clasped in modest and seemly fashion. This is almost certainly why the Virgin Mary is depicted so frequently in similar pose. Otherwise it would be Whoops-a-Daisy and, 'Oh give it here, God—you're making a right pig's ear of it. Call yourself a Pantocrator, huh?'

Yale gave me a look that would not have disgraced a maddened bull. I smiled very sweetly, and walked on. One knows when one is not wanted. Valeria looked at me very suspiciously. Maybe I had undone the buttons of my shirt a trifle more than was necessary. Well—what's a girl to do when it is so warm?

'Jeans?' said Roberta, eyeing my outfit with distaste.

Valeria's parents looked at me as if I were a worm.

'Norman Hartnell,' I said conversationally. 'Only things designed by him I've got.' I shrugged and smiled at Mr and Mrs V. 'What's good enough for Princess Anne . . .'

Roberta looked semi-convinced. Mrs V. smiled frostily, quite unconvinced.

'We were just discussing,' said Roberta breathily, bosoms heaving with emotion, 'my Concept.'

'The point is,' said Mrs V, 'that gardeners are not two a penny.'

'The point is,' said Roberta, quite as acidly, 'that we need a promotional angle. We need to burst forth upon the world . . .'

Clamp jaw shut.

'. . . and he is *it*.' She gave herself a good pummelling. 'I shall announce it tonight. Peterkins says it will cohese our mission, purpose, values—and win us universal commitment.'

'And enshrine our vision,' I added promptly.

'Exactly,' said Roberta, startled. *'Exactly . . .'*

The Valerias stared down their noses. Roberta stared up their nostrils. Stalemate.

Roberta was nudging herself black and blue with zealous fire. 'There is nothing English society likes better than to back an outsider. A good amateur is so much more of a draw than a surefire success.'

She gestured at the Celebrity throng. 'It happened for them once. Now they are the past and David Barnes is the future.'

'He is the future of our garden,' said Mrs V. 'And that's that. Boy can't write a book. Boy can barely write.'

'That,' said Roberta, 'is immaterial.' She gestured towards the Celebrities. 'Most of them couldn't write either. Besides—that is what we are here for—to teach! What is the point of giving a scholarship to someone who knows how to do it?'

It was one of those logical moments when you know something is seriously wrong.

She then swung round and faced the glorious west front of Hassocks Hall. She shrugged.

'Without him—I can guarantee the success of nothing . . .' and her gaze was directed in particular at the roof. *'Nothing,'* she said firmly. And she fluttered her dainty little hand.

There was not a lot to choose between being in her lifeboat or the Aged Valerias' when the *Titanic* went down.

We stood there in silence for about half a second. Eventually Mrs Valeria went slightly pink, which was clearly the summit of emotion. 'It took us six months to find him at the Labour Exchange. I simply *can't* let him go.'

I looked at Roberta's jaw. Granite.

I looked at Mrs V.'s jaw. Mere marble.

Roberta would win.

She returned her gaze and did not take her eyes off Mrs Valeria. 'I want David Barnes,' she said. 'And I mean to have him.'

Which was approximately what I was thinking.

The male of the species, Mr V, eyebrows bristling, gazed out to sea or whatever the landed gentry version of this is. Certainly he was no longer with us in any useful or Gainsborough form.

'He will be the Child of Nature taken and civilized,' she offered.

'Or the Noble Savage brought to bend the knee . . .'

Roberta pursed her lips. I smiled innocently. The twin Valerias barrelled us as if we were barking.

'If he cannot write, so much the better,' said Roberta. 'He will be taught. That is what this Academy is for. And taught *properly*. To the point. No nonsense. If he can, anyone can.'

'He is a good all-round gardener,' said Mrs Valeria firmly. 'Not Dickens.'

'That statement is not meaningful,' said

Roberta.

'Dickens was a bottle-washer once,' I offered.

'But hardly out of choice,' said Mrs V. 'We are discussing *gardening*. At which the boy is very good. Is he not?' She gave her husband a corralling look. He refused to come to heel. He was now gazing, steadfastly and with stiff upper lip, at the roof of Hassocks Hall.

'We'll get another boy,' he said manfully. 'But we will never get another Hall.'

Roberta flapped a hand. 'I know I'm right. I can feel it in my bones . . .'

Funny place to keep your bones . . .

Perhaps the Valerias thought so too, for, giving an encore of their excellent impersonation of frozen reeds, they moved off.

From behind me floated an exclamation full of feminine rapture.

Yale had managed the deckchair.

Valeria lowered herself into it as cautiously as a sufferer from haemorrhoids and, achieving the miracle of bum on safestretched canvas, smiled up at him another of those smiles. The sort that I could never manage, the sort that Teddy had never demanded, the silly sort that would make your blood curdle to produce.

And just then, as if it were ordained, I looked across the table of winking fizzing glasses and saw him, and the whale-that-was her, and she was smiling at him in that same disgusting way. My stomach discovered bungee-jumping. I refocused on Roberta, and she, if you please, did the same thing across the addled lawn, to Peter the Bald. All three of them at it. Poor Mary Wollstonecraft might never have been born.

Roberta was still looking soppy as she patted her perfect hair.

'So?' I asked savagely. 'Why Teddy?'

'Why Teddy what?'

'Why is he here?'

She snapped her lizard-like eyes. 'I told you at the dinner, Diana. Sponsorship. And cachet. Men with money love cars. Just go and have a look in the carpark,' she added crisply. 'And anyway—now the baby's on the way it's all in the past, isn't it?'

'Roberta,' I said, 'have you ever had a broken heart?'

'They wouldn't dare,' she said, and bit with large, creamy teeth, right through a brazil nut.

Crack.

I suggested to Fate, with all due reverence, that She make a note of that.

CHAPTER FOURTEEN

It was decided that Erna should go and have a little cool-off indoors. Despite underpinning this entire venture she seemed to have forgotten to underpin herself. She was duly handed over to a waiter and ushered away—though her heels kept sticking in the grass again, and when he paused to haul her out she went for his crutch.

'Must be her little party trick,' I said to Peter the Bald as we watched her go.

'She's worth millions,' he replied.

Which in an odd way *was* a connection. I couldn't imagine her getting away with it if she were on benefit.

His eyes gleamed as she disappeared through the front entrance.

'It's in the bag,' he said softly.

'Or the bag is in,' I offered, by way of jest.

But he was miles away and looking very, very pleased.

The band struck up anew. The girls gave it all they'd got. And the evening commenced. All I had to do was circulate, avoiding Teddy and the Beached Bloater. People kept going up to them and shaking his hand, or kissing her leathery old cheek, as if they had done something special together but really, as I would have pointed out to anyone who might listen, the special thing to do is to stay *un*pregnant. Any woman in the approximate area of thirty years old and in a relationshp will tell you so.

I went over to Sir Randolph Fallow—our tame brewing magnate whose memoirs of his country-house pursuits should have brought down the government—and tried it out.

That Smile.

The transparent one that anybody with half a brain could see through. I looked into his eyes and I gave it my all. It worked. It really *worked.* I think we might have become engaged that night if his wife had not intervened. She was Lady Fallow the second, once a long-legged croupier, and she knew the ropes. The floor was hers. If I had stayed around she would have wiped it with me.

Books, I reminded the Fallows, foregoing the Smile, were the key to it all.

Books, I reminded them, were the panacea for most of society's ills.

Books, I reminded them, could engage and expand the most depraved mind.

They nodded. They listened. They were convinced.

They scanned the horizon, it seemed to me, for a depraved mind with which to do battle. And then, over the system, came Roberta's voice.

'David Barnes to the podium, please. David Barnes to the podium.'

And out from the bushes popped the Child of Nature. With his cap on back to front, his Walkman headphones giving him that mindless lope, his stocky legs and boots ringing loud on the gravel, he could have been tramping off home to his tea. Just for a moment he looked ordinary—until I remembered that he was my route back to Brahms and freedom again.

Then he immediately looked deliciously desirable.

The band gave a flourish of notes. Peter the Bald, all pink and sweaty, stood to one side and gazed up adoringly. She kissed her hand to him, and began.

'Ladies and Gentlemen, Friends,' she said. 'With this wonderful man to steer us through, I am delighted to announce that we have raised full funding. The Academy of Forward Fiction is Fact. I could not have achieved this without such a wonderful partner by my side . . .' She attempted to haul him up next to her, but he was not having any. 'So shy,' she said, 'so very modest.'

He was, indeed, gazing down at the ground, his silly hat pulled well over his head. I put it down to repression.

'But his determination and skill has steered me through.'

Roberta Topp giving full and *public* acknowledgement of his superiority now.

Rock on . . .

Peter the Bald made a little signal towards the back of the crowd, exchanged a whispered word or two with Roberta, melted away, and Roberta stood up. She made the big guns comfortable before announcing proudly, 'And now I want to introduce you to someone.'

Dave Barnes ran from the back of the throng, like a contestant in an American Game Show, spat out his chewing gum, and jumped up on to the podium.

She held his hand up in triumph. 'Friends,' she said. 'Here is Our Star.'

There was a tremendous amount of enthusiastic clapping before she quietened it and began.

'David Barnes. A simple gardener. But we at the Academy for Forward Fiction will take this Child of Nature, tenant of Hassocks Lee, not Hassocks Hall, and we will transform him into the first of our New Generation of Storytellers. We will prove that however humble'—and her tone implied that to be any more humble would be an impossibility—'we all have at least one good book in us.'

Dave Barnes stepped forward. The crowd behind me began to clap. And a lone voice nearby said, 'Christ Almighty, just look at those thighs.'

I turned round. It was Lady Fallow.

'Steroids,' I whispered. And shook my head sadly.

'Shame,' she said.

With luck that had cleared the field.

CHAPTER FIFTEEN

Roberta was not one to let an audience go. And, to be fair, this audience did not seem inclined to depart. They had paid their dues and they wanted their money's worth. Dave Barnes stood next to her trying to look like a star. In the distance, Mrs V. wrang her hands and when a tray of drinks appeared, most unusually, she grabbed a glass and downed it in one shuddering swallow. Mr V. appeared much interested in something stuck on the sole of his shoe. Mrs V. took another one. Well—it was a hot day . . .

One of Roberta's great skills, one I truly admired, was her showmanship. She might not be the most accomplished writer in the world, but she could certainly deliver a speech and her timing was impeccable.

She praised the Academy's setting: '. . . this Adam House set in a Council Sea . . .' and told us that here, at Hassocks Hall, we would be Guardians of the Good, Defenders of Demystification, Promoters of a Modern Literary Armageddon, relegators of all novels without a proper beginning, middle and end, all novels that allowed the Writing of the Understood to swamp the Writing of the Explicitly Pointed Out. All novels that got too convoluted, lost the plot or made you look too often in a dictionary.

One was moved to speak up for the Bible but one opted for cowardly silence. In the war one would undoubtedly have been a collaborator.

Roberta rounded the speech off by reminding the assembled that without

Florentine Medici patronage, Sandro and Leonardo (she was, apparently, on first-name terms with the passed-on artistic genius of Renaissance) would never have got anywhere. That what they produced under their Medici patrons was quite recognizable, not a bit hard, and certainly none of your arcane tricksy stuff.

She glowed with Revelational fervour. Now for writing. And then there was Dante.

Dante also being the name of a particularly vibrant new aftershave, this caused a little confusion among the listeners, who thought perhaps this was another of the sponsors. What was it, Roberta continued, about the *Divine Comedy* that people remembered and *liked*? Hands on hips, she waited.

The assembled were still considering aftershave. Lady Fallow, a game girl, called out Give Us A Clue. Roberta told them. What they liked and remembered about Dante, she opined, was the Love Story. Right?

Right.

Next to me a lilac Lauren polo, with moustache, shrugged, looked relieved, and said that it certainly wasn't the smell.

The question of Value For Money was dealt with. Roberta went quite pink on the subject of under two hundred pages being just not worth sixteen pounds.

I wondered about the value of Basho's:

This road:

no one walks along it.
Dusk in autumn.

Less than a bottle of Dante, very likely.

Roberta was nearly at the end and extolling the visionary virtues of Mr and Mrs V. for their enlightenment in the use of this noble house. How good it was to see this fusion of ancient and new, this happy marriage of culture and setting . . .

Mr and Mrs V. looked more inclined towards a divorce and Mrs V. had definitely gone ruddy. There was about them less of the Medici, and more of the Savonarola. And Valeria, stuck with a party on the far side of the crowd, looked unhappy enough to be the product of a broken home. She was going giddy trying to keep an eye on all three of her responsibilities, Yale, parents, patrons—very much in that order. When I sought shade and arrived next to Yale she went demented, sending him long, loving, mournful looks across the throng. He gave the odd little wave, and once blew a shifty kiss in response to hers. She responsed with That Smile.

Behind us stood Peter the Bald with his arms folded, henchmanlike. In his beige linen suit of vaguely military cut, he only needed an armband with a black lightning motif and proclaiming Steward to complete the picture. Apart from the silly hat. He had an odd expression on his face. Just the slightest bit shifty, I thought.

Everyone was now completely enraptured at the thought of being on chummy terms with Sandy and Len the Florenteenies. Even Teddy, in the distance, looked convinced.

I leaned towards Yale and said, '"What is the use of a book?" thought Alice, "without pictures or conversations . . . ?"'

Yale smiled awkwardly, as well he might. 'Needs must,' he said abruptly.

Valeria was staring hard again, hungry as ever.

'She's a jealous little thing isn't she,' I said. 'I think she's afraid I'll jump on you.'

He laughed. 'I don't think so.' He gave her a little wave. She lit up with pleasure. 'You being of a different persuasion.'

I opened my mouth to protest, but he put up his hand. 'Well, you got so friendly back in the rhododendrons, I had to say something.'

'Only because that was my ex I was talking to.'

'I realize that,' he said coldly. 'Well—if you wouldn't mind leaving it the way it is with Val—I'd be grateful. As you say—she can be jealous.'

I looked at him in genuine amazement. 'Are you two really an item?'

He gave another little wave and smile.

'Looks like it,' he said.

'You cynical shit.'

'Everyone has their own agenda, Diana—

what's yours?'

But we were interrupted.

'Behold,' he said with sideways whisper. 'Here comes our very own Catherine de' Medici!

Erna, accompanied by Peter the Bald as Stormtrooper, made more little molehills as she walked, hoicked, walked, hoicked, her way to the podium. Roberta led the applause. The band did another little antiphonous salute for silence. The Child of Nature, who had been standing by, gave an odd little dance as Erna climbed up next to him. I thought I saw her hand do something unmentionable, but it could have been heat haze.

My mind wandered. I was plucked from a pleasant reverie in which Teddy suddenly flew to my side crying, 'It is all a terrible mistake and I love you, I love you, I love you,' by a gasp from Yale.

He was beyond speech and could only nod towards the declaiming La Topp.

I made to speak. 'Ssh,' said Peter the Bald as Stormtrooper. 'Ssh!'

I saw Mrs V. take one more glass. I knew how she felt.

La Topp lowered her voice. 'Yes, David has a dream. And I, too, have a dream . . .' She did more deep, dark, saurian lid-closing, looked about her, embraced the world again, and added, 'We all have a dream.'

Along with raising the Medici we now,

apparently, had the second coming of Martin Luther King.

'This, surely, is madness?' I whispered.

Yale shook his head.

'We can't let this happen,' I said.

He shifted uncomfortably. 'If we weren't doing it, somebody else would.'

Now where had I heard that argument before?

Roberta invoked one more call upon the Having of a Dream.

'Somebody shoot *her*, will you . . .' Yale whispered.

Getting a vague flash of Peter the Bald's disapproval, and looking neither to left, nor right, I fled.

Tripping over the adulators as I went. By now they were practically speaking in tongues. Even Teddy.

I was across the hallway and halfway up the stairs when I heard the distant burst of applause: Roberta had succeeded. The Dream was Fact. The band played, excited voices were raised and jabbering. The Academy was born.

I went to the bathroom, putting my wrists under the cold tap, reading the Sanilav bottle, that sort of thing, and feeling very ashamed, but justified. Yale's words were very comforting. If not us, who else?

I stayed in there for quite a long time.

Which accounts for my missing the juiciest bit of the evening.

CHAPTER SIXTEEN

Afterwards Yale christened me in a rather grudging homage to Mitford as 'The Bolter' and told me with some irritation that in future I should stay the ground. 'And maybe calm down a little . . .' he added, with feeling.

This because he had found me hiding behind a Tudor outbuilding in tears. The tears, of course, were on account of my not having avoided Teddy and the French Bloater as they left. And Teddy shook my hand. *Shook my hand!* And said, 'Well, we're off,' as if they had been married for a thousand years. You'd expect a girl to make salt tracks after that.

Yale, of course, assumed I was just highly strung . . . You know, the way men do if you show any kind of emotion above hearty surprise.

Anyway, as he reiterated, he had his own agenda to deal with. So far as he was concerned, it was head down from now on. *I* said I didn't think that was a very polite way to talk about Valeria, but he was not amused. He walked away very briskly.

The fireworks lit up the sky in a heedless round of noise and bravura. The folks of Hassocks Lee retired to bed, no doubt relieved, and at the end of the evening Roberta and Peter the Bald took Dave Barnes off for a meal with selected Celebs, so there was no debriefing over little Japanese cups.

There was no sign of Mr and Mrs V. Valeria draped herself around Yale as if he were a hall stand and took him off out of it. Which left me to wander home alone. But at least the contact was made. At least now I had a plan. A Project, as my mother would have it. Though it was hardly one of which, I was glad to say, she might approve. I had no more duties for the time being, not until the Heritage people's caring builders had done certain internal works to the place and I could begin setting up the library.

'And that,' as I said to Pearl the next day, 'is that.'

She merely pursed her lips and asked me prying questions about the youngster and my plans of a personal nature. When I told her she went pale and said she didn't think I ought to go whisking innocent young boys off to Foreign Parts.

'Who says he's innocent?' I asked her. After which she was unusually quiet.

I felt remarkably bullish that day and when a woman complained about our lack of Deepest Sympathy cards I said shop policy was that Death Was No Bad Thing. Pearl was exceptionally out of sorts and wouldn't even laugh. 'Go to Spain,' she pleaded. But I just raised my chin and said *No*.

*   *   *

Roberta was very clear on the kind of modern library she wanted installed. The literary equivalent of easy listening. Which was fine by me. Pearl refused to have anything to do with it and even refused to take wholesalers' messages on the phone. Apart from this the shop ticked over much as usual. Book sales were better than expected, if anything, due to the laziness produced by the pervasive heat. I felt a great deal happier now that I had a plan.

After a couple of weeks, I was invited—or maybe summonsed—back.

By now Yale had moved into Hassocks Hall, though not, strictly, into Valeria's apartment. He had a bedroom of his own in the attics and a substantial study in the west wing looking out over the lawns. These were now in even worse shape—what with the yellow marks of the execrables and molehills and barbecue burns. I remembered that beautiful, golden first evening. It seemed we had already begun to sully the place.

Playing the English Gentleman, Yale gave a sherry party shortly after taking up residence, and for it he dressed in slightly too tight English tweeds (in all that heat) which was a great mistake. As I told him.

The jacket pulled and the leather patches on the elbows should have been scuffed. 'Just like jeans have to be faded,' I pointed out. He merely smiled, I believe the term to be *loftily*, and said, 'You don't say.'

Valeria scarcely left his side. If she did she devoured him across the room, while he talked of New American Trends and the blandness of UCLA.

His plan was to get his own work out of the way before Forward Fiction commenced. He might make it; the room was neatly settled with bookshelves, reference files, WPC settled upon a solid mahogany working table (at which, I was told by Mrs V. the Prince Consort had once sat and peeled an apple while waiting for Victoria to complete her toilette) and shutters at the windows which he closed to stop him admiring the view while writing.

A serious man.

Roberta wanted him to be Dave's Muse, what lesser beings would refer to as Dave's Ghost, but he refused.

A brave boy.

At his sherry party, Roberta threatened, cajoled, woggled her substantials until he was red in more than his face, but he would not budge. He wanted what free time he had left for his own work, and that was that. Roberta sighed and shrugged. She had planned, she said woefully, to keep Dave's Dream within our inner sanctum (that meant us) but she would not be able to do the fundraising and organize tutors, courses and all the ills that creative writing is heir to, as well as Forward his Fiction. The shoulders are broad, she said, but not that broad, which drew attention—as small women will—to her daintiness.

'Employ someone,' said Yale airily.

Peter the Bald, who handled all the money, appeared to wince at this.

'Don't think the budget will stretch, old boy,' he said quickly.

Yale merely shrugged.

Roberta went all velvety and showed her teeth again. 'I appeal to you,' she said.

Always risky.

'All the publicity centres on him and his book,' she wheedled. 'We really need you.'

Peter the Bald said, 'We would value your input on this one, Jim.'

Yale merely shrugged again and did a pretty good James Mason lip curl. 'Sorry,' he said. 'No teaching before commencement. Space to do my own thing. Or it's back to the States.'

Valeria went pale.

'We're in enough trouble with my parents as it is,' she said, looking very positively at Roberta, who—astonishingly—backed off.

'Trouble?' I asked, but Roberta just flapped her hand again.

'Don't ask,' she said, and returned to Yale, fluttering. 'We've—er—had a lot of interest from one of the—er—Royals. Private tutorage, that sort of thing.'

'No!' shrieked Valeria. So we all knew immediately who she guessed it to be.

I liked the idea of A Windsor Saga. An everyday story of Regal Folk, with crowns. 'I'll do it if you like,' I said enthusiastically.

Roberta looked as if she had just stepped into something unpleasant. 'Please Jim. If not HRH, will you help Dave Barnes? For me?'

Yale had shown a flicker of interest at the mention of Royalty—as Americans will—but conquered it. He shook his head.

'David will need a lot of help,' she pleaded. *'A Lot.'*

He shrugged and backed away. 'Well, there you are,' he said firmly. 'I just don't have the time . . .'

'Ah,' she said as if to clarify. 'Ah—well—not *that* much. He already has his storyline. All he needs is some help with—the—er—*filling* . . .'

'You mean writing it?'

'I most certainly do not. The boy is a natural. That outline he delivered is a magnificent first attempt.' She looked quite puzzled. 'Magnificent. It proves *conclusively* that everyone can do it. And that is our thrust and our mission. To prove that it need not be hard.'

'That's not what my mother says.'

'Diana,' said Roberta with exasperation. 'Your mother thinks she is Louisa May Alcott, Muriel Spark and Proust all rolled into one.'

I thought that was quite amusing but didn't say so. One has to stay loyal even if the recipient of one's loyalty doesn't deserve it.

She refixed her zealous gaze on Yale. She believed her own propaganda. She would make it succeed. The nation and the world would become flooded with demystified stories, a terrible landscape of blandness, peopled with folk whose countenances bore no trace of the struggle to understand, embrace, celebrate the higher ground.

The prospect was horrible—evil—to be spurned.

'I'll help Dave Barnes if you like,' I said.

Roberta ignored this.

Valeria was called away to the other side of the room. She went as if she had been summonsed either to Heaven or to Hell. With a backward glance at me more searing than Medea's.

'David's book will just need—well—*tidying up* a bit—that's all,' wheedled Roberta.

'No,' said Yale, rubbing a sulky brogued toe across the faded Turkish. 'I have to finish mine. It's imperative.'

He said this so firmly that I gazed up at him in admiration. Quite suddenly there was the rushing of many wings. Roberta opened her mouth to say more, but Valeria, apparently blessed with fuel injection, was again at Yale's side.

'Come and talk to Pussy,' she said pleadingly. 'I've told her all about you.' He went with humility, Valeria holding on to him as if he were precious porcelain. I gave her a smile which she did not return.

Pussy, I was relieved to see, was not a revered and furry feline but a juiceless old woman of about ninety who had some trembling difficulty in getting a sherry glass to her lips but, once there, knew how to run it dry. Yale stood to attention in front of her and looked ridiculous and uncomfortable in his tweeds. Pussy, when the glass was quite drained, peered up into his face and said, 'Why are you talking like that young man. Are you Irish?'

He shook his head.

'Very glad to hear it,' said Pussy. 'They should all be shot.' And she handed him her empty glass.

Roberta watched him go and then, looking distinctly rattled, said more or less to herself, 'We *will* have to get in an outsider, then. Damn.'

At which I pricked up my ears.

'Er—Roberta,' I said. 'I'm quite serious. How about me?'

She gave a little abstracted shake of her head.

Just then Desmond arrived at her side. 'Darling,' he said, and kissed the air surrounding her cheeks. He was short, neat, grey hair cropped to his head, and nicely suntanned. His dark little eyes flashed. He took her hands. 'Lots to talk about—India *divine*—lots and lots—where shall we go?' His button eyes winked with pleasure. 'Now you must tell me everything about this—it all sounds absolutely fabulous. Diana! Darling—you too! Heaven!' And he kissed my cheekly air too.

Peter the Bald, bearing his shifty look again, disappeared immediately. Presumably on the assumption that if he hung around he, too, would have his air corridors attacked.

'And what,' said Desmond, bringing his head into very close proximity with ours, 'is really going on? What's all this I hear about grabbing the aristocracy by the nuts? And is there anything in the fact that Dave the Dreamer is young and hunky, and you are (pause) mature and (pause, pause) womanly?'

Aristocratic nuts? I wanted to say.

But, 'Hush,' said Roberta quickly. 'Peterkins will hear.'

We all looked over at Peterkins, who looked flustered and quickly turned away.

'Come on Roberta. Tell. Dave the Hunk?' said Desmond suggestively.

Roberta went pink. Batted her breasts. Shook her head. 'Oh you may as well know,' she said. 'But keep it to yourself. We are going to be married.'

'Married?' We both gave a good imitation of a St Winifred's Choir two-part.

My heart hit the floor. This was the only man to stir my dormant libido. He and none other. And now he was off the menu?

'You mean you and Dave?' I said weakly.

She fairly bounced me twixt her baubles. 'I do *not*,' she said with irritation. 'I mean me and Peterkins.'

Desmond mis-swallowed his sherry and then both our mouths hung open.

I had a passing thought, that it was a pleasure to see Desmond speechless, before following Roberta's fond gaze across the room to where it lighted upon the back view of her affianced's glowing head.

Desmond's eyes snapped open and shut like the camera he was. 'That?' he said. '*How* extraordinary.' And then, staring much harder, he said, none too pleasantly, '*Really?* Well, well. Perhaps I'd better go over and talk to him.'

'Oh Desmond,' I said. 'You are such a lookist.'

But he did not share the joke.

The object of Roberta's heart was engaged by a demotic Mr V. in extremely earnest conversation. His pink head nodded soothingly as he listened. Mr V. was wearing the right kind of tweeds and brogues, without a hint of body heat. They looked moulded to him and much as if they were handmedowns from a charity shop. The leather patches were completely devoid of shine and the brown brogues had soles as thick as a slice of Mother's Pride. I made a note to point this out to Yale when I had recovered from this dazzling piece of news.

Roberta in love? *And* getting married?

It was monstrous.

Mr V. also appeared to be finding things monstrous. He pointed out of the window, down on to the sullied lawn. He fulminated. He insisted, very loudly, that he would Never Have That South African Woman Here Again . . .

'That's a bit strong,' I said to Roberta.

She gave me a look, the love light all gone now, and said, 'That's my *other* problem.' And a rare touch of humour entered her voice. 'Honestly Diana—you'd think Lord Hartley would enjoy the joke. You really would.'

I remembered the dinner party. I remembered Dave Barnes's little dodging manoeuvre on the podium. 'Oh my God,' I said. 'Not Erna? Not Valeria's father?'

Desmond said, 'Old Pretoria custom I believe. Hear jazz. Drink taken. See Man. Swing-on-balls.'

He was staring at the two men again, wrinkling his brow and looking far less amused than expected.

'And then, of course, Lady Hartley took exception and brought out the shotgun. Fortunately *not* loaded . . .' Her gaze travelled back to the angry animations of Mr V. 'This time . . . Peterkins took it away from her. It wasn't very nice.' Roberta sighed. 'You see, Diana, the problems I have to deal with. First that. And now I haven't got a Ghost for Dave Barnes.' She put her hand to her mouth. 'I mean *adviser* . . .'

'Ghost-schmost,' I said, to coin Pearl's phrase. 'I'll do it.'

But Roberta simply gazed anew at Peterkins and gave her head a little shake.

Roberta *married*?

Valeria and Jim together.

I looked across at Desmond's lover—beautiful Indian boy in white.

And back to Roberta. She was glowing with love.

And then I looked across at Pussy. Tremble, tremble went her aged hand. Down went another sherry. Out from her beak came another sharp remark to be met by mild eyes that knew they need not take her seriously. One day that would be me. I broke out into a sweat.

No Teddy, no life.

'Oh don't look so miserable, Diana,' said Roberta sharply. 'No need to sulk about it.'

'I'm not sulking,' I was moved to say. 'I am practically suicidal.'

She narrowed her eyes. 'I had no idea you took it so seriously.'

What did she think I did? Get broken-hearted for a hobby? A little sob escaped. 'It was all I ever wanted.'

I felt the tears swim up.

She peered again, her voice went slightly

softer. 'Oh very well then—have him.'

I bridled. Have him? Have him? Easy to say . . . I glared at her. Out came the lip.

Yale and Valeria stopped mid-listen to Pussy and stared. Pussy, oblivious, went banging on about the way the Irish bred and then took over our churches. An interesting image.

Roberta, taking stock of the lip, looked unnerved. 'No need to get so upset.' She backed away slightly. 'If you *really* want to, there's nothing stopping you!'

How dared she? The dam broke.

'But he's MARRIED, Roberta, M-A-R-R-I-E-D—'

'Well—' conciliatory now. 'That doesn't *necessarily* mean it will be difficult. It might be a positive advantage.'

'A positive advantage? Are you mad? Oh excuse me Diana I've just got to go and ring the wife and see if the baby's come yet?'

Roberta looked even more unnerved. 'Baby? Baby?' she repeated, as if about to launch into a Buddy Holly number.

Yale looked concerned.

Valeria looked at him and looked concerned.

Peter the Bald, also concerned, looked like he was on a short piece of elastic—moving in the space between Mr V. and us and never quite making it to either.

Desmond looked exhilarated, already with

his notebook in his hand.

Mrs V. stared pointedly out of the window. Mr V. put his hands behind his back. Pussy went on talking to nobody-at-home, fondly remembering the bonny Black and Tans.

'Well—' said Roberta. '*I* didn't know about the baby, I suppose it might make a difference . . .'

'Might, *might*? And you didn't *know*? No one gets that gross on chocolate creams, Roberta. She was out there like a blob of walking oestrogen and you didn't know?'

'I didn't see her.' She moved towards me, her bust full of pity. She lowered her voice. 'But if I organize it all properly it will be fine.'

Organize it? Was the woman really barking?

'Oh, I think Agnes bloody Yaudet has already organized it, Roberta, thank you very much. With a sperm too far.'

Silence rent the air.

Roberta was beyond even the comfort of her upholstery.

'Agnes?' she said sharply. Her mouth was a perfect circle. 'I thought we were discussing David Barnes.'

My mother and Pearl have both been known to call me single-minded. Not to say, occasionally and quite wrongly, self-obsessed.

'Dave Barnes?' I replied. Also a perfect circle. 'Oh.'

In the distance I heard Pussy say querulously, 'And then walk off in the middle of whatever it is I was saying—and don't ask *me* what it was because *I* don't know . . .'

Roberta was still frozen with astonishment.

'Misunderstood you,' I said. 'Sorry.'

Yale was there, handing me a handkerchief. It was not white like Teddy's, but better than nothing. Probably Gieves. I dabbed at my eyes and blew my nose. Quickly Valeria took her precious piece of porcelain off once more, whipping the hankie from my hand as she went. None of your Desdemonas for her.

'No more muddles,' said Roberta when I had rearranged myself. 'You can be in charge of David's book but you know the brief. None of your arcane nonsense.' She flapped her hands and gave her bosom a bit of rough. 'He's got a perfectly decent plot which fits his image, and we don't want any fiddle-faddle to muddle him. Clear?'

I nodded. I looked grateful. I looked like a woman who would be struck dead rather than tempt any mortal with fiddle-faddle. Words of four syllables were out and there would be none of this reaching into the soul nonsense. Narrative arcs and story structure with a cliff-hanger ending each chapter.

And Amalfi.

I feigned nonchalance. 'I shall have to take him away somewhere quiet for a little while—just to concentrate his mind.'

More sweat of the out-breaking variety. She'd see through that for sure . . . But

Roberta merely continued to flap her hands. 'Yes, yes,' she said, her little chin poised towards her affianced, who appeared to be suffering.

Mrs V., now back from gazing steadfastly, was extremely cutting. 'There are still some things worth fighting for. And this is one of them.'

Mr V. took a sudden step back and let slip the dogs of war. 'And if that woman ever sets foot on these grounds, let alone in this house, again—I'll shoot her.'

'Excuse me,' said Roberta, and floated like a piece of ironbound gossamer in their direction.

'And a budget . . .' I called after her.

Flap, flap, went her hands. 'Yes, *yes*,' she called impatiently over her shoulder. 'Peterkins will deal with all that later.' She reached his side. 'Won't you my love.' She turned towards Lord Hartley, standing twixt him and her beloved. 'Hit my boy, and I'll hit you,' was the silent message. Out loud she said, We will do our best to keep her away. But it will be difficult. Extremely *difficult*.'

'First our gardener, and now this,' said Mrs V. tragically. Marie-Antoinette travelling in her tumbril could not have wrung more hearts.

Sanest cocktail party I've been to for a long time, as I said to Yale on leaving. He had Valeria still clamped to his side like a baby koala. Well, if he felt a bit rattled, I felt astonishingly good again. Got my own way with Roberta. And all that screaming in public held a certain cathartic quality.

I was smiling over this when I felt a poke in my ribs. There, staring up at me, was Pussy. 'Hear you're a lesbian. Vita was One of Those. Apparently. But she'd never talk about it. Tell me.' She sidled nearer. 'What exactly do you people do?'

I told her we just pressed flowers and went on hikes.

She looked a bit puzzled. 'Sort of thing I did when I was a girl,' she said.

'Well, there you are then.'

And I Bolted.

CHAPTER SEVENTEEN

Peter the Bald became rather shifty when I approached him for money. Not surprising, I suppose. Even I thought it sounded a bit tall. But I had Roberta's agreement so I stood my ground.

'I need to take him away. Somewhere peaceful and atmospheric.'

'Where for example?'

Nothing for it but to plunge in.

'Italy,' I said. 'Amalfi as a matter of fact. He needs setting.'

'He can bloody well need a week in a jelly mould for all I care but he's not going to Italy.'

This was rough stuff. One must needs counter it.

'Roberta said.'

'Ah.'

'Congratulations, by the way.'

He blinked and then gazed out of the perfect eighteen-paned window with its damp-rotted frame, past the perfect rake of gravel, across the hideously defiled lawn, beyond the ha-ha, to the sweetly grazing cows.

He, too, had secured workspace within the Adam gem. Roberta was somewhat jealous on her affianced's behalf after Yale's sherry party because, a few days later, her beloved was given this very nice room on the first floor east, and a desk at which—so said Mrs V.—the Empress Eugenie had sat to write her plaintive little notes to Louis Napoleon after he ditched her.

'Thank you,' he said perfunctorily. 'And No Way, Italy.'

'But Roberta agreed.'

Just for a moment I thought he was going to say something rude, but he changed his mind.

'Italy is necessary. It really is.'

He brought his eyes back from the pasture. 'I've got a flat in Caterham,' he said hopefully.

'Peter,' I said kindly. 'We can't get a Terminatrix in the true Terminatrix mode if we have her striding down Caterham High Street in studded thigh boots and bumping into shopping trolleys.'

'Oh very well.' He passed a hand over his head as if seeking out new growth. His brow cleared. He smiled. 'We'll reimburse you. Just keep all your receipts. OK?'

'What's my budget?' I asked.

'Anything reasonable,' he said, and flapped his hands just like Roberta. Rather sweet.

Well that was easy, I thought, as I left the room.

'Thank you,' I said.

He gave me an odd smile. 'Don't mention it.'

I went in search of Valeria's aged P, female.

Things were hotting up.

* * *

The tussle over Dave the Gardener and Dave the Dreamer was not yet resolved. He still had some hoeing time to put in. When I asked Mrs V., whom I found in the sunny rose garden where she appeared to be squeezing individual aphids between finger and thumb and enjoying it, when he would be free to go, her expression changed to one which made me glad I was not of green hue and bewinged.

'Impossible,' she said. Squeeze, pop, ooze. 'We need him until the end of the month.' Squeeze, squeeze, squeeze, lots of pop and oozings.

'Fine,' I said.

She looked surprised.

'He's an extremely good gardener,' she said. 'A natural with his hands.'

Nothing to say to that. Not really. 'Oh good,' I said, and skipped off.

*   *   *

The lad himself was in the shrubbery. Early summer had turned him more golden and though he was not Teddy he would certainly do. The libido stirred. A great relief. I approached cautiously. How to get him to adopt the thin line between respect and becoming my rampant sex slave?

I sat down on a bench. It was not my usual kind of problem. He joined me, removing his headphones. 'All right?' he said.

'All right' is an interesting linguistic phenomenon. It can mean, How are you; it can mean, Sorry your poodle died. It can be merely a cheery greeting, or an outbreak of hostilities. In this case it meant, apparently, Can I Show You Something?

He removed a much bigger wodge of paper than before from his back pocket.

'My notes, like you said.'

'We can deal with all that when we are in Italy.'

'Ah,' he said. 'My Nan says that the food in Italy gives you belly-ache.'

'How silly of your Nan.'

'Ah,' he said. 'My Nan's all right. And I

don't like foreign food much. Except curries.'

'You like pizzas don't you?'

He nodded.

'You like pasta?'

'We-ell—I like macaroni cheese,' he said grudgingly.

'There you are then.'

Teddy used to say that if I got an idea, the rest was history. He was right.

* * *

I returned to the shop to relieve Pearl.

'Your mother rang,' she said. 'She wanted to know what you were up to and if you were well. I really do think you should go.' Pearl sounded almost soft, and ever so slightly desperate.

'That's so typical. All she wants is good news.'

'I said you were looking after yourself—keeping fit—eating yoghurt.'

'What did she say?'

'That you must have a new bloke in the pipeline.'

So poetical, Pearl. This is the trouble with having a novelist for a mother. They run ahead of themselves.

'Well don't tell her anything else.'

'Don't you worry,' said Pearl, oddly fervent. 'I wouldn't dream of telling her half what you get up to.' She paused and looked really disapproving. 'You aren't really going through with it? Not with a boy?'

'Well, I'm not going to do it with a hamster,' I said crisply. 'Anyway, you're only jealous.'

She sniffed. '*That* I am not.'

'Are you off to your country cottage for Whitsun, Pearl?'

My little joke. It is probably a shack. Pearl is very circumspect about her private life. Since her husband died she says she likes to be quiet. He made her go to the British Legion every Saturday night, apparently, and she never forgave him. Apart from the six pints of Watneys Red, it was all gossip and rumour. Nowadays she keeps herself to herself.

'Maybe, maybe not,' she said. 'And where will you be, Miss?'

'Oh, the flat. I've got these notes to go through.'

She took them, scanned them, handed them back. 'Sometimes you really shock me,' she said, and I believe she meant it.

She tied her scarf under her chin. How often have I told her to knot it *on* her chin—but she just won't listen. 'Never mind all that,' she said, when I again pointed out this stylistic faux pas. 'Just go and see your mother. Before you get into real hot water.'

'Good afternoon, Pearl,' I said, and picked up Dave's notes.

'Don't forget to cash up,' she said, and banged the door.

Something had got on the wrong side of her all right. Maybe it was jealousy? I felt quite bucked at the thought. I settled down to read.

*　　*　　*

The story was profoundly moving. So was the spelling. But then—so was Chaucer's spelling. Spelling, as I reminded myself, is not Story. It concerned a beautiful young woman with an hourglass figure and sweet ways whose new husband is mistakenly shot by hoodlums in suburban crossfire. Why change the plots of a lifetime?

Not surprisingly, given the detailed descriptions of hubby's agonizing end and her close proximity, she then goes into the psychiatric wing of a hospital to recover and while there she overhears a doctor telling another doctor, as doctors will, about a new wonder drug that makes you practically immortal (the technical stuff here was very impressive for one such as myself, to whom the molecular pattern of an egg, boiled, is as mysterious as Mars). This new wonder drug does things, in combination with rays, to the outer layer of the skin, so that all physical attacks can be repelled. Only the mind can be got at so she must wear a special helmet with ear plugs (!). Fortunately she cannot read since the shooting. This is psychological trauma and is also useful for plot.

It is her sole aim in life to Get Those Hoods, and we ain't talking *Pixie.* One minute she might be queuing up in Sainsbury's—the next she will observe through the window one of Those Thugs lurching by—Thugs apparently hang out in supermarket carparks—and she bravely leaves all her shopping *behind*—and nips off to take a wonder pill. She then has a quick lie-down in what looks like a sun bed and *isn't*. Next thing you know she's got conical breasts, thighs like a scrum half, plum-coloured lipstick and an invincible look. Men who call out to her as she passes in the street get smacked round the ears and die. She shows no mercy in her invincible lust for power . . .

Which includes the sweet-faced young boy who carries her groceries from the supermarket on this particular occasion and arrives just as she has returned from shooting down a couple of Apes in porkpie hats and floating them off down the river. An activity that, apparently, would go quite unnoticed by Hassocks Lee police.

Love begins to blossom in the time-honoured way after he—surprise, surprise—surprises her in the kitchen in the middle of the night in her negligé. Interesting, these old-fashioned adolescent fantasies.

I made a quick note to buy a negligé. Did they still make them?

After this, slowly, hesitantly, our heroine's

skill of reading begins to return . . . Sex removes the scales from her eyes.

The sweet-faced young boy, to cut a long story short, persuades her (after quite a lot of urban mayhem and gore and negligés) that the real target should be the Root rather than the Branches. And off they go to make it happen. In the course of which the Root and Branches attempt to bend our Terminatrix's mind with reading material writ large, after giving her Ecstasy (nothing if not topical, our David) to keep her eyes open. Since her brain is new-washed so far as reading material is concerned, this is very dangerous. This is also very deconstructivist, and very Serendipity.

What the reading material might say is not detailed at this point but the attempt nearly succeeds. It is foiled by sweet-faced young boy turning into a sweet-faced young technocrat and busting the lights.

And then, with miraculous reincarnation of *Silence of the Lambs*, the sweet-faced young technocrat, plus two pairs of infrared glasses, saves our Terminatrix who then saves the day by shooting everyone who can't see her.

The world (though the threat is unspecified) has been saved.

No more Thugs in Sainsbury's.

After which they settle down to happily married life. She stays home and becomes ordinary and he becomes a policeman.

But We Know that if the world gets nasty

again—there will always be the Terminatrix.

END

'Excellent beginning,' I wrote on the notes. 'Now let us consider *location* . . .' And I went off to the local travel agent.

CHAPTER EIGHTEEN

Oh those golden days. It was one long, warm feast of time that summer. The British at Large walked around with bemused smiles, surprised eyes and a nasty feeling lurking within their breasts that they were losing their comfortable, cold insularity and joining the sweat and garlic of Europe.

Even the term 'Becoming Mediterranean' was mooted in the watering holes of Middle England. Of course, Knights of the Shires went on wearing ties to cricket matches but then, they had the wearing of armour on a sizzling desert plain in their genes. Yale stuck to his tweeds, which was remarkably silly, and no one pointed out that a decent crumpled linen would do. He wanted to be an English gentleman—and he would be. Valeria adored him. It was sickening to watch.

Amalfi was booked. For the date the Baby was due. Just a coincidence.

That bit of my diaphragm above the stomach and below the heart, through which

Teddy punched his way, had not closed up. But I was determined that, after Amalfi, it would. Meanwhile Brahms remained locked away in his drawer. I would not open it. A contagion of sadness was too likely. He sat there, arms folded, glowering, waiting to come out to play. Not yet, Johannes, I would mouth. Not yet. Soon.

By now everyone connected with Forward Fiction, except me, had a private space in Hassocks Hall. The builders had the roof, Yale his two rooms, Peter the Bald his office, Roberta *her* office. All I had was the library now it was cleared.

Mr and Mrs Valeria and the Little Valeria lived in one wing and Little Valeria had taken up her art in the porticoed summer house. This was in direct line with Yale's study window. Each morning she gave him a pathetic little wave before he closed his shutters in defence of his work. She then put her hand under her chin and gazed into space.

She was supposed to design the Academy's logo, diplomas, letterheading and stuff. When I sneaked a quick look at what she had done that day I found a pencilled motif of the initials J and V intertwined with garlands. When I popped my head round Yale's door he neither heard the knock, nor noticed me. No garlands or loveknots for him. He was glued to his screen and typing away.

I went to the Hall quite often once Pearl

returned from the Whitsun break. She was very definitely snarky about what she called 'the goings on up there' and refused to visit. Which was just as well because I left her in charge of the shop. She was quite good at assuming responsibility for brief periods, though inclined to get uppish about the stock. She never re-ordered anything of which she did not thoroughly approve. And that included the Roberta Topps. Best keep the two of them apart, really.

Amongst its many other charms, Hassocks Hall was cool. The summer's heat was fairly blistering now. Once I caught Yale splashing about in the lake, early in the morning, but when he invited me in, I declined on the grounds that carp like our tender bits. He and Valeria had a row about this afterwards. She was woken, apparently, by the sound of our laughter. If there was any splashing to be done thereafter, she did it.

It was not hard to keep up the interest in Dave Barnes. It was not hard to keep up an interest in anything other than handling the books for the new library. Roberta was thrilled as the shelves began to fill. I stared out of the window at the Child of Nature and his moss raker. I was really impatient to put Amalfi to the test—after which, I told myself firmly, all my sorrows would fade. Brahms and the Requiem would be mine.

The builders were also preparing the space

for classrooms in those semi-underground caverns where the pointilliste pigs had so lately hung. Next would come the student residences, in the Tudor outbuildings. The project was taking shape at alarming speed. Money and the tame Grandees helped. Roberta was already turning candidates down. Anyone well known was definitely out which, apparently, HRH approved as very democratic. Personally, as I said to Pearl, it was more likely because there were no unpublished celebrities left.

One afternoon I left off cataloguing to watch a crimson half-tester being carefully dismantled for removal. The fabric was so faded and thin in places that the young man conducting operations wore gloves to handle it. Even so, as he touched it a small piece of worn silk fell away to the floor, almost crumbling to dust. I watched him take it up gently, fold it in tissue, and stow it as safely as if it were alive. The bed, it seemed, wished to stay put.

I looked behind me at the library.

Goldsmith, Johnson, Gibbon, Hazlitt were all gone, replaced by material that so astonished my usual wholesaler he had rung to see if I was having a post-Teddy breakdown.

'Not *all* the Roberta Topps?' he pleaded. 'Not in triplicate? And the Dan Costellos? Surely one of each would be enough?'

'I'm giving them what they want,' I said

firmly.

He then asked if I had been supplanted by an alien.

Roberta was pleased and at this stage that was all that mattered. She came to admire and stayed to pray. She actually ran her fingertips over the spines of her bookjackets and nearly transubstantiated. 'We will change the world,' she said. 'Peterkins says it is my mission and my goal.'

I nodded and heard a cock crow.

She very likely would. Patronage was still pouring in. Even Lottery money had been seconded. It was one way to get them off the streets.

The builders got on very quickly with the roof, at which Mr Valeria would stand and stare with a fixed look of approval, sometimes for hours.

* * *

Erna came into the library one morning with two mugs of coffee. Given her startling emerald trouser suit, her even more startling scarlet polo neck, and the quantities of gold and pearl festooned all around, she was close to a starring role in Diane Arbus meets Joan Collins. How she got past Mr Valeria and his roof watch in that lot was impossible to say.

She knew nothing of his threats. She had simply been told to stay away while the work was happening so that we could surprise her.

Roberta dealt with it by giving her lots of treats—'She likes treats'—and arranging for a chauffeur. His itinerary included a few trips to prime literary sites. The house in Highgate where Roberta Topp was born, and where she completed her first manuscript among them.

In she pottered. Given the sweetness of Erna's disposition I had no heart to tell her she was likely to be shot on sight, so I welcomed her. At least Mr V. was unlikely to come in here now his own books had gone. Erna stood looking up at me on the library ladder. Being before noon, she was reasonably comprehensible.

'I'm so glad to get back here.' She looked around in delight. 'I just love this place. Oh, you have no idea.' She woggled one of the mugs at me.

I came down the steps, took it and thanked her. 'I need a break,' I said. I sipped. It had floaty bits on top.

She squinted at the shelves. 'Well isn't all this lovely?' She ran her fingers along some of the thick bold spines. 'My, that is a lot of books,' she said admiringly. 'Something to really get your teeth into.' I held my breath but she did not oblige.

I suggested we move into a cooler part of the room. 'You English,' she said. 'Always on about this heat. It's glorious. If I'd known I'd have settled in England sooner.' She gestured so that some of the coffee slopped on to the tiled floor. She looked down at the classical patterning. 'Great for dancing,' she said. 'You like dancing?'

I shrugged.

'You got children?' she asked. I winced. 'Me neither,' she said. 'We wanted them. Who doesn't? But we were never blessed.'

I refrained from saying that I knew of one on the way she could adopt if she wanted, and we sat down on the blissfully cool tiles.

'Sad,' I said.

'Well—it was.' She wriggled her bottom to get comfortable. 'Yes. Sad. My late departed Howie lost it in the army.'

'Ah,' I said. 'Bomb?' I said.

Erna laughed her naughty laugh and shook her head. 'Mumps,' she said. 'Firing blanks ever after . . .' She gave me a wonderfully wicked look. '*Lots* of blanks.' She slapped her knee and wiggled her rings. 'He gave me the world to make up for it. You got a boyfriend?'

'Nope,' I said.

A change of subject seemed appropriate.

'Don't you just love Adam?' I offered.

She slapped her knee again. 'Sweetheart, it's all over for me now. But you go right ahead. Which one is he? Not the one with no hair? I don't care for him. The other one now, with the smile, I *do* like.'

'Ah,' I said. 'Well he belongs to someone else.'

'So did Howie once,' she said, taking a big drink. And she winked.

I sipped at the floaty bits.

Erna looked up at the ceiling and around all the walls. 'This is a *great* room,' she said. 'Good for parties.' She returned her slightly swimmy stare to me. 'Howie was my baby,' she said.

I wish women wouldn't do this. I wish women would not, in my present state, try to *confide.* I mean—what could I say? 'Very interesting pass the flask?' People have no right to go bleeding everywhere. They should just *do* something about it. Like me.

Footsteps echoed across the floor. It was Yale and Valeria. Yale paused at the door and sniffed the air. The scent of whisky hung upon it. He raised an eyebrow and sniffed again, like a keen and disapproving hunting dog. I thought sourly how tolerant Teddy had always been. Even if he had found me at half past two in the morning sitting on a dustbin sipping cider and singing 'Annie Laurie' he would have smiled.

'Hi,' said Erna from the floor. 'I was just admiring this lovely room. You must be so proud of your family home.'

Valeria had given up the koala bear and was now clinging to Yale like a raft. Surely she felt safe now? They were incontestably mated. Mind you, she ought to be careful. She wore a long, lilac-sprigged frock and he could be forgiven, in the light of this, for buggering off. It was not her best colour.

Did I imagine it or were her eyes even larger, even hungrier, than usual? Certainly they were more frightened than a drowning woman's.

Valeria replied nervously. 'Oh yes,' she said. 'But times change. We really don't need all this space . . .'

'Hell,' said Erna. 'I don't *need* all my jewellery but I like to have it.' And she wiggled her beringed hand.

'I wondered,' said Valeria, giving her a flustered smile, 'if you would like to come for a drive with me?'

'Where to?'

'Oh—anywhere. You say. Just for something to do.' She looked from Erna to Yale with eyes of pitiful misery.

'Well?' said Yale.

'Well?' said Erna.

'Well,' said Valeria.

'No well without water,' I said.

Yale came right up to me so that his stupid brown brogues touched my outstretched feet.

'Pathetic,' I said, studying the shoes.

He looked down severely. He then turned to Valeria and said, in a voice not unlike a frozen lake, 'Get her out of here. *Now!*'

I looked up. 'Who?' I asked. 'Me?' And made to rise.

Both Yale and Valeria looked disapproving.

Neither returned my smile. And at that exact moment I had a shaft of understanding about something completely different. I turned to Erna and said, 'Oh—I *see—that's* why you grab their balls. It's psychological. Howie's blanks . . .'

Erna giggled. 'I like a reaction now and then,' she said.

Yale yanked me to my feet. It was definitely winter around his bouche. 'Shall we just go over here for a minute?' he said, pulling me out of earshot.

Valeria helped Erna to her feet and proceeded to make little encouraging stabbing motions into her back to get her moving. Bit like playing cattle prods. At the door Erna turned. 'You two be as long as you like now,' she said, and winked. Valeria began playing cattle prods for real.

We watched them and then he turned to me. 'For fuck's sake why are you encouraging her? You know if Val's father sees her here, he'll *shoot* her.'

'Be serious.'

'I am being serious.' The grip on my elbow sharpened. There was real emotion in that grasp.

'But he can't actually shoot her. *Droit de Seigneur* has sort of vanished from the Twickenham area nowadays.'

'I don't know if he would or he wouldn't. You English are a law unto yourselves. All I do know is she shouldn't be here. You might try thinking of someone else once in a while.'

How *dare* he?

He pushed back my lower lip with his fingertip, as one might push a button. It was very gently done and a gesture not lost on Valeria as she hurtled back round the door.

'Cave!' she began, 'Cave! My father's coming up the stairs.'

And then she stopped.

Yale removed his fingertip.

I retracted the lip.

Valeria's mouth hung open and she changed colour—not a very fetching shade of peony with the lilac. She gripped the side of the door. 'Oh,' she said.

From behind her popped Erna's smiling face. 'Aah,' she said.

Yale sprang to life. I have never seen brogues fly. He arrived at his beloved's side, with me following, still attached. Footsteps echoed up the wide marble staircase.

'Valeria, Valeria,' called Her Father's Voice. 'Could you move your car, my dear, I can't get out.' Erna was leaning over the gallery rail, looking down upon the advancing silvery head. I remember much of this in slow motion—I remember thinking how pink Mr V.'s scalp looked beneath the thin covering of hair, how stiff his shoulders while his arms swung as if he were on manoeuvres—and how he began to look upwards.

And then it speeded up again.

Yale grabbed Erna, by the shoulders, and thrust her at Valeria. Valeria thrust her at me. Erna giggled a little perplexedly and clung on. It was to be hoped she would keep her teeth in.

'Valeria, are you up there? What's going on?'

Thank God Robert Adam liked long, lavish staircases.

If the term Collective Panic Disorder does not exist, I hereby patent it.

We all started moving around each other, tripping up, that sort of thing, and squeaking a bit. Mr V.'s footsteps advanced. It was not unlikely we would all become doubly incontinent when Valeria suddenly went very still, reached out for something on the wall and, hey presto, a door, well disguised, opened.

'The po cupboard,' she said, I thought just a little too cheerfully, and with surprising force she thrust Erna and me inside.

* * *

Nowhere in Pevsner is there mention of the eighteenth century's more delicate approach to a full bladder. Hitherto, and before Adam, country houses had alcoves for chamber pots, but these had neither doors nor privacy and were usually provided only at a discreet distance from the dining table.

Robert Adam, perhaps in the century's new anatomical, as well as spiritual, enlightenment, saw that man's bladder, like his soul, was weak. Women, as in so many other spheres of activity, were expected to exercise control. They were furnished, after all, with childbearing muscles and a natural propensity to endure. The po was not for them. But men required a ready receptacle.

Here at Hassocks Hall, Robert Adam spread his visionary light to embrace the chamber pot. No longer was it enough to provide a visible (and hearable) means of relief only for the brandy and cigar-ers. In future, in the best and most decent houses, he proposed a shut-off place in which man's urinating, like his conscience, was a matter between his God and himself.

The Age of Enlightenment, as it were, provided the first guest cloakroom. And we, Erna and me, had just got ourselves shoved into it.

Fortunately it was a beautifully proportioned thing, dimly lit by discreetly slatted holes, and neatly finished with very nicely turned architraves. On a broad shelf, mid-thigh height, stood a large and ornate chamber pot—a veritable Jeroboam of a potty—decorated with puff-cheeked reliefs of naked young nymphs who breasted outwards, their nipples tipped with gold.

To anyone who has heard a patient and demented mother attempting to get her little boy to pee into a drain, the breasting naked nymphs came as a surprise. Discreet plain white would, surely, have been less intimidating? Blokes probably hung around in this delightful architectural offshoot for hours attempting to clear their minds and get on with it.

There was time to mull over such things, for the look on Valeria's face as she ushered us in suggested that if we didn't come out until the Millennium, it would be too soon for her.

Fortunately, Erna was a very amenable internee. As we became accustomed to the gloom, I just kept my fingers to my lips and rolled my eyes a lot, and she followed suit, perfectly reasonably, by touching her own lips and rolling her own eyes like billy-o. The naked breasting nymphs appeared to change colour but that may have been a trick of the light.

When we weren't doing the Marcel Marceau stuff we took swigs from the flask. The incarceration had all the makings of a grand life.

Beyond our door, Valeria, whose voice had taken on a touch of steel, began to expound a seemingly passionate desire for her beloved to be introduced to the various pop-eyed ancestors hanging about on the walls. 'Oh, Daddy,' she said, and I bet she bulged her own smug eyes towards our hiding place, 'why don't you give Jim a little run-down on Sir Finborough Hartley before we go? And Lady Angelica and her friendship with Dryden.'

Yale, torn between the knowledge of our incarceration, and needs of his own, eventually opted for politeness. 'Do, sir,' he said. 'If you don't mind.'

Lord Hartley, apparently, did not. 'Well,' he said, 'this fella here now. Married to this gel here. Lady Angelica. Who met John Dryden, the poet fella, at Twickenham in the sixty-eighth year of his life. Shortly afterwards he and Sir Finborough fought a duel . . . Missed each other, of course. But the gel died. Overcome with anxiety.'

'So that's where Valeria gets it from,' I risked whispering.

Erna winked. We were sitting end to end, quite comfortably, on the floor now and a nymph or two peered over the edge of the shelf near our heads looking distinctly mocking. And well they might. For any time it sounded as if Mr V. was wavering, or if he said something like, 'Well, must be getting along,' Valeria would say perkily, 'Oh tell him about this one Daddy—Lord William—didn't he hang a vicar from the belfry? Or Julius, the one with the carp.'

Bloody ole hungry eyes was Showing Off. She was telling Yale that she had a pedigree and that it was gilt-edged—never mind giltnippled. I leaned back and took a swig of whisky. Valeria knew what she was doing all right. She was also showing who had control.

She asked her questions.

Mr V. rattled on, and on.

And I vowed Revenge.

Dryden—the iniquities of Popish clergy—the first ancestor to put carp in the new pond—by now even Yale was getting desperate. Erna, fortunately, fell quietly asleep.

After a very long while I considered using the vessel of the nymphs, but resisted. It is good for one's pelvics to be put on overtime, strengthening, helpful in old age when incontinence looms. What it is not good for is one's temper. By the time we finally came out to the empty grandeur of the landing, blinking like a pair of bunnies, I vowed, as I smoothed myself down and shook Erna properly awake, that I would get even with Valeria one day.

One Day.

Somehow.

Really I would.

CHAPTER NINETEEN

Fax from Roberta Topp:

To all team members.

(ABSOLUTELY CONFIDENTIAL)

At our Business Review Meeting I asked you to go away and consider your *personal* overview and do some deep and shared strategy thinking. Thank you for sharing that with Peter and I. As we said, if any of you feel strongly about something we will understand your withdrawal from the scheme.

Peter and I are open to any comments or criticisms.

We want to unite in an enshrined vision (something I cannot repeat often enough) and to win Universal Commitment. We also have to be sure that our venture is properly project-managed to minimize non-chargeable resources.

Feedback on the question of 'What Is Culture?' was very interesting and quite diverse. Peter is analysing the results. My view is that there is nothing wrong with an undemanding novel, providing it is *thoroughly* undemanding. I expect the analysis of your opinions to match this Overview or we would not all be here together. We must remember that many of our students will be tender shoots and easily open to influence.

Our 'As-Is Analysis' showed a healthy baby in need of a change of nappy.

OTHER MATTERS (HIGHLY CONFIDENTIAL)

As you know, for the time being, Mrs Erna Werner is not encouraged to spend time at HH. If any of you *do* find her here, please act speedily and accordingly.

On a much happier note, David Barnes has now finished his gardening duties at HH and is a fully fledged student under the wing of Diana. Should you see him engaged in any tasks of a non-literary horticultural nature, please inform me at once. Lady Hartley's confusion in this matter may be referred to myself or Peter.

HEAVEN'S GATE

And finally, I am thrilled to share with you the information that we have surpassed our Budget Strategy Target. The Academy is on course to be viable. Congratulations to you all.

On the final page of this document I list the tutors who have agreed to join us. Term dates, projected class sizes, course structures, etc.

Our ability to reward ourselves in the way we would like depends on our performance. There is still considerable opportunity to improve the present situation if we can

Over-Perform.

FORWARD FICTION!

Note left on kitchen table from Dave Barnes to his Nan:

Dear Nan

Here is the £20 for the use of Ladybird. We will clean up afterwards and I will take sleeping bags.
Thanks for the pen and pencil set.
Love Dave

Fax from Beverley at Travel Italia:

To Diana at Bookland.

We confirm that we have also arranged the rental of the Romeo and Juliet House, for the first two nights of your stay.
Please do not hesitate to let us know if we can be of help in any further way.
May we take this opportunity of wishing you a very enjoyable honeymoon.

CHAPTER TWENTY

It was a bit like having 'flu. Every time I thought I was cured and leapt out of bed to greet the beautiful day, something would happen to make me go wobbly again. Like seeing them together, spontaneously, in the distance. Which was the worst of all. My hope-filled heart nearly stopped.

It was in a road near my flat, and Teddy helped her out of the car so sweetly, so like he used to help me, that my knees buckled. She looked so large and so smug and such a balloon that if I had a pin I would have rushed up and stuck it in her. Then she would have been borne away on a long, loud fart, never to be seen again.

They went up the path of somebody's house. Somebody I did not know. A new friend. Once this happens, the making of new friendships, you know you have lost. There is nothing more painful than evidence of your ex-lover constructing a new social life. I hid behind a lamppost. Well, I *thought* I did. Looking back, the lamppost was considerably narrower than me, but at the time I operated on the principal that if *my* eyes could not see *them*, *theirs* could not see *me.* I must have looked fetchingly insane. The experience stayed with me for several days. I very nearly capitulated and fled to Spain and my mother. But fortunately there were the delights of Hassocks Hall, a place I had grown to enjoy and where things were moving along nicely.

Soon after this particular lamppost incident, I was standing near the lake watching the carp gliding about and generally feeling pretty miserable, when up stomped Roberta in Gauleiter mode.

'Tears?' she said sharply. 'Oh not again . . .' In the old days she might have been a bit sharp but she would have shown a degree of kindness—or at least tolerance. Love and Glory had brought her a new-found severity, as in If I Can So Can You. The usual cry of the untouched. You just wait, I felt like saying. You just wait . . .

'I'll be all right in a minute,' I said. 'It's just I saw them recently and it was a bit upsetting.'

'Tosh,' she said. 'It's been ages. You are simply wallowing, Diana. Rally!'

The lake was flecked with little pearly ripples from the slightest of breezes and the carp bore a look of welcome about them. I had a very strong urge to push her in. It wouldn't matter if she could swim or not because she'd float a treat. No Mae West required.

'Oh come on, Diana. I've given you a Mission to help you through all this. Think of the greater good. Think of helping the world to write nicely.'

'Nicely?' I said. 'Is that what we're doing?'

She spoke in almost sorrow for my ignorance. 'Of *course* it is. We don't want to teach people how to write nastily, now do we?'

'Put like that . . .'

'Absolutely.' She nodded. '*Nicely.* Without the characters shooting off or dying of unmentionable illnesses.'

'Up,' I said.

'What?'

'It's shooting up, not off . . .'

She flapped her hands, woggled her bosoms, and looked like she was about to do a bit of shooting off herself. 'Well, whatever it is. It's Street Life or some such and very, very dreary.' She peered at the water. 'Good Lord,' she said. 'What an amazingly big carp.'

At that exact moment Peterkins came trotting up on his stubby little legs.

Nowadays he did have something about him of the gasping fish. He was not good in the heat. Sweat poured from his bare, steamy brow and his shirt was sticking to his tubby torso. He seemed to be more and more under stress, which was odd since the Academy had done so well. I put it down to Roberta Fatigue. He was certainly playing it very low key about their engagement.

Desmond had tried to interview him on several occasions, but he pleaded too busy. Roberta guarded him.

She, of course, gave enough interviews for several fiancés—her face and views were everywhere and there was a worrying response to the notion of Nice Writing. It seemed to me it fell into the same category as Victorian Values. Not that I was dissuaded from aiding and abetting. It was disgusting of me really but I suppose I was working on the principle that if the world hurt me, I would hurt the world. I'd be better once I Got Back Brahms, I promised, I would, I would . . .

'Beloved,' said Roberta, and seemed to have no squeamishness about kissing him, though personally I would have preferred to kiss a toad.

'You are looking wonderful as usual,' he said, and took her hand to kiss. It was *extraordinary* how such flatteries worked. Not least because she did look rather wonderful. All glowing and rapturous. As she said, *often*, it is important to be a woman and loved. Just the kind of thing I needed to know.

Peterkins did not like me very much. His quick sideways look was a very creditable combination of damp prawn and gigolo as he bent over her hand.

Roberta turned to me. 'You see, Diana, there is always someone out there,' she said smugly. 'Who would have thought I would end up with someone so clever, so young, and so businesslike after all those difficult creative types? Could I ask for more?'

I wanted to say that a bit of hair might not go amiss but managed to hold back. No point in upsetting anyone before Amalfi. Even so, just for a moment I was grateful to be free. If compensation could arrive in such packages, then a small convent in Reigate, or a touch of the 'Great Railway Journeys: Anna Karenina', still held charms beyond rubies.

'Come along to the office and sign some cheques, dear one,' said Peterkins, 'before the day gets too hot.'

'Oh,' I said. 'Perhaps you could reimburse me for the Amalfi tickets?'

'Ah yes. Good choice,' said Roberta grandly. 'People like exotic locations. Lifts them out of their humdrum lives. I don't see why not if we're going up there now.'

Fair play to Roberta, she has always been generous of nature. I could say many things of her, but that she is mean is not one.

Peter the Bald looked sweatily irritated. 'Not at the moment,' he said. 'I haven't got to that side of the accounting procedures yet. Submit all the expenses *afterwards*—as I asked you.'

On the other hand, *he* was as mean as Scrooge. Without the Revelation. He never even bought a round on the rare occasion when we all ended up in the Hassocks Arms. Even Yale, who was prepared to tolerate anything in the name of getting his book finished, made the odd jibe in the Bald One's direction over the Rolling Rocks. To no avail though.

I remembered Nietzsche. As you do. Only because it was one of the tags my mother had pinned up in her study. 'He who cannot give anything away cannot feel anything either'. I looked at Peterkins, little pink oily runt, and I wondered if this might be true? He certainly fawned on Roberta. But was that feelings? I supposed it was. I have always found it hard to imagine the unattractive sharing the same depth of emotion as the physically blessed. Pearl says I will get my come-uppance about this one day. Maybe I had.

Roberta put her hand to her mouth. 'Sorry,' she said. 'Mustn't interfere in the business side.'

He looked mollified and gave her a squeeze. 'Perfectly all right,' he said, and laughed. 'Remember—You Creativity, Me Finance.' And he imitated an ape scratching his armpits. I thought this was something of an improvement. They went off laughing.

Meanwhile, in the distance, I saw Dave Barnes. He was sitting on a bench chewing a pen and looking constipated. Beside him a bed of scarlet and white pelargoniums burgeoned in the sun—a warm, peppery smell that I decided was extremely sexy. It was important to keep up the erotic tension. He thought only of his book, and I thought only of my bonk. It made for a kind of harmony. I decided to redouble my efforts and expunge the temporary memory of Teddy and La Barrage and the lamppost.

Side by side on the nice warm bench we squinted smiles at each other. This was the time to break the news to him that our trip to Amalfi was now booked. And then it would be, Oh dear—*what a silly mistake—the Romeo and Juliet House is a double*—well, well—I suppose one of us could sleep in the bath.

Close to, he did look a bit pimply, but then, so do all very young men. Probably a sign of virility. I moved even closer. Our knees touched, or rather stuck to each other, the morning being quite advanced and the bench being in full sun. He looked away, screwing up those adorable blue eyes and giving a remarkable impression of a writer at work.

'Fuck me, it's hard,' he said.

Nothing wrong with a little Shakespearean bawdiness.

'We need to talk location,' I said.

'Yeah,' he said, 'I know.'

There was an irritating confidence in his voice.

'Amalfi,' I said, 'is perfect.'

'That place in Italy you talked about?'

I nodded. 'I've booked it.'

He removed the pen from his mouth. He gave me a look. Peevish. I recognized it from somewhere. 'You said writers should write about what they know. Well, I know Sheppey. I went on all my holidays there in my Nan's caravan. So I've booked *that*.'

'But it's hardly exotic,' I said.

'It's what you make of it, my Nan says.'

Here was a strong reason for repeal of the entire Education Act. Give the proles a ruddy inch, as I often pointed out to Pearl.

'Look,' I said humouringly, 'Amalfi is lovely, beautiful, and—'

'That settles it,' he said. 'I don't want beautiful. I want rough.'

I knew what he meant.

He then, to my horror, developed a dish-effect lip. 'And who's writing this book?' he said. 'You or me?'

Me, actually, I muttered. But I knew I had lost.

'Anyway,' he said, 'I don't like flying. I like roads. And I like Sheppey.'

I took a deep breath. This was no time to have a lovers' tiff. 'Is the caravan very big?' I asked.

Without a hint of a leer he said, 'Plenty. I used to go when I was little. There's a club on the site and a shop and fish and chips and everything.'

He then looked down at my knee (I was wearing shorts) and reached out.

I nearly passed out with fear. I was not ready for this. But he only said, with the kind of interest a boy might show on observing an ants' nest, 'What's those?'

He was pointing at a little cluster—a very tiny and delicate little cluster—of broken veins.

'Veins,' I said shortly. 'Look—about Amalfi—'

'I thought only old ladies got them. Like my Nan.'

One more mention of her and . . .

'Sports injury,' I said, with sudden inspiration. And was rather pleased.

He gave a very wicked laugh, and a not altogether respectful one, to match his not altogether respectful look. He had become quite uppish since acquiring the title Author. 'Get away,' he snorted. And then he turned and stared me fully in the face. 'Here,' he said, smiling like Alfred E. Neuman, 'how *exactly* old are you?'

'Sheppey,' I said, 'is possible.'

He folded his arms and looked pleased. 'That Desmond bloke sent another photographer yesterday—took my picture for the brochure—with a cheque for the advance you call it.'

'Oh good,' I said. 'What are you going to do with the money?'

'Oh, it was only a pretend cheque. I haven't got it yet.' He stood up.

'Better get on.'

He looked at the pelargoniums, then reached down to feel some of the powdery soil. 'Bit sorry for themselves. Too dry. Perhaps I'll come back when Miss Topp's gone home. I only live over there.' He cocked his thumb at

Hassocks Lee. 'Don't say anything if I do will you?'

In the distance, waving a trug and a pair of very large secateurs, was the brown and green figure of Valeria's mother. Even on a day like today she wore an old cardigan, just the colour of my carpet, and a shapeless skirt in that peculiar non-green that smacks of well-used quality. Her hat was an exquisite cartwheel of old straw, and if it were not for her fearsome expression she could have stepped straight out of an Augustus John.

'Hi, hi' she called, as one might address cattle. 'Don't just stand there, there's work to be done.'

And she arrived at the bench neither breathless nor sweating. 'Put that absurd notebook away and come with me,' she said. 'And good morning.'

This last was to me as she hauled the lad away.

I watched them marching off and then a voice close to my ear said, 'She's under starter's orders. She's off.'

It was Yale. Beaming his college boy. Bursting with joy.

'All's well with the world,' he said happily, and patted his chest in self-satisfaction. 'Oh to be in England. And what a glorious day.'

He yawned and stretched and then gave me a sideways look. 'Nice kid,' he said. 'How's the book coming along? I hear you're going off to

Italy with him soon?' The teeth continued to dazzle in the sun. '*Nice* work.'

'Oh fuck,' I said, suddenly remembering.

He put up his hands. 'Please—no swearing on such a golden day.'

'You're in a good mood. For a change.'

'And you're staying in one spot for more than half a second. For a change.' He smiled even more broadly. Here was a man who was determined to love the world.

'But that's not what's put you in a good mood?'

'Nope. What's put me in a good mood is that I have finished the first draft. I knew I was right. This place is *fantastic* for getting on with things.' He looked about him. 'The grass, the sky—He pointed at the flower bed. 'The—er—'

'Pelargoniums,' I prompted.

'Pelargoniums,' he agreed. 'England. I love it.'

'Sheppey,' I said. 'I'll hate it.'

'Sheppey?'

'Sheppey. Sheppey is not Amalfi.'

I flopped down beside him.

'Sheppey is—er—a dog?' he hazarded.

'You could say that. Yes. Sheppey is a *Dog*. Another one.'

He shook his head. He leant back against the bench, crossed his arms and said, 'You know, if I had the time I'd like to do a study on the elliptical in your speech patterns.'

'Pardon?'

'I mean, what do you mean?'

'I mean that I've just realized I've spent all that money and now we are not going on location to Amalfi. We're going on location to Sheppey. In a caravan.'

'Like a gipsy?'

'Not like a gipsy.'

'Where is it?'

'It's on the south-east coast of England and is made, I imagine, largely of mud. Instead of *saltimbocca* we'll be eating whelks, and instead of *vino rosso* we'll be on brown ale. Or, more likely American rubbish.'

'Thank you,' he said.

'Don't mention it.'

'Why there?' he asked. 'If you prefer Amalfi? I can't imagine you giving in over anything you want.'

'Dave Barnes is better at it,' I said. 'Younger and stronger. He has a Look. And he can stick his lip out further than me.'

Yale looked impressed.

'And he only likes travelling on roads.'

'Fear of Flying, eh?' he said. 'So what about the Zipless Fuck?' He laughed.

I could feel myself going pinker than ever.

'Sorry,' he said. 'That was crass.'

'Don't be silly,' I said, in a sudden desire to shock him out of his bonhomie, 'that's the whole *idea* . . .'

He sat bolt upright, stared and said, 'You

are *kidding*?'

I put my hand over the little cluster of veins. 'I am not,' I said.

'But why?'

'Primal urges. Need there be any more than that?'

He relaxed, crossed his arms, shrugged and said, 'Guess not.' I waited.

He remained quite silent, as if staring across the sunny parkland was all he had on his mind.

Once or twice he shook his head and said softly, 'Shoot . . .' And then he said, smiling again, 'Well—are *we* a pair? So this is *your* agenda?'

And then I told him. All about Teddy and the baby, and Brahms and everything. 'Just a little rearrangement of the memory,' I concluded. 'Why not? You've got your plans.'

'Not the rape of innocents, I haven't.' He looked across to the lake. 'You're nuts,' was his thoughtful comment.

I waited. I was longing to hear about Carrie and his own heart and to show him what a wonderfully sympathetic listener I could be. But he didn't say a word. There is no standard quid pro quo in the exchange of confidences between men and women. He just stood up, and without so much as a decent goodbye, said, 'Well, I wish you luck.' And wandered off.

'Whatever gets you through, too,' I called.

He turned. There was that smile again. Saying nothing, covering all.

Later, walking back to the car, I saw Dave Barnes kneeling by a patch of spicily scented stocks and Sweet William.

He looked nervous. 'I *planted* these—grew them from seed—and they're already getting smothered. Bindweed. I'll do a bit more to the book tomorrow. Anyway—the old girl's in a right two and eight.' He went back to the weeding. 'Oh—and I shouldn't go down past the woodstore . . .'

'Why?'

'Bit of a ruck going on.'

'About what?'

'That Australian woman.'

'South African.'

'Whatever. Well—she was caught in one of the raspberry cages. Couldn't find her way out. Lord Hartley went off to get his gun. Miss Topp practically wet herself. Went for him like a bull terrier but he wouldn't budge. "If that woman remains connected with the Hall, this whole arrangement ends." She spat a bullet and all he said was, "Money, Miss Topp, is not everything," in that plummy voice of his. Well, they all say that when they've got it, don't they?'

'I don't think he would shoot, not really.' I said this more to bolster my own courage than out of conviction.

'I've worked here for nearly two years,' said Dave Barnes, as if it were a splendid record of achievement, and, screwing up his face into an expression of the utmost seriousness, he added, 'My money's on him.'

* * *

Pearl said, 'I'm sure Sheppey will be very nice . . .' And then she laughed so much she had to hold her sides and added, 'I'd like to see it.'

'Well, you can't.'

'No?' And she laughed and laughed again.

This is not normal behaviour, even for her.

When she calmed down and had dabbed her eyes with the duster—filthy habit—she said, 'Well, you'll be giving the whole thing up now, then?'

'Not on your nelly,' I said. 'I've still got the Requiem and I've still got Dave Barnes. Amalfi would have been nice—but you can't have everything.'

That wiped the smile off her face. She sat down on the top of the Hoover and looked at me and shook her head. 'Well I'll go to the top of our stairs,' she said. 'You'll actually *go* to a caravan on Sheppey?'

'Of course. And you, Pearl, can go where you like. The shop will be closed for two weeks.'

'Lady Bountiful, I'm sure,' she said. But she wasn't her usual happy self at the prospect.

'And now I think I'll choose a couple of nice books to take with me.' I paused and looked at her across the counter. 'Just in case I get a bit bored . . . Unlikely though.'

I gave her a really lascivious grin, knowing I was safe with customers in the shop. 'Care to recommend me something?'

'You won't need books where you're going,' she said thoughtfully. She wore such an odd expression on her face that I wondered, again, if she was jealous.

The very last consignment for the Forward Fiction Library arrived and I began to check it against my list. Pearl made me do it in the small back room, out of sight of the customers. I told her that everything comes with a price but she wouldn't let me out until the task was complete.

'All loss is gain,' I told her. 'Just as each gain is a loss.'

She was not impressed.

I reminded her that Absolutely Nothing comes free, and ticked the very last title. When they were all boxed up again, she let me out. She was still looking at me very oddly. I decided that she definitely *was* jealous.

Poor thing.

CHAPTER TWENTY-ONE

After the raspberry cage incident Erna was under round the clock surveillance. Roberta was very snappish about it and we were all on red alert.

Personally I found time spent with Erna very restorative. After a day out with her I always came home feeling refreshingly sane. She had no time for Lord Hartley's taking offence. 'Only a bit of fun,' she said. 'When you get to my age you've saved up your wild side for long enough.' She laughed her ginny laugh again. 'Only, by the time you get to indulge it, nobody wants you . . .'

I felt a little icicle touch my spine. Wild? I could be wild. And I had better get cracking.

Erna was also grateful but puzzled at the way we kept her so busy. 'So *very* busy,' she said, just a little doubtfully. But she loved us all, she said, and felt very cared for. She would make England her home.

Frankly, if she had been busy, we were all exhausted. Cracks were even beginning to show in Roberta's Mission Embracing, which was something of a relief after her unnatural and endless joy in new-found love.

It had not helped, apparently, that *Wotchacock* took some pictures of the Happy Couple on the announcement of their engagement at the same time as the Dave Barnes photo-call. Peter the Bald had been quite put out. He had already stopped one picture of himself, momentarily hatless, with the Polyfilla Actress, in a previous edition, and I could see his point. If I looked like him I wouldn't want to be featured either.

Desmond said it was too late to do anything about the engagement photo because the magazine had gone to press. Roberta had been calming ruffled feathers ever since. Her affianced seemed not to approve of mixing the Academy with their private affairs.

'Oh,' said Roberta gaily, 'the more publicity the better . . .'

'Yes my love,' he replied, definitely waspishly. 'But for the Business, not for Us.'

A distinction which Roberta found understandably incomprehensible.

I don't think Yale came out of his room for twenty-four hours after the engagement picture incident, which had Valeria prowling around like a cat on heat. I have to say that her third finger left was still very bare. And I have to say I was pleased. Time spent in a po cupboard does not fade from memory

I came upon Roberta kicking a tree trunk one morning after Erna the Pariah had somehow managed to persuade the chauffeur, who was taking her to Longleat, that it would be fun to collect a few folk from Hassocks Hall on the way. Mr V., coming out of the side door, had been very surprised to see a large Daimler streaking past with a green plaid blanket bobbing about on the back seat.

'I'll call Tree Line,' I said.

I felt extremely sorry for the tree. She packed quite a kick.

Her eyes registered real fury.

'Roberta,' I said. 'Calm down.'

'Diana,' she said. 'Shut up.'

I took a deep breath, against my better judgement, and said, 'Sorry.'

'Good heavens,' she said, genuinely surprised.

So was I. Apologizing was not my strong point.

'Do you realize,' she said, 'that everything is ready to go—only the final touches needed—Desmond's got us a huge spread in *Wotchacock* about Dave Barnes; the courses and the tutors are all organized; Phase I of the building work will be completed on time—Lord Hartley is about to sign Phase II, which is the completion document for the lease. And it could all, *all* dissolve because of one silly incident.'

'Well, I don't think Lord Hartley thinks it's silly'

'Clearly,' snapped Roberta.

'I mean, men have a view that there is a time and a place for having their testicles pulled. And in the grounds of one's stately home with a jazz band accompaniment it seems—well—unlikely to meet with approval. Not least if it is done in front of his wife.'

She contemplated her nails crossly. 'I know, I know—I think he really does mean it,' and shook her head. 'Poor Peterkins—no wonder he's ratty.'

'It's hard for all of us. And we're doing our

best. But you can't keep Erna away from here for ever. At some point she's going to notice she gets shot at every time she cruises the lawn.'

Roberta chewed her finger.

'It doesn't have to be for ever, pea-brain. It only has to be until Phase II is signed. Your being away doesn't help.'

She chewed her finger some more. 'I just need someone to mind her until then. After that we could bring in a troupe of Turkish belly dancers and he couldn't object. *Three* troupes . . .'

'Roberta,' I said, 'your engagement has coarsened you. Pearl would tell you to wash your mouth out with soap.'

And then a very odd thing happened. Her brow cleared. Her eyes grew tender. Her lips curved in a matching smile. And she embraced me. It was not pleasant but I bore it. Sapphic I would never be . . . She clasped me firmly into her chest, and said, *'Pearl!'*

She could mean me.

She could mean my cleaner.

I decided not to hang around and find out. I took Erna off to the Canadian Trade Commission where she made a completely incoherent speech and presented them with a book on the South African wine industry. For which, in return, they presented her with a case of Canadian Club Whisky. On the way back Erna winked. 'Fair exchange,' she said, and, settling back into the spongy leather for a snooze, she added, '*very* fair.'

*   *   *

After this, Roberta's temper improved, despite Peterkins suddenly having to go away on some kind of business trip. She just flapped her hands and rallied the foreground when I asked her what kind and where.

'Oh, don't ask so many questions,' she said peevishly. So I took it that she did not know.

We were checking the final list of books in the library. Roberta strutted around calling out names as she slid the very last lurid beasts into their respective holes.

'*High Fever*,' she called. 'Two.'

'*The Magnate*,' she called. 'Two.'

'*Hollywood Games*,' she called. 'Two.'

'*The Good Sex Guide*,' she called. 'One.'

She paused, book in hand. '*The Good Sex Guide*?'

'A mistake,' I mumbled, reaching out for it.

She looked at the jacket, opened it at random, closed it very quickly and said, 'Yes, well, I might keep this myself.'

Damn.

'All done,' she said proudly, and she gave the sheet of ticks a last flourishing signature.

The Hassocks Hall Thoroughly Undemanding Library was born.

She looked around the room at the tracts of

vulgarity lining it, and congratulated me.

'Mephistopheles,' I muttered.

But she was deeply engrossed in Good Sex.

*   *   *

Alarmingly, Dave Barnes did not fulfil his early promise.

Whereas the whole Terminatrix outline—if absurd—at least followed a logic with start, middle and stop, and had a touch of invention, nothing else he attempted showed any sparkle at all. He frequently said that his brain hurt and looked with increasing yearning at the gardens and distant orchard muttering things like, 'Plum sawfly' and 'Boron deficiency'—and I can tell you, these mutterings were a sight more interesting than his jottings on the page.

The full horror dawned on me. In Getting Back Brahms I was actually going to have to write the thing as well. And nothing Ghostly about it.

I missed Teddy. And though I nodded and smiled and looked dazzled at all Dave Barnes's pronouncements, I had not quite got *into* older woman mode. Pearl said it was because I wasn't one and should give the whole thing up.

I might have done if she hadn't told me to.

As it was, the only consolation for sitting with Dave Barnes in the garden while he pencil-chewed was that the weather allowed my mind to wander off into a Tennessee Williams fantasy. All steamy heat, oppressive air and mumbling. It only needed a rather sweaty satin slip, off-shoulder, a lank lock of hair hanging in one's eye, the curl of cigarette smoke through glistening ruby lips and a line like, 'God, this heat—if only the rain would come . . .' to make it complete.

Satin slips, I had discovered, were a great deal easier to purchase than negligés nowadays. I began to daydream about palaces of ice.

Increasingly, Yale came out to wander around the shadier parts of the garden, or sit, typescript in hand, correcting pen in the other, and perched on his nose the most contrived pair of thin-wired academic spectacles. Poser. But even he had abandoned the tweeds at last and reverted to perfectly sensible T-shirts.

I found it quite hampering. Especially since, on the rare occasions we did get talking, Valeria would appear, miraculous as the shoal of fishes. I suspected that she spent most of her time watching him through a telescope.

To get Dave Barnes's mind off the garden, and to gain a little privacy, we spent a few days in the Hall's basement rooms, those of the pointilliste pigs and nose-punching. They were the only truly cool places, but the builders' noise eventually drove us away. The main rooms were *quite* cool but not peaceful; there was always a whirl of activity as sponsors, potential pupils, tutors, were lunched, or dined or squeezed in for tea.

The day Roberta announced that Royalty had agreed to open the place, Yale just rolled his eyes and walked away saying, 'Ah well . . .' As if none of it had anything to do with him.

When I called him Pilate he just said, 'You can talk.'

He took himself too seriously, I decided.

We went into the New Library.

'That stuff about albatrosses wanting to be in the wrong place?'

'Yes?'

'If you don't mind my saying so,' I said, 'aren't you?'

'Nope,' he said, with irritating certainty—'I am in the right place and doing fine. Work completed. Know where I'm coming from. *You*, on the other hand, have a distinctly albatrossian air about you.'

'Tell me about Carrie?'

He shook his head. 'The past, as they say, is another country.' He went over to the window to look out.

The lawn was getting dryer and yellower with no Dave Barnes in attendance. And the sculptural shapes had scarcely recovered. He said it reminded him of New England summers. 'Eliot was an exile, too. You know "Little Gidding"?'

'Small town in Tucson?'

'Touché.' At least he smiled. 'Small town in

Northamptonshire. Big poem, big subject.'

'I know it,' I said indignantly.

'Well—good. Then you should re-read it some day.'

He turned back from the window.

'You make a better albatross than dyke by the way. And a better dyke than *femme fatale.*' He wandered round the room looking at the shelves. 'Yards and yards of crap.'

'Not all of it,' I felt obliged to say. For I had sneaked a few of my mother's in.

He stretched and yawned. 'I feel really at home here,' he said, looking up at the embellished ceiling. Nowadays he was altogether relaxed, pompous even. 'Well—the end justifies the means in my case.' He stopped yawning and gave me a look. Of serious puzzlement. 'But I'm not so sure about you. Don't you think the Brahms Requiem is a bit heavy for what you've got in mind?'

'You wouldn't understand.'

And did he say, as he would in a film, Try Me?

He did not.

He just traced the beautiful, simple, concentric tiles with his toe. And then ran his fingers over the shelves, feeling the spines, his mind somewhere else.

'Is your book anything about—um—what happened before you left the States?'

He looked up and laughed. 'Nice try,' he said. 'And no.'

I have always been good at wheedling. My father was a sucker for it, and so was Teddy. I came up and stood very close to him and put on my best wheedling voice. 'Tell me about Carrie. Go on.'

He pulled out a fat volume in white and gold called *Doing It All* and made a great show of being interested.

I took it from him and put it back.

He took out another one.

'Or shall we just pull out a few of your teeth? You'd probably prefer it.'

He stopped touching the books, and gave me a long, hard stare, shoved his hands in his pockets and walked away.

I ran after him. 'I hope you know what you're doing,' I said. 'If you think I'm being too heavy. You could end up married.'

'I could,' he said. 'That's my business.'

He began to take the stairs two at a time.

So did I.

'And I hope you're not going to follow me round doing this all day,' he said over his shoulder. 'You could end up unmarriageable.'

He ran out on to the sunny gravel.

I pulled his sleeve saying, 'Tell me, tell me . . .'

He stopped and turned. The sun was so brilliant that I could not see his face. His hands were clenched though. I thought that was a good sign. If men talking about their feelings was akin to tooth pulling, at least he seemed close to sitting down in the dentist's chair . . . I was about to suggest we took a walk in the rhododendron shade when out of her dignified little pavilion sprang Valeria—pen in her mouth like a carnation for a Spanish dancer, ancient white smock smeared with paint.

'Darling,' she said breathlessly. 'You must come at once. I've just finished the book jacket.' She looked at me as if I were a slug.

He moved towards her. His face visible once more was smooth and smiling, and he took her hand.

'Excuse me,' he said. Polite to the last.

She could not have looked happier if Monet had just popped in to congratulate her. They walked away.

I was really hot from all the running. Enviously I watched them disappear into the shady portico of the summer house and I thought of its cool, grey interior. They might have invited me. I considered this. Why couldn't *I* go and see the book jacket? After all, without me there wouldn't be the book. I thought some more. The sun was irritating in its intensity. And it looked so cool over there. They wouldn't mind. After all it was work. And just a welcome break. They'd probably value my opinion on the design. Sure to, in fact. So I followed.

I went up the steps, enjoying the shade, and peered through the side window. There was

Valeria with her smock up over her head, thrust back on her drawing board and being given what in impolite circles is known as a damn good rogering. Yale had not even taken off his shoes—I mean, *really*—it was just shirt tail, sock tops and a pair of wrinkled English flannels cast aside on the worn stone floor. I knew how they felt.

I retreated hurriedly. Roll on Dave Barnes and the caravan, I thought. Roll on Dave Barnes and *anywhere.* Even just roll on Dave Barnes. But the truth was I was not, entirely, convinced. Something approaching rapture had shone out of Valeria's myopic, unfocused eyes and it made me ache.

On an altogether more pragmatic note, I registered that Yale had a very nice bum.

CHAPTER TWENTY-TWO

I was packed. I was waiting for the cab to the station. And thence Sheppey and the caravan. I must have checked about ten times that I had the Brahms cassette safely tucked in my bag, and that I had my cassette player with me. Nothing could be left to chance. I had even managed the special box of chocolates—Italian—from Harrods of course, because I did not expect the Isle of Sheppey to go in for anything other than very pink sticks of rock.

Pearl, apparently, was going somewhere new for a change. I could only guess this because she helped herself to a few books which all appeared to be Guides for Great Britain.

'Not going to your shack then?' I asked.

'Shack-Schmack,' she said. 'Maybe later.'

The weather was bliss and the portents were good.

Pearl was no longer interested in discussing my holiday, location or hopes. She just pulled her mouth into a disapproving line and said she had other fish to fry.

*   *   *

I went down to the caravan ahead of Dave Barnes. I needed time to prepare it. I told him that I needed time alone there, to commune and let the ideas rise from the centre of my being like yeast. Not only did he believe it—but he jotted it down. He was getting desperate.

I went by rail, which I prefer. Dave was to have the loan of one of the Hassocks Hall cars the next day. He had given me all his notes to read on the way down, which I threw out of the train window.

*   *   *

In railway terms, the journey from Victoria has

to be one of the most dreary routes anywhere. If you didn't have the hump, as Pearl would say, you'd soon get it. This was what Dave Barnes called going into the country. Flat, dull housing and square, unyielding buildings that mistakenly thought modernism was a cue for brutality. Clear away the rubble of the past, someone said, between Bromley and Sheerness, and put up any old thing in the name of The New.

It is the equivalent of a second marriage—hope triumphing over experience. Bromley, Chatham, Sittingbourne—it cannot get worse, you think, it cannot get worse.

But it does.

Queensborough.

I kept my spirits up by remembering that a good number of my friends who had babies forsook marital or partnership joys soon after, both in bed and out, and eventually found themselves stumbling alone on the wasteland of lost hope. Well, I thought, looking out over the sunlit wastes of my destination—Teddy knew where to come if the *chaudière vieille* let him down and he started stumbling alone.

In the meantime I had the challenge and the excitement of the task ahead.

I tried to feel challenged and excited. Actually I felt much as I had on the eve of my sinus operation. Nervous but ready to get on with it. Not a *particularly* sensual analogy.

I imagine Brahms would have liked the Isle

of Sheppey for its brownness. It pertains to the same tonal qualities as Mrs V.'s gardening outfit, but minus the quality, being largely, as I suspected, founded on mud. By the time the traveller alights, the traveller is inclined to be overjoyed. By the time the traveller alights, there is but one way, and that is up.

What I did not need when I arrived at the station was the offensive garrulity of the ticket collector who was drinking from a can of lager and took the point of view that I was single.

'My boyfriend is coming on later,' I said coldly.

'Why wait?' he said, swigging away, 'when I'm here and coming on now?'

He thought that was ever so funny. His eyes beneath the peaked cap shone with uncontainable joy at the wit.

'Can I have your name?' I asked, with suitable hauteur.

'Not unless you marry me first,' he quipped. 'Nice tits.'

Backbone of England.

How could Teddy leave me to face these things alone? I got into the taxi, disregarded the whistling, and never looked back. The taxi driver remained mute, apart from asking, 'Where to?' At least he had heard of the Happy Holiday Nest.

It was not a very long drive, and suddenly, there it was. On the cliffs, sprawling towards the edge. Mathematical rows of bad-taste capsules lined up to salute the duskening blue sky. Dogs barked, children screamed, and the smell of frying onions was everywhere. The taxi passed beneath a wooden sign arched across the entrance which, quite without shame, announced we were in the HAPP OLIDAY EST.

A clever invention, the English caravan site, for quieting the potential mob. It is the holiday equivalent of a fast-food burger bar. If ever one were on a quest for the heart of the English working class at play, you can find it alive and well and pumping its little arteries out in a place like the Happy Holiday Nest.

Whoever Nan was, she was part of a great tradition. That of the lowest common denominator, the tabloid world. Here was everything the fun-loving and peaceful proletariat required. A clubhouse where the men wore blazers and flannels, the women shiny black frocks, and where all the participants knew how to enjoy themselves. Wives and girlfriends drank gin and tonics, men drank beer or lager, and the food was served in a basket. I always say this is very hard on soup-lovers.

We stopped by a little brick shack. The unedifying modern version of the honourable coach house. Just for a moment, as I gazed from this to the parallel lines of caravans, I thought about Hassocks Hall with new understanding. And it goes without saying,

Amalfi it was not.

The woman in charge smiled and directed us to where *Ladybird* was berthed. The taxi driver bumped his way slowly along the impacted grass and mud.

Children in grubby swimming gear stopped and stared as we passed, dogs dropped their tails and got out of the way, parental onion-fryers stood at their little square windows and stared through fancy nets.

'Just a minute,' I said, tapping the driver's shoulder. He braked so hard that he could have been going for gold.

'What?' he said nervously.

We were passing the octagonal ranch-style clubhouse.

'I want to pop into that bar.'

His eyes widened. For the first time there was a hint of life. 'Oh—mine's a—'

'No, no—not for a drink. I just want to ask them something.' And off I went, returning a moment later with everything arranged. The staff of the clubhouse stared out after me as if I was deranged.

The taxi set me down at *Ladybird*—a grey/green monster with not a hint of red or spots about it. And I opened the little door.

I remember, distinctly, that I curled my mouth in disdain as I prepared to cross the threshold. A curl that went suddenly flat as yesterday's perm. All my expectations, all my sociological ruminations, shot to hell.

That this huge, wonderful, terrifying world can go on surprising us is an extraordinary thing. In a thousand years of progress I would never have expected to find in that caravan what I found—in that caravan.

I should have known what I would find as soon as I opened the door. I should have known without looking. I should have known, of course, by the smell.

CHAPTER TWENTY-THREE

The other thing my mother likes to say is Never Judge A Book By Its Cover. She even said it about Teddy when she was trying hard to find something to commend in him. Never Judge A Book By Its Cover, she urged, though later when she got to know him she said she thought in his case it might be inappropriate. It was always very odd to have a mother urging me to get a little more excitement in my life and saying things like You Only Live Once.

She would certainly have liked this visual little twist. It was Never Judge A Book By Its Cover in earnest.

The interior was dim because the windows were shaded. The air was fusty from being shut in. But the smell was both second nature to me and totally unexpected.

The caravan was six or seven metres long

with a little kitchen area to my right, and to my left, past the lavatory and shower, a sitting area with neatly fitted cupboards, benches and a central table. It was so neat that it looked like a *sculpture* of the perfect caravan interior with a place for everything . . . As if an artist had taken a cast of one. But the familiar smell, and unexpected surprise, was because every possible bit of the spatial jigsaw held rows and rows of *books*.

I had foreseen sticky lino, formica, ancient copies of tabloid newspapers, the odd issue of *True Confessions*, *Hello!* and *Wotchacock*, a couple of well-sucked babies' dummies and an old jar of instant coffee. If I were asked to create a still-life of my expectations, that would be it. I had come down here determined to rise above. What I found was something resembling the perfect erudite bookish retreat. I breathed in the smell again. With it, faint on the air, came the smell of onions wafting out to sea. A child cried, a dog barked, a door banged and somebody swore.

I rolled up the shades and wandered around feeling both amazed and deflated. You forget just how neat neat has to be in a very confined space. The kitchen drawers and cupboards contained the basics in plain white and no nonsense. I had expected something beige and floral. Do not say anything, I warned my mother, who was hovering about with a *very* superior smile. But she did anyway. Judge Not

Lest Ye Be Judged. I believe I heard the Oracle laugh. Brahms would not be out of place down here, after all. Sometimes one has to rearrange one's prejudices.

It wasn't even an Elsan out the back. The loo and shower were tiny and clean, with one of those mincing machine pumps attached to the lavatory—the sort that, after an initial attempt at use, are guaranteed to make the weak-hearted caravanner constipated for their entire stay. The sitting area, which had the full benefit of triple aspect, was booklined above seated head level and had built in drawers that contained everything from polishing cloths to pen, paper and ink, all perfectly ordered.

Just for a moment I forgot why I was here and took a childish delight in the double bed which pulled down from a central position in the wall. On the shelves there were tilley lamps, though I had brought candles, and on the benches some nice squashy feather cushions covered in red velvet. The window blinds were dark blue and a transparent sliding contraption in the roof could be opened to the stars. It was directly over the bed. Why ask for the moon when we have the stars . . .? I thought about opening it, since it was very warm, but its locking complication had the same appeal as the lavatorial mincing machine and I was not ready. Anyway—warm was nice. It was to be hoped we would dance all our hot way to hell.

I watched from the window as the dusk finally darkened to night and I felt almost happy. It was like playing house, or a pre-wedding eve from olden days—a girl's last night of purity and freedom and a little like being in a fairy tale. I thought about Brahms and Clara Schumann. Forty years of worship. And where did it get him? Better by far to have a go at shortcircuiting it like this. I stretched and yawned and gazed at the stars.

When it was too dark to see anything but the outline of the empty caravan next door, and when a distant bass beat indicated that the clubhouse had livened up, I took a book from the shelves and went to bed. They made an odd collection. Mostly secondhand. Light novels like Barbara Pym, Margery Sharpe, Joyce Cary; collections of essays by Chesterton, R. L. Stevenson, Hazlitt; some classics—Suetonius, Homer, Juvenal; much from the nineteenth century in paperback—Russians and Victorians mainly—and a good amount of contemporary fiction, including what is known as the Literary Mafia, though oddly nothing by Bill Brandon. I looked high and low but not one Brandon could I find. Pearl was the same about him. No better than he ought to be, was the way she put it.

I chose the Muriel Spark short story in which the young heroine stands at the crossroads, both symbolically and literally. She is deeply confused, deeply unhappy. So she pleads with God to help her out of this mess. At which point God takes pity, and has her shot.

One way of looking at things, I thought, as I yawned and settled down into the nice squashy double bed. But better, perhaps, to take your fate in your own hands like me. I was soon asleep.

CHAPTER TWENTY-FOUR

Morning. Dave Barnes was due to arrive at one o'clock. I thought we should take a good long walk with a picnic lunch, to get the feel of the place before settling down to—um—*work*. I wanted us back in *Ladybird* by six that evening, with good reason.

Morning. I awoke to the sound of what seemed to be rather large fairy feet dancing over the roof of the caravan.

Morning. After several weeks of heat and dust, it rained.

And rained. Worse, it was chilly.

Not very chilly but chilly enough to make Tennessee Williams seem a little ridiculous. And I had pinned quite a lot on him. One brand new satin slip, hair-tousling equipment and a louche cheroot to be precise. I could feel the first creeping hint of a sulk, something that tends to show very distinctly in my face. The more I am aware of this, the more I glower.

And attempting to use the lavatorial mincing machine had not improved things. Women are not made to wreck their femininity with alternative sewage inventions. If I wanted to be butch, I would have stayed that way.

I made toast, found I had forgotten milk, drank black tea, and glowered some more. In a vest and sweat shirt and leggings to be precise, which was all the warm clothing I had. With luck the day would warm up so that I could wear the *Night of the Iguana* satin slip with impunity. I needed the boost.

At around eleven I had had enough. There was a packaway waterproof in one of the drawers, and as I needed new trainers anyway, I went out into what was, effectively, mud.

I passed the clubhouse, where the manager and his assistant worked their way slowly through the detritus of the night before. I waved. The manager responded with a thumbs up. And started humming 'Happy Birthday to You'. I smiled as much as I could and walked on.

Children are amazing. There they were, in their swimming gear, hurtling around in the rain, happily turning blue. Glum parental faces looked out from rain-dashed windows. I walked to the edge of the site, and peered over the cliffs down on to the muddy brown shore, where more children swarmed, dodging the waves, shrieking with delight, dogs dancing along in noisy joy. So much for our solitary saunter and picnic anyway. The place did look rather good from the point of view of a hideout for villains, especially in the driving wet. What it did not look like, alas, was the mossy bank of love.

After about half an hour I turned back, convincing myself—as we English do—that a rain-drenched, windswept struggle against the elements is a bracing walk and therefore good for you.

I splodged back down the running mud track to base. Fixed to the door of the caravan was a note.

> Got here early. You out. Gone to get
> something to eat.
> See Ya, Dave.

It wasn't even noon. Glowering continued. Well—that was just great.

I made a huge sandwich of smoked salmon and cucumber and washed it down with more black tea. I had even forgotten to buy some sodding milk from the camp shop. I climbed back into bed. Chilled, damp and very, very miserable. The table by the window mocked me. I had put out some books, a pen, some paper, and I was *supposed* to be sitting there by the window when he arrived, in my satin slip, one strap dangling, smoking the louche cheroot and looking dangerously available.

So much for forward planning.

It was a great bed though. All squashy and big and cozy and warm. I picked up the Muriel Spark, turned to the next short story, and fell asleep immediately.

*   *   *

Brahms was not much good in wet weather, either.

When Clara Schumann had a stroke, in her seventy-eighth year and living in Frankfurt, Brahms was resident in Vienna and not well himself. When he heard of her death, Brahms was inconsolable. It was the final, great disappointment. Despite his own frail health, he began the arduous journey by train to her funeral in Frankfurt. He travelled overnight but was not woken at Linz for the connection and had to take a later, slower train instead. Arriving in Frankfurt, exhausted both physically and emotionally, he was told that the funeral had taken place, that Clara's body was now on its way to Bonn to be buried by her husband's side.

Given his own frailty, he could have given up at that point. But not Brahms. He was determined to be witness at her grave, his last duty as her lover. He made the further laborious journey, a day and a half of travelling, to Bonn, and arrived in time, though weary and wet through, to stand in the driving rain and cast his handful of earth before the grave was closed. He returned to Vienna, with the sense that all purpose had gone from his life. Not long afterwards he died.

*   *   *

The rain decided it had made a friend of the HAPP OLIDAY EST and was not inclined to desert it. I woke up wondering where I was, still to the tune of the faery clogs, and fully dressed. It was just after four. How much did Dave Barnes *eat*?

I pushed the bed back up, checked that the cassette was in the player, and that the player worked, congratulating myself on aforethought. And went to have a nice long warming shower. I found a little fan heater which helped, and was just putting the final touch of scent in cleavage, when there was a noise over and above the rain dance. The noise of someone knocking at the door.

Perfect timing. I smiled and opened it as planned in my satin straps, hair too short for tousled but suitably mussed, and, thanks to the heater, with only a very mild case of goosebumps. But what I saw dealt rather awkwardly with the louche cheroot. I coughed and had to be thumped on the back.

Thumped? you will say. Surely a *Thump is* not seemly from a potential swain, even if the potential swain does not yet know he is one?

And, of course, you would be right.

But it was not Dave Barnes who took the liberty. For he was not the first to cross the threshold. He was there all right. But he was not alone. In the circumstances it was not surprising that I choked. Because, although one member of the group accompanying him was a stranger, the other two were familiar. Very familiar.

And it was with lots of happy familiarity that In They Came.

CHAPTER TWENTY-FIVE

'Erna! Pearl!' I said, with the joy born of madness.

I looked searchingly at Dave Barnes. Next to him stood a very small creature, even smaller than Erna, in a baseball cap and very wet jeans. 'And who is this?' I asked politely, trying to peek under the hat.

Dave Barnes shuffled forward and smiled rather self-consciously. 'My girlfriend,' he said shyly and with pride. 'Pauline.'

I extended my hand. Hers was very small and very wet. In fact, I thought sourly, *she* was very small and very wet.

I could hear my mother again, laughing softly, somewhere in the ether. Of *course* Dave

Barnes would have a girlfriend. You only had to look at him to see that. How could I ever have imagined he was free?

It was Pearl who thumped me.

She looked me up and down, and there was something about the way she said, 'Oh—you going to bed then?' that made me very suspicious.

'We've all come down to say Hi,' said Erna. 'Just for the night. It's a little adventure.' She gave me a radiant if slightly unfocused smile. 'Pioneer spirit.' She tried counting a couple of times but gave up. 'Four of us. Any room at the inn?'

'Come in, come in, all of you,' I said joyfully, trying to hide my upraised satinate nipples—either from fear or low temperatures the erectile tissue was doing its stuff—with one hand, while not doing anything too awful with the cheroot with the other. 'Come in before you catch your death.'

Pearl sniffed and eyed me up and down. 'Boot on the other foot, *I'd have thought.*'

Dave Barnes looked all around him, and whistled. 'Hey,' he said, not entirely approvingly. 'This is all a bit different. Where's the bunches of plastic daffs I got free with Fairy?'

* * *

I hunched over the little hob waiting for the

kettle to whistle. At the other end of the caravan, Erna, in a vivid royal blue ensemble, largely comprising zips, and quite useful if flying a Fokker, was holding forth to Dave Barnes and his girlfriend about the cuteness of the place, the Englishness of the rain and the fun of having English tea. And what a *Wow* of an idea it was of Pearl's to come down here to the English beach.

Well, Wow!

Pearl was with me and also hunching over the kettle . . .

Pearl was with me and in danger of being throttled.

It is very hard to conduct a conversation with any form of privacy in such confined space. Nevertheless I attempted it.

'You're fired,' I said. 'You realize that?'

She snorted. 'Can't do that. I'm on my holidays. This is free time.'

'Why here? *Why?*'

'Roberta Topp. Her idea.'

'She sent you? Why would she send you when she knew we were coming down here to work?'

Pearl coughed very deliberately and gave me that Look.

'As far as Roberta is concerned, that's all we've come down here for. Work on the book. So why would she interrupt us? It is *very* unprofessional.'

Apart from a deep suspicion, I could feel

the tears rising. Pearl opened a cupboard under the little sink and took out some kitchen roll. She handed me some and then put the rest back. Very neat is Pearl.

'Her fiancé returns today and she wants the place to herself. Milord, Milady and the little Mistress have gone to Scotland for a family wedding—three or four days—though the young Miss wasn't too keen.'

I *never* knew if Pearl was being ironical.

'The American didn't go to Scotland because he said he was out of sorts.' Pearl did not bat an eyelid. 'He hopes you're enjoying Brahms.'

'I'll bet he does. Out of sorts! He was well enough yesterday.'

'Well he isn't well enough today, Miss. In fact he's looking green all over. Pass us the tea.'

She pointed at the cupboard above my head, and I obliged.

Oh, the *ignominy* . . .

She gave me a sharp look and flexed the corners of her mouth. She went on counting in the spoons of tea. 'We asked him if he'd like to come with us, but he said no. And I don't blame him.'

The tea was set to brew. Pearl took from her bag two packets of biscuits. 'I thought we might have a drink,' I mumbled.

'This is a drink,' said Pearl firmly. 'Milk?'

I shrugged. 'I forgot it.'

She opened a cupboard and took from its depths a packet of UHT. She plonked this down with a look that would have made Einstein feel inadequate.

'Roberta Topp asked me to look after her'—Pearl jerked her head in Erna's direction—'and I am. And I am *not* having her drunk all over the place. Not while I'm in charge. Sugar?'

Sugar was found.

'Never known anything like it,' said Pearl. 'She's getting that fiancé of hers to sleep with her in the rose silk bed—you know—the Queen Elizabeth one.'

She ripped open the sugar packet and proceeded to pour it into a dish.

'Personally it looks like one snore and it'll fall apart. But there you are. Likes of her doesn't think about future generations.'

'That's wicked,' I said, remembering the precious bit of crumbling gossamer.

'Wicked,' Pearl said positively. 'Calls herself the Queen of Fiction and *that's* not royalty.' She opened a drawer and removed a little sugar spoon which she plonked into the dish. 'And she's planning some sort of dinner for the two of them in the dining hall. Oh, it was all going on when we left—polishing the silver, getting out the French china and whatnot. She even told the builders not to come in today . . .'

While talking, Pearl was getting pinker and pinker. 'I must say I do find her an arrogant woman. Can't write and now *this* . . .' She gave the pot another vigorous stirring.

'And you! All this wasted energy of yours, my girl,' she said, pointing the spoon at me. 'Give it up. Waste of time. Carpe Diem.'

'Pearl,' I said. 'Don't talk Latin.'

I looked down the caravan to where the three visitors sat. And I heard Dave Barnes say, 'The Terminatrix. A very, very powerful woman. Of course, it's only a fantasy . . . My Nan started me off on it. But she says I'm on my own now.' He looked towards us, I thought rather pleadingly. 'And it's *hard*,' he said. 'Without her.'

I looked back at Pearl.

She was bending down.

'Pearl?' I said.

No response.

'*Pearl!* How come you know where everything is?'

She straightened up from removing a tray from the side of a cupboard. She looked at me. And she laughed.

Well,' she said, with her hand on her hip, 'either it's Magic Realism. Or it's my caravan.' And brushing me aside, she added, 'You don't know *everything* . . .'

'Did *you* write that stuff for Dave?'

'I did,' she said firmly. 'I thought it would stop all this—' she cocked her eyes towards Dave Barnes, who appeared to be posing for Mark II of Rossetti's *Jesus in the Temple with the Elders*—'nonsense of yours. And I never, ever, not in a million years thought you lot would fall for it.' She put down the pot and shook her head. 'How daft can you get?' And she took a cup of strong, sweet tea down to Erna.

Just then there was a knock on the door.

'It's probably the Pope,' I said. 'Can we squeeze another one in?'

But it wasn't. It was the manager from the clubhouse.

With the champagne.

Bang on the dot of six o'clock.

*   *   *

Roberta may have been halfway to barking with love, but she had not entirely arrived. The party was booked into the best hotel on Sheppey and Erna, surprised and not a little sobered by the tea, offered to buy us all dinner there. Seemed like a good idea. Anything seemed like a good idea.

For the first time since I met him, I saw the correct light of lust in Dave Barnes's eyes.

'Think we'll just stay on here. Me and Pauline.'

Pauline, now dry and, I would say, definitely shrunk, said, 'OK.'

'Rubbish,' said Pearl. 'You'll come with us. Both of you.'

Dave drew himself up to full height. 'I'll just

stay here and do some writing.'

Now I knew where I had seen that Look. It ran in the family.

She cuffed his ear. 'Writing-Schmiting,' she said.

'I'm the Core of their Mission,' he said, with wonderful grandeur.

'And I'm Diana Dors,' she said. 'Get your anorak.'

Erna was smiling from among her zips and fingering the champagne bottle as absently and expertly as a whore in a clipjoint. Once or twice I saw her eyeing Dave Barnes's crutch, but she resisted. Must have been the sobering effect of the tea.

'Anorak,' said Pearl again.

Dave glowered. But Pauline just fluttered those underdeveloped lashes of hers and gave him a smile. Yup. *That* smile. How could I ever have dreamed up such a scheme with him? The combination of me in a satin slip and Brahms in all his glory would have had Dave Barnes running for home. Anyway, it would probably have had me running for home, too. Now I came to look at him he was a bit gauche: heavy round the jaw and with one of those chins that betoken too much willpower in one so young. Erotically speaking, he suddenly fell flat.

Progress nil.

I looked across at the cassette player. It had the air of betrayal about it. I was suddenly aware of standing in the centre of a HAPP OLIDAY EST wearing only a satin slip and a pair of Janet Regers and attempting to commit madness. I was very, very glad to look up and see Pearl. With Pearl around things have a way of staying distressingly sane.

She had sucked in her lips. 'You,' she said to me, 'had better get something on.'

'Why didn't you tell me?' I said. 'You've let me make a complete fool of myself.'

'Ah no,' said Pearl, raising her bony finger, 'you made the fool of yourself. I've just got you out of it.'

'You wait until we get back to the shop,' I said.

It could have been worse. I could have been the woman at the New York party who sidled up to one of the guests after he burst spontaneously into song and said, 'That was great. Ever thought of taking it up professionally?' To which he replied, '*Sì*—my name is Pavarotti . . .'

I looked at her. 'Why didn't you tell me? And how could you feed him such drivel?'

She now pointed the same long, bony finger at me, showing a distinct relation to the Oracle. 'You didn't have to go on eating it, though, did you?'

Buck-passing. I despise it.

'I never dreamed in all my years that there were so many silly people with so much money to waste.' She looked genuinely shocked. 'And as for Amalfi . . . Well!'

'It might have worked, Pearl.'

Might, schmight,' she said, and looked at the shrunken Pauline. 'None of it would have worked. Even if it worked. If you see what I mean.' We both looked at Dave Barnes. He was in love.

Pearl sniffed. 'Now—you get a shift on so we can all go and eat.'

I looked across at Erna, who was blissfully drinking champagne from a milk jug. Dave Barnes and Little Pauline held empty glasses that had not even been wetted. They were leering at each other—or as much as the young and unformed can be said to leer.

'You could give a great party in here,' said Erna, coming up to Pearl.

'I've only just got it the way I want it. Thank you.'

Erna went to peer out of the window on to the sodden vista of caravans, grey on grey. 'It's got a lot of potential,' she said.

'I've been coming down here for thirty-five years,' said Pearl. 'First thirty with Dick. Last five on my own. I've just got it the way I want it. My way. And I'm not about to give it up.'

'Not give,' said Erna helpfully. 'I'd offer you a real good price.'

Pearl shook her head. 'Don't be daft,' she said contemptuously, rattling up the cups.

It was while I was struggling into a skirt and tights that Erna began to beep. Short of waiting for a ping to say she was done, we galvanized. It took the concerted efforts of us all to undo the zips and finally locate the right compartment for her mobile phone. She answered it.

After some difficulty about who she or anybody was, she handed it to me. 'It's for you,' she said, 'I think.'

I was halfway into a pair of tights when I took the call. It was Yale.

'Are you there? Who is that?' He sounded slightly panicky.

'I'm here, I'm here,' I said. 'Now what?'

'Who *is* that?'

'It's Diana.'

'*Diana?* What the fuck are you doing with Erna's phone?'

'Good evening and how are you, too?' I said, hopping and poking at my tights.

There was a short pause. I managed to hook my toe into one leg.

'Yes?' I said testily.

'Have I—er—disturbed anything?' he asked.

Trying to get tights on single-handed can do things to a girl.

'I'm dressing,' I said.

'Ah,' he said.

'It's not what you think.'

'No?'

'No. It's just that we're all going out for dinner.'

'All?'

'Yup,' I said, looking around. 'Would you care to make a selection? There's quite a lot of us. Erna, Pearl, Dave Barnes, Dave Barnes's girlfriend, Pauline . . .'

He laughed. 'Dave Barnes's *girlfriend*?'

'So glad you find it amusing.'

'Best laid plans,' he offered cheerfully.

'Sometimes don't get you laid.'

'No Brahms?'

'No Brahms.'

'I'm sorry.'

'You sound it.'

'You'd better finish dressing.'

'Thank you.'

'And then all of you better get back here right away . . . Can you hear that?'

In the background I could hear an operatic kind of wailing. Could have been *Tosca*, could have been Roberta. I finally got the tights up to my waist, breathed a sigh of relief which was not very long lived, and said, 'What have we got to come back *for*?'

He lowered his voice further.

He waxed poetical, as do all great messengers with news of portent.

He said, 'Shit's hit the fan.'

And rang off.

CHAPTER TWENTY-SIX

I wanted to say Go On, Give Them a Nudge, like in the old days, but even I knew when to stop. Roberta was in a place beyond her breasts. And from the look of her it was a place where none of us would choose to be, and whence I had recently escaped. Or very nearly. It was the Land of Heartbreak, or, worse, its Continent.

If you can imagine a raven-locked Miss Havisham minus the Nottingham lace, several years, and swathed in burgundy silk, you would not be far out. She sat, tousle-haired, bare-shouldered, smouldering, at one end of the long, gleaming dining table, amidst winking crystal and shining plate. One of the winking glasses held a little red wine and beside it was a dark green bottle upon which she drummed her finger-ends quietly. Like water torture.

Over by the wall, on a great carved chest, probably Stuart, stood an unopened bottle of champagne in a silver cooler. What had once been a bottle of white wine now lay empty on its side, the contents dousing the floor. A little silver dish of assorted nuts had also tipped over and spilled on to the chest-top. My stomach, betrayer, spotted these and growled. I realized I was very, very hungry. It is a terrible thing in the midst of such suffering to want a snack. But I did. It was, I realized, the first time I had truly felt hungry since Teddy left me. But the significance of this, if any, would have to wait.

I pressed sternly on my stomach and looked back to Roberta. So grand was the setting that she looked like a tiny jewel in a sumptuous crown; a very unhappy and tiny jewel. She had lit the hall with candles, lots of candles, which were now dripping from the various sconces and candelabra around the lofty dining hall, their spills of wax matching, rather grotesquely, the tears that flowed down her cheeks.

I took another look at the nuts and wondered if I could make a run for them. Roberta was still staring ahead, eyes like soggy diamonds, and scarcely seeming to breathe. Her fingers continued to drum. Erna, I noticed, was staring very hard at the champagne. The rest of us had our eyes fixed on Roberta as if she were a display tableau in a museum. None of us wanted to make the first move. Somehow it seemed rather crass to bound across the room and speak.

'Well,' said Erna suddenly, under no such constriction and bounding her zippered way across the room. 'What a great place to have a party . . .' She stared about her in wonder as she grasped the neck of the bottle. 'Wow,' she said, looking up at the pale and shadowy plasterwork ceiling. And while doing so she popped the cork as casually and expertly as before.

Roberta blinked at the noise and her fingers stopped. She took a sip of wine and then looked across at first us, then Erna.

'Hi,' said Erna, and gave a little wave, indicating the room. 'And you all on your little owny-o. Mind if we join you?'

At which point Roberta dropped her head on to her hands, sobbing loudly.

And I made a dash for the nuts.

At which point Roberta removed her head from her hands and glowered at me, just as I popped in a salted brazil.

'How could you?' she said. 'How *could* you *eat*?'

Why is it, somehow, always me? Why is it that anybody else can pop champagne, do handstands, anything, and they are not singled out, but if I make one false move, bite on one small savoury, somehow, *somehow* it sticks out like a deeply painful digit?

'Sorry,' I said.

'Sorry,' she repeated. *'Sorry!'*

Dave Barnes advanced a little uncertainly. The girlfriend also advanced and held his hand. She gazed at him proudly as he addressed Roberta.

'I'll—er—be going back down there in the morning like,' he said, 'to finish the location stuff. And then it's'—he smiled and made a scribbling gesture—'write, write, write.' He stood confidently to attention in front of her.

Roberta picked up the bottle near her glass and poured some more wine. Staring bleakly over the rim she said, not very nicely, 'Write, write, write—'she drained the glass. *'Bollocks.'*

'Now Miss Topp,' said Pearl.

'Now Miss Topp,' mimicked Miss Topp. 'What, Miss Topp? *What?*'

She ran her hand through her hair, which now resembled a black mop, fixed Pearl with a Look—one, I am happy to report, which matched the recipient's own—and stared down at the table. 'Nothing,' she said. 'All over . . .'

'I think you'd better go,' whispered Pearl to Dave and Pauline. 'Go on, hop it.'

They needed little encouragement.

As did not I.

I began to sneak off but Yale came up behind and sort of shoved me back in line.

'Oh no you don't,' he said. 'All for one, and one for all.'

Erna sat herself down at the corner of the dining table and poured the champagne rather messily into glasses. Including Roberta's, which fizzed over the top in a froth of pink.

'Here you are dear,' she said, all concern.

'Thanks,' said Roberta, and raising the glass to her lips said, 'Bastard.'

Yale looked at me.

'What's going on?' I asked.

Pearl ignored me, tutted her way to the table and began to wipe up the puddles of champagne with a serviette. Then she also sat down. Roberta Topp was flanked on each side by an odd pair of guardian angels. Erna put her chin in her hand, or approximately, and urged Roberta to have a good cry; let it all out. Which seemed a strange piece of advice since Roberta already was. Indeed, if she let any more out we could expect a visit from the Noise Abatement Society.

Pearl, while nodding encouragement at Erna, was actually encouraging Roberta to speak, rather than howl.

Then came the sound of my growling stomach.

'Come on,' said Yale. 'Let's bring in some of that food from next door.'

'Good idea,' said Pearl.

'But I want to know what's happened. I've never seen Roberta shed half a tear before.'

He took my arm. 'I'll tell you,' he said.

I looked back at the table and wondered if I should desert them. But Erna and Pearl seemed to be coping.

My stomach growled anew. The word Food was suddenly up there in neon. Odd to have that sensation back again.

There was another odd sensation too, I realized.

One of absence.

We tiptoed out.

'Why Yale dear,' I said, 'you aren't wearing Valeria tonight.'

'She's still in Scotland. For another three days.'

I got the distinct feeling he spoke with relief. I wondered if there were suction marks on his shoulders where she had to be prized off.

Behind us it was one nil to Erna. Roberta had started yet again to keen.

*   *   *

Greater love hath no woman than she prepare everything in advance, no matter how incongruous it might appear.

The pretty pale grey antechamber which once held poor Caroline of Brunswick while she waited to be received by her horrible husband, and in which hopeful refugees, fleeing Madame La Guillotine, sat waiting to learn if the English Lord would hear their pleas for asylum, now held a hostess trolley, a microwave and a fold-up table with several sorts of cheese. Thus did modern appurtenances come to Hassocks Hall.

I fell upon the cheese. Yale looked at me in amazement.

'What's up?' I asked through a mouthful of Brie and biscuit.

He looked away. 'Nothing, nothing.'

'Have some,' I said.

'I couldn't eat a thing.'

He sat down, leaning his back against the

wall, and picked at a piece of Stilton. He did not look happy.

'Not very well?' I asked. And then had a rather mischievous thought. 'I know—you're pining for Valeria.'

He gave me an even less happy look. And shook his head. 'Nope. Peter has done a runner. With all the money. Milked all the bank accounts and gone. Roberta found out tonight.'

I stopped chewing.

'You're kidding.'

'A beautifully turned phrase,' he said wryly. 'No—I'm not kidding. He's gone. And that'—he popped a valedictory grape in his mouth—'has just about blown it.' He paused. 'Or certainly for me.'

'And me,' I said, suddenly not wanting any more cheese. 'Dave Barnes may have turned into a fiasco, but I really liked this place. I was looking forward to having a long relationship with it.'

'Yup. That makes two of us.' He stared bleakly at the hostess trolley.

'Pity about the Brahms,' he said kindly. 'How did they find your little love nest?'

'Oh—Pearl is Dave Barnes's grandmother. And she owns it.'

He looked interestingly aghast. 'She *pimped* for you?'

'No,' I said. 'Probably the very reverse. I think she's been trying to protect me.'

I began to peel a grape. He gave a roar, which I think was amused, and which was loud enough to make me jump, and said, 'Protect you? Christ, woman—put you in a ring with two lions and a gladiator and my money would be on you. Protect *you*? You're crazy.'

'Thank you,' I said coldly. 'And what would you prefer? Valeria the clinging vine?'

'A happy medium would do,' he said.

His face had a sort of collapsed look, even in profile. I suppose he did stand to lose quite a lot—ivory tower, adoring ladylove, new world, magnum opus.

After a while he said conversationally, 'So you didn't manage to deconstruct yourself either, after all that?'

I shook my head. 'We've both failed. Sorry about that.'

'I'll just have to go back to the States.' He kicked at nothing in particular. 'Ah well, there's always the beauties of Fall.' He did not sound like a man happy to be At One with Nature.

'You're not going to stay on?'

'How can I?' he asked. 'After this? The place will just continue to fall apart. If I stay I won't be able to write. They'll be asking me to run up ladders to put a tile back in place, or fix a gutter, and next thing I'll be the handyman. No thanks.'

'When are you going?'

'Soon I guess.'

'What about Valeria?'

'She'll get over it.'

'And you had the nerve to criticize me?'

'Dave Barnes is young,' he said. 'Valeria is a big girl.'

'So far as you're concerned, she's about two and a half.'

He rubbed his face thoughtfully. 'If I can't have my side of the bargain, then it's no bargain. There has to be gain on both sides. I didn't come to England to be a janitor. When the Chinese strike a deal they don't bother to make it into a big legal contract—and that's because the Chinese say a bargain should benefit both parties or it won't work.' He smiled again. 'Valeria will be fine. Besides,'—he handed me a grape—'All Women Are Bastards.'

Grape-peeling is quite a good activity if you want to produce slow and careful thought, because it is both sensual and to a point. I put the denuded fruit in my mouth. The process had worked. I had a sudden and alarming revelation.

'I've still got the Amalfi tickets,' I said. 'If you feel like a detour on the way home.'

Having said it, I broke out into a cold sweat. *What?*

'With Brahms?' he asked.

'Naturally.'

And then he really did laugh.

'Well why not?' I said, a little offended.

'One of us could get what we wanted out of this.'

'Wouldn't it be easier to get yourself hypnotized or something?'

'It might be,' I said, feeling warm again, 'but it wouldn't be such fun.'

I thought about kissing him.

I thought about it very hard while I rolled another grape around in my mouth.

I think he was thinking about it, too.

But from the other room, noises off, came more drawn-out wailing.

'All Men Are Bastards. Where's the fucking food?'

'Poor Roberta,' I said.

'She's not the only one,' said Yale, with a little shake of his head.

We thought about it all over again and then Pearl appeared, cross-armed at the doorway, eyes glinting coldly.

'You,' she said, 'I expected it of. But you,' she pointed at Yale, 'I thought would know better.'

'What Pearl?' I yawned as convincingly as possible.

'You get in that room and take some responsibility,' she said. 'Start thinking about somebody else for a change.'

She looked really fierce.

'And you—' she said to Yale, who had jumped to his feet. 'Take some of this stuff in so we can get some food inside her. She's in a terrible state. Erna's on the phone to her banker and *she's* in a terrible state. And now *he's* in a terrible state. And I come out here and you two are sitting around as if it's nothing to do with you. Get going the pair of you.'

She stopped and looked suspicious.

'What's been happening?'

'Nothing,' I said, picking up the fruit bowl. 'Yet.'

Yale was picking at the Stilton again, and lost in thought.

CHAPTER TWENTY-SEVEN

Well, it was pretty bad.

Wotchacock came out that morning, and *Wotchacock* had all the photographs of the Hassocks Hall project, and of the happy, newly affianced couple. Which is what must have occasioned the wily Peter's departure. Roberta saw them, screamed, and went back to her office.

Peter the Bald had planned well.

Not a halfpenny of the loot remained. Fortunately, people were not cruel. Roberta was seen to have suffered enough. Indeed, she looked seriously deflated. As if the air really had gone out of her. Everybody helped to protect her from the flack. I thought, rather miserably, that no one had shown me half so much care and attention. Pearl said they had.

The telephones were non-stop with warnings from well-connected people nationwide who seemed to have no shame when it came to admitting that they both recognized the man and, surely worse, subscribed to *Wotchacock.*

'Do not trust this man,' said a landowner from Wiltshire.

'This man is *con parfait*,' said another from near Crewe.

'So I was right,' said Desmond, pleased with himself. 'Now deny me the freedom of the Press.'

He, apparently, thought he recognized the miscreant from an earlier run-in—being a sharp-nosed, disbelieving kind of an individual. But Peter was clever. Knowing that the monied circuit was small, and that his last venture in a little matter of shares in several race horses had been quite recent, he shaved his head.

Desmond could not be sure, so he got round it rather sneakily by inventing a column called How Would They Look If . . . and putting hair on him. Hence Mr Crewe and Mr Wiltshire and their kind.

Desmond was delighted because he had his scoop.

Roberta did something remarkable. Generous and professional to the last, which reminded me of why I *sometimes* liked her, she telephoned to congratulate him before collapsing in more floods of tears and taking to her bed. Cries of 'Give me more drugs' echoed about Hassocks Hall, where we had made her up a little day couch in her office.

We sent her off to *Ladybird* to have a rest. Just as well because over the next few days the telephones did not stop and we were worried about Roberta causing a world shortage of Prozac. Indeed, rather than reduce the Prozac Mountain, Roberta was threatening to turn into it.

Mr and Mrs Valeria and the little V. were still mercifully up in the Highlands, which gave us just enough time to tie up ends before exiting gracefully.

Dave Barnes showed remarkable fortitude, not to say relief.

Things that have taken months or years to build up, take but a few days to tear down.

Erna flew back to Cape Town. She was quite well-oiled by the time we put her on the plane, but because she flew first-class nobody bothered.

'I am very upset,' she said, 'and I want to help you all. We were just like one big happy family, weren't we?' Her eyes were in their usual swimmy condition and I thought I detected real emotion there. 'I really thought I'd settled down at last. I love England. And that Hall was real fun. When they let me in it.' She sipped her Bacardi thoughtfully and looked about her. We were in the VIP lounge.

She smiled. 'Even I don't think we could have a great party in *here*,' she said. And then added ruminatively, 'But we certainly could have *there*.'

Builders were laid off. All progressive activity ceased and Hassocks Hall became very peaceful. If you listened hard in the starry moonlight, you could almost hear the termites munching.

* * *

'I always said he and Roberta made an unlikely couple,' I reminded Pearl. 'I thought he was a little shifty at the time.'

Pearl just sniffed and said Benefit of Hindsight. But just for once, it wasn't. It was sound judgement, about which I felt rather proud.

We were packing up the library at Hassocks Hall at the time. I thought if I managed to get the books back, in pristine condition, the suppliers might waive some of the bill. To be honest, I didn't really care. Teddy's baby was due any day now. What was a few thousand pounds here or there compared with that, and who needed the deposit for a flat anyway?

'But I did spot him, didn't I? I mean, who would really have taken up with Roberta for a romance?'

She paused for a moment. 'Love is blind,' she said. 'Just as well in your case. Now—pass me them books. If we're ever going to get this done before you bugger off to Amalfi.'

'And you bugger off to Sheppey.'

'No swearing please,' we both said in unison.

Pearl had volunteered to join Roberta down in *Ladybird.*

'It was kind of you,' I said.

'What was?'

'Offering to look after Roberta.'

Pearl paused and looked at me. 'Kind-Schmind,' she said. 'Somebody's got to do it.'

'Yes, well, thanks.'

'Good grief,' said Pearl. 'I think I need a lie-down.'

The sun had returned—the land all steamy after rain. Out of the window I could see Dave Barnes with his shirt off kneeling at the side of a chrysanthemum bed. The dark gold torso flexed and reached and reflected the hot light and I gazed at it for a while. It did nothing for me at all—not a thing.

Which I thought was very odd.

Perhaps I had turned into a lesbian after all?

There had, however, been something in Yale's smile the other night that quite hit the mark. Just a smile.

Also, my appetite had come back completely. Another odd thing.

I tried humming a bit of the Requiem beneath my breath but before I could know whether it still held its contagion of sadness, Pearl thrust a huge armful of gold-embossed books at me.

'And don't you go saying anything to Roberta Topp about how unsuitable you always thought she and him were. Or you'll regret it.'

'Oh, why?' I asked, perhaps a shade belligerently. 'Everybody said it to me about Teddy.'

'Not at first they didn't,' she said. 'So don't try it.'

'She did,' I said with triumph. 'Roberta. And my mother. She said Teddy and me were unsuitable.'

'And they were right, too, as it happens. Put that lip back.'

'I have a mother for that, Pearl,' I said with dignity.

'Well go and see her then.'

'I just might,' I said. 'On the way back from Amalfi.'

CHAPTER TWENTY-EIGHT

Late September on the Amalfi coast is the nearest thing to heaven that I know. But it is not for pragmatists.

It was not really Brahmsian terrain. There is too much of the pagan fancy about the place, not enough human realism. Wagner came, of course, and finished *Parsifal* and much else, feeding off its lores and atmosphere. I could imagine Isolde standing like Ariadne at the rocks and surveying the sparkling sea. But not the Chorus from the Requiem.

Sex though, sex was in every jutting crag, every lemon grove, every twisted olive branch that clung to the sunbaked hills. These hot-blooded Neapolitans, tinctured with Arab, were not like their Northern cousins of the mountains and lakes. They were fire and earth, which suited our situation perfectly.

A boat ride from the little town of Amalfi, deceptively near, Capri shimmers, beautifully guarding its history of cruelty, piracy and betrayal. A floating jewel, bargained for throughout the ages, a final resting place for many, whether they chose it or not. Including the Emperor Tiberius.

Tacitus says Tiberius was an evil-doer and half mad; Suetonious says he was a wanton Libertarian with orgies and gluttony and the usual Roman jollies. I'd say neither. I'd say Tiberius was a sensible plodder who left anything nasty to his Prefect of the Praetoria. Tiberius did his job for a while, and eventually retired to the peace and beauty of Capri, from which he could see his enemies coming from a long way off.

The Villa Jovis, which he built, is a vertical hike from the shore, and it was from here that

I had imagined the Terminatrix should overcome her pursuers' desire to plunge her into the rocky sea below. I doubted that Dave Barnes could have failed to be moved by the heart-spinning fall.

As I stood there looking down and telling Yale all about it, I felt my stomach turn over. But whether it was for the swirling deeps below, or whether it was for the excitements to come, I couldn't say. We hadn't actually kissed yet. Odd. But true.

'Did you really mean that about all women being bastards?' I looked at Yale, who was staring down at the foaming water.

'The way things are,' he said cheerfully, 'we could both do ourselves a favour and jump.'

This from the man with whom I was to make sweet, as well as Brahmsian, music that night.

'That's not very flattering,' I said.

He muttered something about not getting him wrong, and being beautiful. I thought he said that I was beautiful and thanked him rather bashfully. He was looking out across the water and, somewhat heedlessly for a swain, said, 'No—not you—the view.'

I waited for him to suddenly slap his forehead and say, Oh My God, I Didn't Mean That The Way It Sounded—only he did not. Jumping began to take on a certain attraction.

Yet we made the perfect couple: leaning on the crumbling outer wall of the villa as

Tiberius's guards once did, and looking across the water, back towards Amalfi. You could not have painted it better. Sun in our faces, wind in our hair—spread out beside us a half-finished picnic of mozzarella, tomatoes, olives and bread—wine glasses in our hand with the rough *rosso* of the region. Well, it was a start. If you look the picture, I reminded myself, you are halfway to success.

'Pity the Romeo and Juliet house wasn't still available,' I said. We had passed the little ochre cottage clinging to the Amalfi rocks on our boat trip earlier.

He put his arm round my shoulders. Nice enough gesture, and natural.

I jumped a mile.

'Given Romeo and Juliet's fate, I think I'd rather sleep in the main hotel. Anyway, we're too old for all that.'

'Speak for yourself,' I said.

He looked at me. 'Correction. *I* am too old for all that. You are, of course, eternal.'

We then sat on the dry, tufty grass and proceeded to kiss. I was entirely willing, and jumping a mile was out of the question. In between we finished off the fizzing Gragnano which enhanced it all quite nicely. I began to feel better about it all. There was even a moment, in the silence and the warmth, when we nearly joined the Suetonius school of thought and had our own orgy. Just as well we didn't, for a party of thoroughly good-hearted

English came stomping up the gulley.

I believe in the nuclear family.

I believe in society's salvation through a mum, a dad, a sister, a brother and four grandparents. It is just that when such harbingers of future goodness hove into view somewhere like Capri, I could wish them and their hearty, stout defence of global order to the moon and back.

We just about managed to adjust our clothing before they turned the corner and came upon us. From the way they stared, I bet those children had their television rationed.

'I'm sorry,' said the cheerful Dad, who was wearing so-cool-it-was-embarrassing Marks and Spencer gear. 'Did we disturb you?'

'Oh no,' I said pointedly. 'We normally lie around in the grass like this and . . .'

Yale interrupted, very politely, and glared at me. 'Not at all, sir,' he said. 'Have a nice day.'

How is it that Americans are so polite under stress?

How do they fight wars? Apologize in advance for any inconvenience caused by the flame-thrower?

'Honestly!' I said, removing his hand and watching their cheery backs go cheerfully on. *'Honestly.'*

'It wasn't their fault,' he said, quite unruffled.

'Well I don't suppose it was the Viet-Congs' either.'

He stared at me, and shook his head again.

'Come on,' I said, giving him a little hug. 'Let's wander back. Get the evening ferry before it's too crowded.'

It is considerably easier coming down than going up and we were in good spirits really. I suppose, though we said nothing, we suddenly felt it was going to be all right. We even sauntered around some of the expensive boutiques on the lower slopes. Shopping solo can hold a mirror to life's emptiness. We bought each other little terracotta wall plaques, in the sunburst shape of Apollo's head, and caught the late afternoon ferry. Driving back along the sheer ribbon of road towards Amalfi I reminded myself to keep *this* as a memory because it was all so beautiful.

The evening sun was low and benign as we pulled into the hotel carpark. When we had set off that morning we were quite wary and nervous—now we were easy, relaxed, almost like any ordinary couple from anywhere. We even laughed to remember the embarrassment of the English family and how reckless we had nearly been. I think our laughter must have travelled all the way across the water, danced over those rocks and up to the Villa Jovis.

I hope so. It was to be our last laugh for a very long time. As the evening unfolded into the all important night, we were about to find that out.

CHAPTER TWENTY-NINE

While Yale was getting ready I made a phone call to Pearl. Amphibian Features had gone into labour that morning, exactly on the date predicted, about an hour or so after we left for the airport.

Just in time.

According to Pearl—all those hours later—the Frog was still at it.

'That sounds hopeful,' I said. 'Perhaps her strength will give out.'

Pearl tutted but said no more.

On the subject of Mr and Mrs Valeria and the little V. she was forthcoming.

'They're back. And in shock. Not surprisingly. Valeria is running around like a headless chicken—or she was earlier this afternoon. Just as well Roberta is safely off out of it. That Lord Hartley has a wild look in his eye. You can see him from any window pacing about, sometimes staring down at the grass, or standing on the gravel, staring up at the roof. He either sighs or swears. Says things like, The Barbarians are at the Gate, over and over again. Lady Hartley is not so upset. She found my Dave doing the soft fruit so that bucked her up. I had a word with her about a few things. Gave her some advice.'

She paused.

'What advice, Pearl?'

She ignored this. 'It's got a bit chillier up here. Lady H. is not so bad. Now, do you want me to telephone you when—er—the news comes through? I'm back off to the caravan tomorrow.'

'No,' I said, thinking it might be at just the wrong time. 'I'll call you. And look Pearl—I'm really sorry to leave you with all the mess to mop up. Especially Val.'

Remembering that dark cupboard and the breasting potty nymphs, it was hard not to sound pleased.

Pearl said drily, 'Are you gloating?'

'Would I?'

'You would.'

'Promise not to tell her where we've gone? I've only borrowed him.'

'In my opinion that's as good as saying you only borrowed a peach when you ate it.'

'She can have him back.'

'What rubbish you do talk.'

I wanted to say that this was me being existentialist, but such things are lost on the ill-educated.

Pearl said, 'And it's no use trying to dress it up in anything else. It's just plain *wrong*.'

If Pearl had been Bertie Russell's auntie, or Sartre's grandmother—it beggars thought.

'Well,' she said, 'you'd better get the picture anyway. Angry is not quite the word. Last time I saw her she was sitting on the floor in the old library shredding her shawl end and screaming that she was forty-two. Did you know that? Well preserved I'd say . . . Still—never known a hard day's work I suppose.'

I had the smallest, creeping feeling that Pearl was actually enjoying some of this too.

'Oh dear,' I said.

'Very much Oh Dear,' said Pearl. 'You still going to go through with it?'

Forty-two? My heart sank. That really *was* old. Could I truly do what I was about to do to a woman who would probably never have the chance again?

Just then Yale came out of the bathroom wearing a white shirt and knotting a red silk tie. The sun had added more colour to his face and he was whistling. He looked—well—quite presentable really—for an American academic mid-thirties. And I had the oddest sensation in my stomach. It was called the Hots.

Forty-two was not so old. And she could always take up macramé.

Was I still going to go through with it?

Yes, was the answer to the question. Yes, Yes. Just like Molly Bloom.

'Bye Pearl.'

'Did you know,' I asked, removing his hands from his tie and putting them round my waist while I got on with the red silk. 'Did you know how old Valeria was?'

He looked uncomfortable.

'Yes,' he said. 'Thirty-six.' He suddenly

seemed really stricken. 'That wasn't her? She's not called? Thank God I moved everything out. She'd have destroyed the lot.'

'Got a temper has she?'

He looked at me. 'She could be wild.'

I remembered the sight of them together in the summer house.

'So I noticed. Don't worry. Pearl is the only one who knows where we've gone. And she's completely trustworthy. A bit like Juliet's nurse,' I said cheerfully.

Yale gave a little grimace. 'Juliet's nurse,' he said, 'fucked up.'

'Did she? Well, don't worry. Pearl won't let us down. She's on our side.'

'So was the nurse,' he said.

I took his arm.

We descended to Flavio's.

The full ritual had to be observed. Besides, food is of the utmost importance for a long, hard night. Soldiers and priests will tell you so.

CHAPTER THIRTY

Our balcony faced the sea. The night was suitably inky and starlit, with a high, round moon inclined to be generous. Looking out across the expanse of such prettily spangled light, the whole seemed as perfect as any to which a painter might aspire, and fail. All this and the long, intense contrapuntals of the Fugue reaching up to Heaven and perhaps into the very deeps of Hell itself.

'But the Righteous souls are in the hand of God . . . How lovely is thy dwelling place . . .'

Should any late passerby look up they would see two naked figures, sitting on a hotel balcony, staring out to sea, sipping from small glasses and with an air of both separation and harmony about them that betokens the aftermath of bedroom love.

If asked, one of them would say that she felt as if someone had just rolled a great stone from her shoulders. She would say it was as if she could breathe properly again. But she would also say that with it, of course, came the bathos. What had once seemed so important and urgent now seemed capable of having the question asked of it: So What? Hindsight, of course, makes rational beings of us all.

The other, if asked, would take on the glaze of I'm Not Receiving You—and look as if someone were trying to pull out his teeth.

I was thinking Sponge. I was thinking, as I sipped Amaretto, that I wanted to be like a huge Sponge, and absorb everything. I wondered, looking across at him as he tapped his chin with the glass rim and stared at the night, what he was thinking. I thought, perhaps, it was kinder and more diplomatic not to ask. Nothing really mattered any more, in an easy kind of a way. And if I felt a bit foolish over it all—well—it was worth it now—to be here and to be listening to Brahms.

On the table were chocolates and a bottle of liqueur. Without looking he said, 'How can you eat those and drink this at the same time?'

I had persuaded him that Amaretto was one of those drinks that tasted really good in its country of origin, and really terrible anywhere else. He said, 'In that case, let me tell you, Amalfi is very much Anywhere Else.' But he kindly obliged. Who could not, with the waves slapping and the occasional far-off sound from a fishing boat?

In bed, I had thanked him for having me. We lay very close and he said, polite to the last, 'Don't mention it.' Which was funny and considerably better than contrived sentiment. I checked his shoulders and back, and when he asked what I was looking for I said, 'Suction marks.' So far as I could see there were none. Neither did I suffer from any pangs of remorse. Also, so far as I could see, my need had been the greater. And it wasn't as if I was going to keep him, I thought with a little pang, nor that he intended to try to stay.

None of it seemed strange. And everything did. The moment of forgetting had come—and I decided it was at that precise moment of loss and pleasure that Teddy and Agnes's baby was born. Don't tell me there is no comfort to be had in ritual.

Of course the memories were not forgotten,

but they had been overlaid with new ones—and the old ones were now just souvenirs of love. Getting Back Brahms represented what those earnest shrinks call Retaking Control. I did it my way . . . It was the grown up thing to do. Only I wasn't *quite* ready to grow up yet.

He poured some more liqueur into our glasses. If I was looking for exchanges of a romantic nature, I was disappointed. 'That set-up was so perfect . . .' he said. 'Bastard . . .'

Like Einstein, Yale obviously found sex cleared his mind for thought rather than softened him up for sentiment.

He ran his hand through his hair in exasperation. 'It all felt so positive. I really loved the place.'

I thought he was maybe a little too In Love with the place, but just smiled. 'Even with Valeria?'

'It wasn't a sacrifice,' he said, giving me a straight look. 'She came with the job. Why not? There have been such arrangements from the dawn of time. Love is a very modern idea and I've got no illusions left. In fact it helped me get over things.'

I held my breath. Boatmen exchanged greetings far off in the bay. Water splashed at the edges of the rocks below.

'What things?' I said as quietly as I could, but I could feel my eyes growing large and my ears beginning to flap.

He looked at me and laughed. 'You really

want to know, don't you?'

I nodded mutely, putting a chocolate in my mouth so that, for once, I would shut up.

'All right. Here you are. I had a girlfriend called Carrie. After three years she just walked. Nobody else. She didn't care for me any more and she was bored with hearing about rejection slips. So she walked.'

'That's it?' I asked.

'That's it,' he agreed.

'Yes, but,' I said.

'That's *it*,' he replied.

I opened my mouth.

He put up a finger and wagged it. 'End of story.'

I supposed it was.

'This stuff is vile,' he said, pouring some more.

'And Valeria?'

'We'd have been fine.'

'She was jealous as hell.'

'So what? I didn't want to go walkabout.'

'She was even jealous of me.'

'I know—stupid wasn't it?'

It was?

'I mean,' he said, seeing my expression, 'given that she thought you weren't interested in men.'

'Don't you realize,' I said, 'that when you really love someone you think everyone else in the world will do the same. That is what that fearful jealousy is. She probably thought I'd ask you to cure me.'

He laughed. 'You did in a way.'

The music rose softly from the room behind us. Far across the water it went, tumbling down the rocks. *'Behold I show you a mystery.'* From now on I would remember an inky night sky and the sound of water lapping against Neapolitan rocks. I felt ashamed to be so happy.

'Valeria would have you back no matter what.'

'No ivory tower, no deal. I told you. The domestic hearth is not for me.'

No wonder there were so many Great Men of Letters. I couldn't imagine, for example, Charlotte Brontë saying such a thing. She wasn't even able to tell her husband that she preferred not to go for a walk in the rain with him and get a chill and die, thank you very much.

The music grew louder. Feeling ashamed just seemed to float away again. I thought of Poor Brahms. Lonely all his life. Even his last attempt at companionship, the singer Berthe Porubszky, married someone else and moved away. He was probably relieved. Too set in his ways by then. When her first child was born, he composed his most famous song, 'Wegenlied', cheerfully enough, and dedicated it to the infant. Nothing ever came close to his feelings for Clara. He remained immured from love for the rest of his life. Not a path to follow.

You have to grab the moment with both hands and all your heart, I thought, because you never know if anything will come within reach again. Carpe Diem, as Pearl would have it.

I stood up. He stood up. Nothing was said as we moved back into the room.

But Valeria? She was far away.

Far, far away.

I lay back on the bed.

Was she not?

*   *   *

Something odd was happening. Something odd which did not seem to have much to do with the something very pleasurable that was happening between us. Well, not unless Yale had taken to female impersonations, yelling blind rage, and tap-dancing with boots on.

We both froze and looked into each other's eyes with astonishment.

I did a rapid calculation. There were, I thought, five doors in our room. The two doors to the wardrobe, the bathroom door, the sliding door to the balcony, and the entrance door. And someone seemed to be knocking very hard on one of them. Well—not so much knocking as beating, drumming and kicking. With voice.

It drowned the Requiem.

It came from someone who should have

been a long way off.

And wasn't.

Juliet's Nurse came to mind. And Pearl. And Yale saying, 'She fucked up.'

Astonishment gave way to panic. We were both lying there, rigid as a couple of boards, staring into each other's eyes with looks that said, 'This cannot be happening.'

But it was.

'Let me jolly well in,' screamed a voice.

Bang, Bang, Bang, went the door.

'Is it?' I said, pulling the covers up to my chin. 'It is,' he replied, placing the pillow over his head. 'Well one of us will have to go.'

'Not necessarily,' he said with muffled conviction. 'Not necessarily.'

CHAPTER THIRTY-ONE

Yale remained just a lump under the pillow next to me, occasionally letting out a soft pleading groan, or a telling phrase such as, 'Oh Let It Not Be Me.'

I felt, approximately, the same. The fulminations and door abuse subdued even the full might of the Baritone and Chorus. Anger clashed with the spiritual, and anger won. Valeria was on the warpath, drawing ancient strengths, it seemed, from her ancestors and their fearless battlings. No tuppeny-ha'penny bit of *Zollverein* composing stood a chance. Valeria was here for the kill.

I nudged Yale, who very slowly and very unhappily pulled the pillow from his head. I wondered, alarmed, whether this would also take its place in my memories. What new images would now unfold when the Requiem next played? I had certainly not bargained for any of this.

'You'd better go,' I said. 'Or we'll all get thrown out.'

'I suppose you couldn't nip out on to the balcony?' he said—I think half seriously.

I looked around the room—which seemed largely to be made up of my discarded underwear and jewellery. I shook my head. Cheltenham Ladies' College might prepare its pupils for the ills of the world by drawing a veil over reality, but it did not give them complete visual impairment. Valeria could draw only one of two conclusions—either Yale had just opened up a whole new world to her of his pleasurable activities with frocks—or he had a woman here.

I had a strong urge to laugh. Hysterics very probably. 'Nope,' I said. 'It won't work.'

The element of surprise seemed sensible. Yale got out of bed, threw on his wrap, strode to the door, banged his toe on the bed leg, swore, and subsequently made what was in my opinion a rather usefully thunderous face as he flung the door wide. Valeria was momentarily silenced.

It was a sticky moment all round really. Not a lot we could usefully say.

Valeria looked amazingly awful. Quite jaw-droppingly beside herself and wild of eye—which, given her eyes, was remarkably impactful. If her hair was up in a chignon when she started, it was in no wise now. One was almost moved to ask if she had enjoyed her several journeyings through a hedge backwards, but one did not. Even one who was not best disposed could see it was dicing with death. Both hers and mine. She was, without doubt, dangerous.

I tried a truthful tack.

'Look,' I said conversationally. 'It's not what you think.'

Lame, I admit, since it was hardly dominoes or whist.

'Shut up you horrible pervert,' she said. And advanced towards Yale who, I have to say, stood his ground. 'How could you?' she said. 'How?' And then huge, noisy tears began, getting all over everything. 'And I love you *so much*.'

Which for some reason set me off too. Valeria was the loudest, I have to admit, but nonetheless, we were a good match. It was the moment she mentioned *love*. The next thing would be fidelity. I could probably overtake her on noise level after that.

Yale took her arm and set her down on the

edge of the bed. She was rumbling like Vesuvius and the mattress began to vibrate. The tears flowed faster, the face looked more and more like an unfortunate accident and Yale, in that manly way, stood there silently chewing the side of his thumb and attempting to touch one part of her soothingly without getting bitten.

This was no time for my tears. What was required was sisterly action. I joggled my fingers to get Yale's attention. He looked at me questioningly across her ravaged head.

'SAY YOU LOVE HER,' I mouthed.

'WHAT?' he mouthed back.

'SAY YOU LOVE HER.'

He looked what can only be described as sulky, though in higher circles it could just be mistaken for superiorly ethical.

'I CAN'T,' he mimed.

'WHY NOT?'

'BECAUSE I DON'T.'

God save us, the Civilized West's science of diplomacy running in our veins and he does this?

'TRY LYING.' I glared.

He glared back. I could practically see his halo.

Valeria looked up. Her extraordinarily pink eyeballs were almost maroon and she looked quite fiendish as she narrowed them. 'What's going on? What are you whispering about?'

'Nothing,' said Yale. 'Nothing.'

Who amongst you with mammaries has not experienced this masculine logic under stress? The Deny What The Eyes Have Plainly Seen syndrome—as in, What woman sitting next to me in bed with nothing but Chanel on, darling?

'Valeria,' he said, reaching out a nervous hand towards the top of her head.

She slapped it away. 'Don't touch me,' she said.

'Um—Dear—' he tried.

She then raised her fist and popped him one on the knee, which was the nearest part of him to her. And oddly enough, he went down. With just a hint of gratitude.

I gave him a look, willing him to speak of love. He merely rolled his eyes as he writhed, knee-clutching, around the floor. Nope. Tenacity and veracity had got muddled up and he was stuck into honour now. The poet in him very probably. Valeria's tears continued. You could practically hear his spurs a-jingling. And the three little words did not come.

The final chords of the Requiem's last movement encircled the room.

'Turn that ruddy music off,' she said sharply. And then, softening her tone, she looked down at Yale, seated on the floor, clutching his bent knee, and said, 'Are you all right darling?'

'I'll live,' he grimaced.

'Fuck that,' said Valeria, and gave him a kick in the other one.

Yet still her eyes shone with love.

I leaned forward, keeping the covers up to my chin, and tapped her on the back. She was puffing like a walrus, a woman scorned.

'He does love you, you know. I just persuaded him to do this as an experiment. It's nothing to do with your relationship . . .' I shrugged as nonchalantly as I could. 'I just wanted to see what it was like. I—er—needed to know for—er—'

What the hell did I need to know for?

'—for *Research.*' This, along with Expert, is a very, very useful word.

Embroidery seemed sensible. Valeria was not convinced.

'But it really isn't my cup of tea. In fact it's horrible. Didn't enjoy any of it—dreadful, dreadful, all that male dominant stuff—can't be doing with it—and so clumsy—I mean—I'll just stick to what I know—all very disappointing but I'm really grateful for the effort.'

I smiled brightly. If they weren't convinced, I certainly was. 'So thanks,' I said cheerfully, 'but no thanks.'

During this monologue, which I thought explained things rather well and left Valeria in no doubt of my personal persuasions, she and Yale had both turned to look at me—the one from the floor, the other from the end of the bed. Yale looked rather pale and had stopped rubbing his knee and Valeria was definitely still in need of some lily gilding.

'Hopeless,' I said shrugging. I was really getting into the part. 'Really hopeless—I don't know *how* you girls put up with it. Yuk Yuk Yuk!'

I gave a passing fair shudder for emphasis.

Yale stood up. He put his hands on his hips. He looked absolutely incredulous, not to say thunderous again, and even paler. I was not quite sure where his mouth had gone. 'Yuk Yuk Yuk?' he said, minus his lips. And then, raising the octave. 'Yuk Yuk *Yuk*?'

'You horrible, horrible warped individual,' said Valeria. And she turned bashfully towards Yale. 'You cannot make bread out of stone,' she said demurely. 'Idiot.'

Yale was still poised and rigid. Not much of the relaxed baker about him. It was an interesting struggle to observe. Go for truth and lose your honour one way. Go for truth and lose your virility the other. And after all, Valeria *was* in love. She needed help.

'We had to get drunk and everything,' I added, just to be sure. And I pointed to the bottle for evidence. I forbore to say that we also had to eat lots of chocolates to keep our spirits up as that seemed a little far-fetched and in line with sardines, rocket flares and an army on manoeuvres.

And then I tugged the scrumpled counterpane from beneath Valeria's bottom, wound it around myself, and went out on to the balcony. 'He is all yours,' I said. 'Thanks for the loan. And sorry for any upset caused.' I could have fallen on her neck in a sisterly way and begged for forgiveness but she would have loathed that, and so should I. It seemed best to stick to the point. There were many shades of grey but, in essence, that was it.

I went back out into the beautiful night. I took the music with me, poured myself another drink, and finished off the chocolates. Behind me, like a chorus, came the raised and lowered tones of the star-crosseds, and then finally the very much raised tone of Valeria saying, 'There is absolutely no point. No point at all. Because I should just follow you, you see. Like I did here. I'll never let you go.'

And if I knew women, and I *did*, it was game, set and match. What lover could resist being told that no matter where he roam, there is no corner of a foreign field where the seeker will not stumble in pursuit; possibly even Croydon. Oh no. He was hers and she had a right to him. Her love, whatever its flaws, was real and strong. I was just an ersatz little thing, I thought mournfully, and shoved in another chocolate.

My mother would have said I was just feeling sorry for myself. But she wasn't here, now was she. So what's new?

Compared with Valeria I gave up on Teddy far too easily. I saw that now. The entire break-up was my fault. I should never have been sitting in my car looking up at his darkened windows—I should have been pounding on the door, screaming through the letterbox, putting itching-powder in her knickers and wreaking bloody war. I wondered why I had not?

I tapped on the window. They sat on the bed holding hands and looking horribly soulful but I needed to know about Pearl. I would have trusted her with my life. Did she, or didn't she?

'Sorry to barge in,' I said, pulling the door aside, and feeling oddly pleased at the way they both jumped. 'Valeria, can I just ask how you knew we were here?'

She looked very smug. People in slightly vulnerable situations should not do this.

She said, 'Your mother rang. I listened in. Pearl mentioned the place and it wasn't hard to find the hotel. I just rang one of Daddy's friends in the Diplomatic Service and they did the rest. Even held up the plane. I was in Naples by ten o'clock.' She looked pink with pleasure at the cleverness.

I found myself idly swearing revenge. But, 'Bravo,' I said, to be supportive. 'No greater love hath any woman than she take Naples airport late at night and alone.'

'Oh I had an escort. Daddy fixed it.'

What though a moat may crumble, a portcullis fade? A thousand years from Agincourt when the bowmen are forgotten, still will there be the protective ramparts of rank and ancient blood. Maybe I'd have poisoned the Fat Frog if there was someone out there to do a Lord Lucan for me. Irksome thought.

'Oh, by the way . . .' Her eyes gleamed with the sweetness of revenge. 'Pearl told her it was a boy. Nine pounds. Mother and baby doing well.'

'Thanks,' I said lightly.

We yeoman stock have our backbone, too.

Valeria smiled. 'Pleasure.' You could see that it was.

Yale looked very uncomfortable. 'Are you OK?' he said.

Best not to speak.

Despite the range Eliot to Topp, sometimes words are just not adequate.

But I felt that Valeria should not have done that.

Not *quite* so cruelly.

She patted her knees with her hands in a gesture of happy complacency. 'Well, well, that's that,' she said. Much as her great-great-grandmother might have pronounced across the tea things on hearing they had cleaned up after Peterloo.

Her big, pink puffy eyes looked at me sideways. I did not like the look in them.

So I turned to Yale and asked him to put his arms around me tight, tight as he could. I don't know which of the three of us was more surprised. And I did not particularly care. It was all true, then, I thought. The big, blowsy, French blip was not full of hot air—it was a real baby—real hair—real fingernails—and a real Daddy.

Truth at last.

Valeria erupted again.

I erupted again.

And the Brahms went on sighing and soaring away. It was quite used to things like tears.

CHAPTER THIRTY-TWO

I looked across the bobbing crowd of heads at Yale who was walking away. He looked back, waved, and was gone, dragged into the crowd by the adoring Valeria. His smile lingered in the hubbub like the Cheshire Cat's. Too late now to ask him if Carrie had been very beautiful. I always think if you have had *one* beautiful lover, then it gets rid of the need to do it again. You know, as it were, that beauty is not necessarily truth.

Valeria was not beautiful but she was willing.

Valeria was not young but she was prepared to be.

If she was not beloved, she was needed, and if he behaved she would bring him peace.

I remembered the tweeds and the brogues.

He was ready for England. Because in England's stuffy old heartbeat lay both the grit to make the pearl, or the peace to make the oyster sleep. And surrounded by a sea of tolerance. Where both he and Roberta Topp could flourish in the living, breathing arrogance that looks upon its turrets and its greensward and says, Everything Changes and Nought Changes; Welcome All. Dark forces might seek to change it. But it would survive. England was ready for him.

All Valeria needed was to convince him that she would be the one shinning up ladders if the roof caved in. I did not tell her this. Why should I help this romance on its way? The po cupboard was bad enough, but to get an escort from Naples and hold up a *plane*? What girl could possibly expect further help after that?

I looked behind me once more but Yale had gone. If he was an albatross, he was a caged one. He would find that out if he ever tried to go home.

I turned away from the barrier and sat down to wait for the flight to Malaga. The announcement of which, I fancied, would be the bell, that summonsed me to Heaven or to Hell.

The Brahms was safely back in my luggage. Mission accomplished, leaving, as missions will, a sense of flatness. The thought of those mushroom-soup walls and tobacco carpet, without Hassocks Hall to relieve them, was not a happy one. I had lost nearly all my money over the library—philosophically this seemed Very Proper Deserts—temperamentally it made me want to cry my eyes out.

* * *

I had seen photographs, of course, and been out to visit a couple of times, but only when winter was upon the land and it was bleak, and barren. I was with Teddy, then, and we drove through the Sierra Nevada, dreaming that one day we would buy one of the white *cortijos* sprinkled about the mountains like rice.

This time it was hot and dry, the light yellow rather than the northern gold of De Cuyps at Hassocks Hall—less golden syrup, more honey and lemon. The red fires of chilli garlands strung from white porches gave a curious neon effect across the mountainside.

My mother had become a part of the landscape. Not a trace of Oxshott remained. It was very shocking.

Her hair, mostly sunshine streaked with grey, blew about her head and neck as she drove us in the open-topped something or other, much more something than other. An old farm vehicle, she said, but perfect for the tracks. Her skin, face, bare forearms, expanse of throat and chest, her feet were all brown as the earth and her mouth was like a curve of chilli peppers—real hot Spanish lipstick, unbelievable when I remembered her smattering of powder and wipe of peachbloom blush. Her eyes behind sunglasses were bright with enquiring blue, and her white frock—a cross between junket-strainer and Indian curtaining—floated about as if she were on a cloud.

I am afraid that my mother looked ravishing.

'You look very well,' I shouted above the noise and the whipping wind. We were bumping about all over the place. I had never known her drive faster than about forty miles an hour, even on the motorway. She was once stopped on the M4 and asked by a policeman if she was used to driving in traffic.

'Well I'm happy to see you,' she shouted back. And revved for a hill.

Further communication was pointless. I had three whole days of it to come. For now I decided to sit back and try to feel as young and dashing as my bloody mother.

'How long will you stay?' she yelled, as we negotiated a donkey and cart.

Nothing else to be seen on the road for miles but a donkey with a cartful of almonds, and the sea beyond.

'Only three days,' I said firmly.

She smiled behind her glasses. 'That's enough,' she said.

And we drove the rest of the way in silence.

*   *   *

It was not until morning, when we were out on her terrace, high above Salobrena, looking across *her* sparkling piece of the Mediterranean, that we talked.

‘How was Italy?’ she asked, pouring orange juice. The sun was so bright its reflection from the tablecloth lit her like an actress on a stage set.

‘Interesting,’ I said.

She bit into honeyed toast. ‘That’s exactly the sort of thing your father would say if I suggested running down the street stark naked.’

‘*Very* interesting?’ I offered.

‘Pearl said you went with a man.’

‘I wish you two wouldn’t discuss me the way you do.’

My mother refilled her cup with coffee, smiling that smile of hers.

‘No you don’t,’ she said matter-of-factly. ‘You’d be very pissed off if we ignored you.’

Pissed off? Since when did she use such language?

‘Well,’ I said, ‘I do feel pissed off actually. And I have done ever since you came out here. Firstly, you did it so quickly after Dad—just upped and left everything behind—and secondly, you haven’t been available for any of the crises in my life. Not for years.’

I was aware that using the word available made her sound more like a consultant, and less like a mother, but it was too late.

'Coffee?' she said.

'Yes.'

'And put your lower lip back in,' she laughed. 'I'm not your father or Teddy.'

I looked out to sea—it really was extraordinarily beautiful—and behind me stretched the mountains and hills.

'Did you ever come here with Dad?'

'Never,' she said. 'Have some toast.' She had buttered it for me, and then put honey on it before cutting it into little squares—just as she used to when I was a child.

I felt loved.

'Are you writing well?' I asked, munching my way through the squares.

She put down her cup and stared at me very hard. She looked absolutely beautiful—still in floaty white with a bright yellow bandanna in her hair. Her skin looked the colour of amber in this light. Up until this moment she had seemed entirely happy.

'Well, well, well,' she said, and really did seem amazed.

'What?'

'In all these years you have never asked me that.'

'Don't be ridiculous.'

'It's true.'

*   *   *

Later, when we wandered down the winding road towards the seashore, brushing against tumbling blossoms and smelling the sun on new-watered grass, I told her that I could now perfectly well understand why she had come here.

She just shook her head.

'You came to get away from the past. All that Oxshott stuff. And Dad. You came to begin again. Somewhere conducive and fresh. The opposite of me going to Amalfi.'

'Oh no I didn't.' She stopped on the road and turned to me. She sounded quite indignant and had her hands on her hips. 'I came because I liked the place. It was a consolation. Not a compromise.'

Then she went all theatrical and waved her arms about, and twirled, and said, 'I love the place.'

Such behaviour in one's mother is distinctly embarrassing.

'Anyway,' she said, 'your Dad's with me wherever I go. So are you.'

When we reached the empty sand she turned and stood staring back up the hill to her house.

'I have a lover, you know,' she said.

I felt very let down. 'Well I *don't*, as *you* know,' I said. 'So thanks for the tidbit.'

'You will, eventually. How's the

deconstructing going?'

'How do you know so much?' I muttered sarcastically, slooshing at the water with bare feet. Little fishes swam happily between my toes and I thought how nice it would be to have no memory except of one's spawning ground, like them. Teddy's face seemed to reflect in the water, and he was holding a gigantic baby over his shoulder—like a Japanese wrestler in nappies. Oh God, perhaps I was going mad.

'Experience,' she said. 'Which is not the same as hindsight.'

We walked for a while.

'How's the dreadful Roberta?' she said, after a while.

So I told her.

'Good,' she said, flinging a pebble into the sea with satisfaction.

'That's not very nice,' I said. 'You taught me to be kind.'

She laughed. 'Up to a point,' she said. 'Only up to a point. But Roberta needs to find the path.'

'I don't think there is any doubt that she's found *something.*'

'Good,' she said, and, turning, waved at a flash-toothed young man who lay in a boat at the shore.

'Coming here had nothing to do with anything beyond the fact I liked the place. It doesn't mean that I can't remember, or don't want to remember, the past because I'm here. I just needed to change—that was all. So did you.'

Her waving increased and I blinked to see her blowing a kiss. I mean, she was well over fifty—*well* over.

'Mum?' I said quietly, watching the young dreamer swing his legs down over the side of the boat. *'Mum?'*

But she went on smiling. 'Teddy wasn't right for you. He was a Dobbin.' She gave me a very straight look. 'You need someone who will stand up to you.' She waved again. 'And fortunately, that's not my responsibility now. It's yours.'

If the young man's smile stretched any further it'd be round the bay. He began to walk along the water's edge slowly, looking down now, slightly shyly I thought.

'You have to face up to life,' she said. 'You are what you experience. You can't deconstruct that away . . .'

'Well,' I said with satisfaction, 'Roberta has had to look into her soul now.'

'And so, my girl, have you.'

Then she went all floaty and female as she took off her sunglasses smiling for him.

Yup. You guessed it. *That smile* again. Sickening.

'You'll get there,' she said. 'I'm not so sure about Roberta. You have to come to any art humbled.'

'Oh believe me, she's been humbled,' I said, feeling rather humbled myself as we stood confronting the downcast smiles of the newcomer.

My mother shook her head. Before she kissed his cheek she said, 'Not humiliated, darling, *humbled.* It's quite different. It's what we call humanity.'

And then she winked at me.

'This is Pepe by the way Pepe—behold my daughter.'

In whom I am well pleased? She did not say.

CHAPTER THIRTY-THREE

In the flower shop I tried to remember what the message behind the various blooms on offer might be. Passing over the thought that lilies were for stinking cadavers and that forget-me-nots were for something else, I settled for chrysanthemums. Seasonal and bland. And I managed to compose a short message without once saying anything unpleasant or questionable. Grudgingly I chose a Congratulations on Your Baby card and just said: 'Best wishes to you all.' And signed it.

It was not 'Wiegenlied' but it would just have to do.

The message wasn't even true.

I did not feel best wishes to them all. But I thought, perhaps, one day I would.

*   *   *

It was packing-up time. No more mushroom soup and tobacco. While I packed I played the Requiem, and a very curious muddle of memory and images it provided, too. Even Dave Barnes was in there. But he wasn't doing anything of an erotic nature—he was just sitting on a bench, chewing the end of his pencil and looking constipated. One hoped this particular memory would fade. Everything else, both new and old, including the white bed, was still there. What was gone was the pain. Or at least, it was vestigial, diminished. As if I were a television set and had added a few more channels.

I was packing because I was moving to a flat in another part of town. Also temporary but nicer. Another suggestion made during that walk on the sands. 'Stop beating yourself up,' my mother said. 'You have to work at being happy.'

I rather thought I had been, as I told her.

Anyway—it really was time to move on.

At some point during the three days, I told my mother about losing money over the Hassocks Hall experience, so she gave me some. What a mysterious bond motherhood is. I wasn't sure if it was the money, or the visit, that had stopped me feeling angry with her. Or it may be because she still had all the photographs of her and Dad and me around, even in the bedroom. It is, nevertheless, very shocking to discover your mother has a sex life. Especially when you don't. Or only a very odd one.

She said that she might need the loan repaid some day. But by then she expected me to be secure and successful. Her tone implied At Last. I did not even have to make her a cup of tea and pretend to ask her advice on something, which is what I did in the old days if I wanted my pocket money. I did, however, pour her a large gin and ask her advice on something, before I left for the airport. Hence the flowers.

She asked me about The American but I told her he was obviously too old for her.

The woman in the flower shop pointed at my bags and said, 'I can see you've had a good holiday.'

I wanted to say that I had been through the most harrowing life curve and if I was a little suntanned it was merely because my harrowing life curve experience had happened to take place near the sea. But I didn't. I had done with battling for the time being. I was exhausted with it actually. Life, I realized, was too short. So I just said, 'Thanks.'

As I packed and listened I forgot to think. It was lovely to have Brahms back.

Outside the sun was still warm. It had been a very odd summer for England.

CHAPTER THIRTY-FOUR

There is, of course, one big difference between me and Brahms.

He is dead, and I am alive.

And I never felt more so than when I entered the gates of Hassocks Hall again. The rain of the preceding week had softened everything and brought down yellowing leaves from much confused trees. Was it or was it not early Autumn? If they did not know, how could I? The grass looked pure and jewel green again and even the lake had a fresh sparkle. It had been a long, dry summer, too long and too dry. I, for one, was glad of the damp.

So was Dave Barnes. I found him on his knees, fixing a net over the ornamental pond, which had begun to spout from its central fishy mouth again. He looked up cheerfully. And seemed pleased to see me.

'Hi,' he said. 'Cop hold over that side will you?' He pulled the net tight. 'Don't know what we'd have done without that rain,' he said, and secured the edge with a bodkin. He looked completely confident, totally absorbed, and quite without constipation.

‘What are you doing?’ I called. ‘Imprisoning the goldfish?’

He laughed, making the final fixture and standing up to brush off his knees. He was dark brown now, all over, and I was happy for Pauline.

‘No,’ he said. ‘It stops the pond getting clogged up with leaves.’

He gathered up his tools and we walked towards the Tudor outbuildings, where the sun was at its fullest. They looked just right and I was suddenly very glad they had not been turned into student accommodation.

In the distance I saw a pair of legs propped up against the back of a bench, but they were so far off I couldn’t tell whose.

‘Dave,’ I said, ‘I’m really sorry it’s all come to nothing for you. I hope you don’t feel cheated.’

I stopped walking. The views and vistas were bathed in morning sun, shimmering, and the old bricks glowed in the heat. You could keep Amalfi, and Andalucia, for moments like this.

‘Nah,’ he said goodnaturedly. ‘I’ve got a job I like. Place has got new owners. And anyway, writing made my brain hurt. But thanks for the help.’ He put his headphones in his ears and went off singing all that stuff about bitches as before. Quite and perfectly mindlessly.

I set off towards the side door to the Hall when a penny suddenly dropped down through the brain-slot and landed like a crashing cymbal. New Owners?

New Owners?

I went to find Roberta immediately.

* * *

She was tip-tapping daintily along the gravel from the carpark. Her awesome frontage was at half-mast. I could not work out whether this was good or bad—were they on the way back up? Or on the way down again? She wore sunglasses which made those other windows of the soul impossible to read. I decided to tread gently.

One should not, I counselled, approach with the merry, Hi there, how're they hanging . . . This was a woman scorned, no matter how she had treated me, and if I had vowed to exact revenge one day, I no longer had need to. There had been suffering enough. Valeria was different, of course, after the cupboard and the baby announcement. I felt she deserved all she got. Even if it did include someone with a rather nice bum. But not Roberta. Kindness was the dish of the day.

I approached in a manner I thought warm and welcoming. She smiled and gave a gracious little incline of her head. Queenly stuff. Not a hint of the suffering soul I had last seen. 'Diana,' she said regally. Too regally. 'You really have been very silly.'

‘Hi Roberta,’ I said with equal pomp. ‘How’re they hanging?’

She removed her sunglasses, raised her eyebrows and gave her breasts a mournful joggle.

‘You have no soul,’ she said.

Coming from her that was a bit rich.

‘Oh yes I have,’ I said. ‘And my mother sends her good wishes.’

‘Still writing contentedly?’ She showed a little more of the old snap and crackle.

‘Yes,’ I said. ‘Very contentedly.’

‘Mmm,’ said Roberta pondering. ‘Shame. No ambition.’

I was about to continue down this offensive path when the cymbal rolled over on its side and gave a reminding tinkle.

‘Roberta,’ I said. ‘Who owns Hassocks Hall?’

But answer came there none.

‘Ah!’ suddenly shrieked Roberta, and she fair gave those bosoms hell. ‘Ah—ah—at *last*.’ And she went skipping off with her white shirt flapping behind as if she were washing on a line.

The object of her greeting was Pearl, just coming through the gate in the distance. She saw Roberta, stopped, if I knew Pearl both shrugged and squared her shoulders before taking a deep breath, and marched on. She was not one to show enthusiasm or emotion in public.

I gave a little wave and turned back to the Tudor sun-trap. I would go and ask the owner of those legs—whoever they were—if they knew anything about anything. And if they didn't, at least I would get to enjoy a seat in the sun.

*   *   *

As I walked past the nice old Tudor buildings and the fruit canes and cages, I saw Mr and Mrs Valeria emerging from the rhododendron dell. At that exact same moment I realized to whom the sunning legs belonged. Something must be done. Without benefit of a modern sculpture show to conceal me, I did the next best thing and crept Hiawatha like, as low to the ground as I could go, until I fetched up at the bench bearing the offending limbs.

I should have guessed the legs' provenance anyway, by the rich odour hanging upon the warm air, which had nothing to do with dying down fruit canes and more to do with well-squashed grapes. The legs were, of course, Erna's. She always liked this bit of the grounds the best. It was the warmest place, apart from the hothouses. I crept right up to the bench to be sure of not being seen, and then stood up.

She was drowsing. On the path by her side was a bottle of champagne, around the lip of which hung one or two hopeful wasps. I shooed them away and gently lifted the glass from Erna's semi-sleeping hand. Immediately she gripped it very hard and sat up, saying conversationally, and still with her eyes closed, 'You don't say . . .'

I was about to assure her that I did, and to recommend she go back to sleep, when round the corner came Mr and Mrs V. And Mr V. was looking very fierce, prodding away at bits of moss in between the cobbles, raising his stick to point out—so I heard—that these particular viburnum needed a damn good seeing-to. One wonders, sometimes, how the upper classes ever manage to reproduce themselves.

They advanced, upright and unyielding.

And then I realized it wasn't a stick he carried. It was a gun.

I recalled Mr V.'s threats. They were very positive.

Erna lay there like a sitting target.

I had an affection for her, and no wish to see her blasted off the face of the earth.

Fortunately she was quite short lying supine, so I picked up the champagne and draped myself along her. I tried to look nonchalant. I had spent time in a cupboard with this woman. Crucial bonds are formed on such occasions.

I removed my sweatshirt from its stylish fling around my shoulders and gave it a stylish fling over her legs. It did not look happy. I just thought positive and smiled bonnily as the pair approached. The champagne, though warm, was good camouflage.

I sipped from the bottle. Behind me I could feel the squashed piece of humanity that once was Erna moving feebly in her sleep. So long as no one tried to remove her glass we were safe.

They arrived, squinting in the sun, straw hats as usual. Mr V. raised his. Decent of him.

'Hi,' I said, looking up at the sky. 'Not going to rain then?'

Since it was cloudless, this was tremendously appropriate. In another culture one of the accosted pair might have justifiably punched me on the nose for the sheer stupid time-wasting quality of the remark. As it was, and being English, we managed to make quite a reasonable little conversation out of it. Not to say philosophical. More than enough blue in the sky to make a sailor a pair of trousers . . . We are, after all, a sea-faring nation.

Mrs V. was looking over her shoulder towards the hothouses.

'Shattered panes,' she said sharply, making it sound like a horse disease.

Mr V. ceased to look fierce and went quite twinkly. 'Add it to the list,' he said triumphantly. 'Add it to the list.'

She plucked a pencil from the side of her skirt, where it hung as if waiting for a dance card, and jotted something down. They both looked extremely smug. I had that feeling about the *Titanic* again. That theirs was the side to be on in such an emergency, but you would have to open a vein to show blue blood pouring out first.

She smiled at me rather vaguely. Then Mr V. raised his hat again, and peered behind me.

'Ah,' he said, 'Mrs Er-Um,' and he replaced his hat. He seemed unconcerned—certainly not murderous.

Mrs V. pointed at the espaliered quince on the wall behind the bench. 'Fruits etcetera,' she said, writing again. 'Ours.'

Erna was blinking in the sunlight. I leaned forward and helped her back to a six o'clock position.

'Ah,' said Mr V., full of bonhomie. 'Enjoying the warmth, Mrs Er—Um?'

Mrs Er-Um nodded drowsily. 'And I always thought England was so cold. Wrong,' she said, emulating a bell. *'Wrong . . .*

She took the champagne bottle from my hands. 'Why it's even warmed this up in the few minutes I've been here . . . I'll have to put out coolers at the parties. Won't I?'

She looked roguish. Just for a moment I thought she was going to take a dive at his masculinity again, but he, perhaps thinking so too, stepped out of reach and made a movement with the gun.

'Don't shoot,' I said. It was out before I knew it. You never know the stuff you have in you until it is tried by circumstance. I prepared myself to stand between the bullet and its target in a gesture of unthinking bravery.

'Please don't shoot,' I added, and ducked.

Erna, blissfully unaware of her impending death, smiled and reached out to touch the barrel. Mr V. seemed much amused. He looked at me as I cowered away, surveyed the item in question—handed it towards me—and said, 'Cherrywood. Replicates the gun used by my father to shoot down nineteen bushmen. Still got the original, of course, notches and all.' Then he did look murderous. Just for a picosecond. '*Might* be useful again. You never know. Barbarians at the Gates.'

Mrs Valeria plucked at his sleeve by way of warning, and gave us an icy smile. 'Now, now,' she said with a horrible attempt at good humour. 'We don't want any accidents, do we?'

And he, with an even worse effort at raillery, removed his hat for the third time, bowed slightly, and said, 'Only larking.' While smiling like a man with piles.

Odd. Very odd.

Even odder was the deprecating way he then excused himself to the half-vacant Erna. 'Just getting the final bits and pieces ready for you and your accountants to agree—and then we can begin. We will see you at luncheon. Good morning.'

And off they went.

' . . . Love the warmth,' I heard Mrs Valeria say sardonically to her husband, and then give a distinctly amused titter. 'Well, well—I expect she does.' And they tittered some more.

I refilled Erna's glass and had another swig from the bottle. All this was most peculiar. Ten days ago, Erna was considered worse than nine hundred and nineteen bushmen and now they doffed their hats? Talk about ten days that shook this world.

'Erna,' I asked. 'Are you really the new owner?'

She leaned back on the bench luxuriously as a cat in the sun, opened her eyes, and nodded, chinking her jewellery. We both said in unison, 'Great Place To Have A Party.'

* * *

Owner was not exact. She was a leaseholder. On a repairing lease. And the Valerians were to continue in their rent-free apartments while overseeing, under the strictest guidelines of the Historical Houses Care Scheme, the complete restoration of Hassocks Hall.

'I've always wanted my very own Stately Home,' she said. She stretched and yawned. 'And now I have. Love this *heat* . . .'

How would the Valerians tolerate it? Ball-grabbing and parties? Bottle banks and helipads? Could they really be so selfless in order to preserve this pile and their place in history? I pondered the impenetrable while Erna debated putting a barbecue on the croquet lawn.

She closed her eyes sleepily and stretched

again. 'Oh boy—are we going to have some fun!' She took out her teeth. Snap, snap, they went, as she removed a floundering wasp from their pink and whiteness.

I excused myself from the bench in case I was tempted to start plucking rosemary, and went off to find Roberta and Pearl.

Someone, surely, had to be able to explain.

CHAPTER THIRTY-FIVE

Pearl and Roberta were sitting in what had once been Roberta's office and was now a Business Empire in the final stages of chaos. Boxes of papers, telephones, fat reference books were piled around the floor, filing cabinets and cupboard doors hung open, half empty, and the waste-paper baskets overflowed with torn photographs of Roberta greeting the Great and the Good at Hassocks Hall. The whole was bathed in dusty sunlight.

Panelling, rugs, tapestried chairs and firescreens stood quietly by, waiting to return the room to the comforts of its past. Next to a half-masted wall chart behind Roberta's desk hung a Fenton of the Hall and Park when it was first created. Sylvan, peaceful, same cows, same light, no execrable lumps. I had always rather envied this room as a powerhouse but I preferred it like this. The end of an Era—one hoped.

The calm did not extend to its occupants.

Voices were raised.

As I opened the door I heard Roberta say, 'I can't do it. I can't.'

And I heard Pearl reply, 'You can, Miss Topp. You can.'

They did not notice me as I entered because they were too busy glaring at each other.

I said, 'Hallo you two,' cheerfully enough. So they glared at me instead.

'Just don't say anything,' said Roberta.

'How was your mother?' asked Pearl.

I decided that age and not brassière size should win.

'My mother is in excellent health, thank you,' I said. 'And bonking the natives.'

Roberta blenched and closed her eyes.

'Now see what you've done,' said Pearl.

'I would have thought, Diana,' said Roberta from behind closed lids, 'that you had done quite enough just recently without adding any more crudity to the world.'

This, coming from a woman who planted smutty sex scenes throughout her work as regularly as Dave Barnes planted his onion sets.

I wanted to say that none of this was my fault, but since this was likely to go down just as badly as a *ballon de plombe*, I tried an alternative topic of conversation. My inner voice of reason, or possibly Pearl's gimlet eye, told me not to bring up the name of Peter the Bald again, not even to spit venom about him as in, He turned out a right toss-pot didn't he, Roberta. So I settled for 'What are you two up to then?'

Roberta opened her eyes. She looked shrivelled and tragic. Her coiffure, which had never righted itself to its normal perfection, was even more extraordinary—like the long, black, straggling tendrils of a drowning woman about her ears. The misogyny of Holman Hunt would have loved it, especially as she also wore a profound sense of slump again. Not just in the chest region but all over.

'Pearl,' she said dramatically, 'is trying to persuade me to live . . .'

'Metaphorically speaking,' added Pearl crisply.

'And I cannot.' She sunk her chin low on her hands, the picture of dejection.

'Of course you can,' said Pearl.

'But it has all been so public. No one will ever take me seriously again.'

Somebody, and it wasn't going to be me, could have pointed out that nobody ever had. Even the Glitz Pots must be pondering her marbles, as they surveyed their execrable lumps and pointilliste pigs.

Pearl patted the top of the desk. 'Well there you are then. Perfect opportunity. Do something to *make* them take you seriously.'

Good old Pearl. It was exactly the kind of

thing she used to say when I threatened to close the bookshop or join Hari Krishna. There was a tone about it that could take you to strangulation point. It was good to see someone else getting the lecture. Especially Roberta. Though she seemed to be listening.

'But that's what this Academy was supposed to be.' She raised her hands imploringly and for a moment, kissed by the sunlight, backclothed with dark wood, she certainly *did* have the air of a Pre-Raphaelite allegory about her. Pride brought low by Cunning, perhaps.

She said, 'The only other thing I can do is write.'

There was an interesting silence following this during which I swallowed hard. Pearl never took her warning eyes off me, and the inner voice of reason suggested it would be foolish to point out the anomaly in that statement. Pearl smiled at her very nicely. 'Then courage,' she said. 'You did it once. You can do it again.'

'Makes sense,' I shrugged. I was a bit fed up with all this sensitivity floating about. 'If the only thing you can do is write—then *write.*'

'Write what?' she snapped.

'Anything you like,' I snapped back. 'I don't know. I just sell the things.'

She looked up, she looked at me, she looked tragic, and a tear welled. 'Parasite,' she distinctly said. *'Parasite.'*

She could talk.

'Now look here,' I said, telling the inner voice of reason to fuck off out of it. 'You may have had a bad time over the last few weeks—but I've been having one for much longer—with no support at all from you.'

'*Diana . . .*' said Pearl, warningly

I rested my hands on the desk and leaned across towards Roberta, eyeball to eyeball. I had waited a long time for this. 'Who was it invited Teddy and that blowsy old bag here without asking me first?'

Generosity, as predicted by my mother, had not yet set in.

'Well, Roberta? And who was it said I'd had long enough to get over it? And who paid no attention to my feelings at all?'

Roberta was blinking those dark, glistening eyes at me. Less with a lizard-like laziness, and more like a panicking owl.

She looked even smaller now.

Good.

I'd give her parasite.

'And now you've had your heart broken—your dreams smashed on the rocks of heedless rapacity—'

'Diana,' Pearl said warningly. 'Mind your metaphors.'

'Oh bugger cool language,' I said. 'Let loose the dogs of war.'

Pearl rolled her eyes.

'The whole of *Watchacock* laughing at you—entirely your fault—'

She *really* bridled at this.

'So perhaps the experience will finally teach you something about humanity after all.'

Pearl made a little noise and muttered, 'Pot calling the kettle . . .'

'Be quiet,' I said to her. 'Two-timer.'

I can never be sure. Sometimes I think Pearl has a very odd way of looking cross. Almost as if she is laughing inside.

Roberta was now crimson, bolt upright, and opening her mouth for her own full frontal. And her bosoms began to receive, apparently with gratitude, a couple of right hooks. I had to get the last bit in. After all, there may not have been many things of which I am proud, but my bookshop was suddenly one.

'And as for being a parasite, Roberta Topp, well—what do you think we've all been? Here? Tell me one person who's doing anything for the greater good. One! Parasite? *Parasite* yourself. And you are worse than any of us because you *enabled* the parasiting activities to take place.'

'Parasitical,' said Pearl absently. 'Not Parasiting.'

'Bugger off, Pearl. I made you. And I can break you.'

'Oh my Gawd,' she said. 'Now that is enough.'

She ran her hand across her face which wiped away whatever the previous expression had been, and then she also opened her mouth—so I had both of them looking like a pair of gasping fish. And then the crimson drained from Roberta's cheeks, to be replaced with white. And she burst into tears.

'Oh Pearl,' she said, seeking comfort by pressing her little heaving self into Pearl's embrace. 'A teensy bit of what Diana says is true. I just want to go back to that caravan and begin all over again.'

I felt smug and vindicated.

Pearl took a handkerchief, a proper one, from the pocket of her cardigan, and wiped Roberta's nose. 'There, there,' she said. 'And so you can. It's never too late.'

I felt extremely smug and vindicated.

I gave Pearl a look which said how smug and vindicated I was. Then she looked up at me.

'Finished?' she said firmly.

I nodded.

'Good,' she said, 'because I think when Miss Topp said Parasite, she was referring to the absconded Peter. Not you.'

CHAPTER THIRTY-SIX

Brahms, of course, wrote the Requiem to confront and to reconcile those twin human emotions, the darkness and the light, Fear and Hope. His is both a cosmic grief and a cosmic consolation for the certainty that is death. And somewhere along the line he touched the Universal Spirit, which is what makes the Requiem a piece of genius, and yet direct and simple enough for each of us to respond to. I understood. If it had been Clapton, or Ella, it would have been poignant but no more. It was because it was Brahms, the highest, that it was so important.

Without our memories we are nothing, we do not exist. We take them with us wherever we go, they sweeten or sicken with age, but they stay in some form and we finally descend with them into the grave. They do not have to be accurate, they just *are.* I told Pearl that I had finally understood all this and she licked her finger, made a mark in the air, and said, 'Chalk it up.' I believe, in proletarian terms, that meant she was pleased.

* * *

We were all assembled in Yale's day room, where once we sipped coffee from Japanese cups and speculated on what lay ahead.

We were here for an announcement.

Roberta sat on a high-backed Hepplewhite, looking pale, composed and determined. Possibly also meek. Her coiffure was immaculate again and she was dressed for a journey.

'They that sow in tears shall reap in joy.'

Pearl, close by, was also dressed for a

journey. Occasionally she would look up at Roberta and give her an encouraging smile. I felt jealous, but did not say anything because Pearl said, if I did, she really would leave the bookshop. She had on her Wise expression.

'See how the husbandman waiteth for the precious fruit of the earth, and hath long patience for it . . .'

Erna was tucked like a tiny black shrew in one of the enormous leather wing chairs, an appalling child who had somehow managed to swap her head for an ancient one. Perhaps she had been to Giza.

Her little feet in their Barbie shoes swung against the seat like an impatient infant's. The beringed hand, liver spots and posy pink polish clutched a veritable cut-glass flower vase of single malt. She, too, was waiting. But she had forgotten what she was waiting for. A shadow passed over the sun, and for a moment her thin little shoulders shivered. She may have been sizing up the room. Great place to have a party. Why was she—the Lady of Mammon—so welcome once more?

'Verily every man living is altogether Vanity.'

The Three Valerians were simply popping with pleasure. They were ranged along the window seat and sipping noonday whisky and soda, all looking smug enough to deserve disaster. But you could tell, you could tell, it would not happen. They were safe on the right side of the *Titanic* doors. They had won. They knew. With God on their side?

I knew why Miss V. the Aristocrat's daughter looked so smug—because she had found, and kept, her heart's desire. She was quite crisp on the subject of having enough love for both of them. She would protect him from anything untoward, defend him against all assaults upon his time, keep his muse safe—Imprisoned was still the word I used. Yale did not stand a chance. Well, not unless a damsel in distress rode by and rescued him.

'How lovely are Thy dwellings fair, O Lord of hosts! My soul longeth, yea longeth and fainteth for the courts of the Lord.'

Yale was leaning against the window shutter, to one side of Valeria, failing to look at ease in his tweeds and brogues. Ridiculous man.

Now who was the albatross? Valeria sat very close to him and I was suddenly reminded of her interest in horses—in bloodstock—he was new blood to feed the line. Whatever he was, he did not look happy.

'Ye now have sorrow: but I will again behold you, and your heart shall rejoice . . .'

And here was I, sitting cross-legged on the floor in a patch of sunlight, picking at the machine stitching on the leg of my jeans and not exactly thinking it was better to have loved and lost.

The Blob had rung me the previous night to thank me for the flowers and to ask me to visit and see the little brute. Teddy came on the line for a few words, such as, 'Sorry to hear about the trouble, Hope everyone (Why not just me?) was all right.' And then he could not stop talking about midnight feeds, the right kind of baby baths and various other compelling subjects. It reminded me of the way he used to go on about cars. Boring.

Then a baby wailed in the background and he had to go. Changing nappies? How disgusting. I tried not to picture its little red fists and vacant deep blue eyes and was glad when he was gone.

All we the assembled needed was Peter the Bald to complete the picture and do an Agatha Christie. No one had told Roberta, but he had actually been spotted in San Tropez. Desmond was on the trail.

I traced the pattern on the rug. It was very faded but was some kind of bird. Perhaps an albatross? I caught Yale's eye. He smiled. A nice smile. His always were.

'Behold I shew you a mystery: We shall not all sleep, but shall all be changed, in a moment, in a twinkling of an eye . . .'

Mr V. rose to speak.

I had never seen him look so happy. I knew he was going to announce that he had, indeed, got two old piles off his hands after all.

He turned to look through the window behind him—soft midday sun still bathed the cows and pasture in a benign light—and the yellow patches on the grass had gone completely. It looked as it must have looked two hundred years ago, and would perhaps look two hundred years hence. I watched Erna who gave a little salute with her glass, rattled her jewellery and burped quite daintily, crossing her eyes apologetically.

Mr V. merely bowed.

He held his glass aloft and declared that we were all foregathered to toast the coming nuptials of his beloved only daughter Valeria, and the fine young man, James Hite from New England.

'To you both,' we all said, and drank accordingly.

'Hic,' said Erna.

'And also to celebrate the signing of a lease which will return this noble house to the proper grandeur that once was.' The glass went up again. 'And her kindness in allowing us to remain here in perpetuity.' A very, very definite line of smugness had crept around his mouth and his eyes and his jaw. 'To Mrs Er-Um. The new leaseholder of Hassocks Hall.'

How could he look so happy at the prospect of a barbecued croquet lawn. How *could* he?

Another shadow of cloud passed over the sun. It was all, suddenly, very autumnal.

'Hic,' said Erna, graciously. And then sitting upright, she added plaintively, 'It's suddenly gone kind of cold in here. Could we turn the heating on?'

To which, as if they had rehearsed it a hundred times, Mr and Mrs Valeria and the little Valeria all said in unison, 'Awfully sorry—we don't have heating. Just put another jumper on like we do.'

Erna leant back, smiling. 'Well—I guess that's one more thing to add to the list,' she said.

'Oh no,' said Mrs Valeria. She was actually glowing with pleasure. Real pleasure. This, it seemed, was her moment. 'Oh no, no, no—I am afraid not. You see, it would spoil the architectural perfection of the Adam Line.'

'Damn Adam's line,' said Erna crossly. 'I want heating.'

'Sorry, my dear lady,' said Mr Valeria, 'the Heritage people will never allow it. Certain tenets were laid down when we received an earlier sum from the State, and those are unalterable. You and your legal advisers *have* agreed all this . . .'

'We did not discuss heating,' said Erna crossly.

Mr Valeria shrugged. He took a document from his inner pocket, planted spectacles on his nose, and gave us the gist.

'Internally the house must not be altered in any way that would detract from the original design. There are'—he turned a page, looking wickedly over his glasses at the squirming Erna—'eight electrical storage heaters in places as advised and grant-aided in nineteen sixty-seven, which maintain the correct winter equilibrium throughout the house. It is recognized that any fiercer form of permanent heating would almost certainly damage the internal decorations and, in some cases, the structure as well.'

He looked up, pleased. 'They make very little difference to the *human* understanding of temperature, of course. They merely allow the correct balance of air temperature and humidity. We mortals are but the transient sentinels of this Great Place and therefore—' he smiled again, and very wickedly—'count for little in the unfolding pattern of time.'

'We'll see about this,' said Erna petulantly. 'My banker will fix it. I'll just get him on the mobile.'

'Nobody can fix it,' said Mr V. gleefully. 'Not him, not the IMF, not even the entire contents of a diamond mine. Some things are above price. Central heating at Hassocks Hall being one of them.'

'Well I don't think so,' said Erna. And she shivered again.

Mr V. continued.

'It would have been just the same if the Academy had gone ahead. Just the same. The students would have got frostbite in those classrooms. It would all have been over by Christmas. There really is nothing quite so bracing as an English Country House in the dead of winter. Why—you have to hack the ice off the bath sometimes. Just like school.'

He spoke with the relish of a captor describing his better lines of torture.

'Not even one little radiator here and there,' she said, puckering up her mouth.

Mr V. shook his head. 'Not one,' he said. 'Houses of Heritage's rules. You'll find the summers a bit tricky too.' He rubbed his hands and smiled delightedly. 'This was an aberration. Oh *quite* an aberration. I believe we're now moving into an ice-age.'

'Then cancel everything, cancel everything,' she said petulantly. 'I want to go home.'

'Too late, dear lady, you are far, far too late.'

And now he smiled with a smile that would have frozen Hell.

'But we can, most certainly, arrange your flight today.'

I looked at Yale, who looked absolutely stricken.

'No *heat*?' he said. 'No heat?'

'None whatsoever,' I said sportingly. And then a rather wonderful thought occurred to me.

'Oh you poor thing,' I said. 'How will you work with *no heat*?'

'Plug-in electric fires,' said Valeria quickly. 'Lots of plug-in electric fires.'

Yale looked vaguely convinced.

'Lots and *lots* of plug-in electric fires.' Valeria gestured as if the Cavalry were, even now, on their way with a crateload of Bellings.

Damn. I watched my wonderful thought fly out of the door.

But Mr V. buoyed up by triumph, quite forgot himself. 'Oh no, oh no—' And he wagged a finger at the rapidly chilling air. 'Can't do that—can't do that, you know—overload the circuit here and everything blows up. Also *insurance.* After Windsor Castle it just won't wash . . . No, no—cold we are, and cold we'll stay—it is our Duty and our Burden. More jumpers—that's all. Put on more jumpers . . .'

He looked terribly happy for about a millisecond, and then he realized that his beloved daughter was staring at him as if he had gone for her with an axe. An air of panic crept into the parental eyes. He looked from Valeria to her betrothed, and blinked. You could almost hear the guinea drop. He took a deep breath. 'Oh, not so bad,' he said shrilly. 'Not so bad. We have the open hearth and occasional electric fires and hot-water bottles and rugs . . . Only six months of the year . . . Hearty walks . . .' His voice trailed off.

Yale did not look convinced. In fact he looked deeply and painfully unconvinced, as if his good red blood had run pale. Valeria was practically concave with despair. She had looked into the future and seen only aimless chinless wonders everywhere.

Something began creeping down towards

my stomach, via my heart, something called Excitement at the Scent of Victory.

Valeria should never have kept me shut in that cupboard.

She really and truly should not.

'I expect you'll be kept warm by snuggling up to your wife,' I said. 'It's traditional.'

Beyond the window, somewhere down in the grounds, we could hear Dave Barnes working away and singing at the top of his lungs from those same, mindless rap lyrics. The Barbarian at the Gate. Green shoot upon the bough.

'Even so saith the Spirit: For they rest from their labours; And their works follow after them.'

I looked at Yale. The prospect of Connubial Warmth did not seem to have done the trick. He just looked bereft.

I traced my foot around the woven picture of a bird that was possibly an albatross and hummed the opening chords of the Requiem to myself. Just to see. As I suspected, it was all pleasure and beauty and forgiveness, suddenly, without a trace of regret.

I looked up and gave him.

You guessed it.

That Smile.